DRAWPOINT

BLAKE BRIER BOOK FOUR

L.T. RYAN

with
GREGORY SCOTT

LIQUID MIND MEDIA

For information contact:

Contact@ltryan.com

https://LTRyan.com

https://www.facebook.com/JackNobleBooks

THE BLAKE BRIER SERIES

Blake Brier Series

Unmasked
Unleashed
Uncharted
Drawpoint
Contrail (Coming October, 2021)

1

By the time Blake reached the bottom step, his resolve had hardened.

His fingers punched in the code with focused accuracy. The familiar *thunk* of the steel bolts preceded the equally familiar whir of the cooling fans.

The positive pressure, created by the hefty air conditioning units sitting behind the townhouse, sent a puff of icy air through the stairwell. It was enough to rustle a lock of fiery red hair across his right eye. He swept it back and pushed his way inside.

Déjà vu.

After everything that Blake had been through over the past week alone, one would think there would be nothing left in the world that could surprise him. Then, there was the note.

A few minutes earlier, he had returned home with a head full of vivid images. A romanticized version of a life that would begin the moment he crossed the threshold of the Alexandria townhouse. He and Haeli. The way it should have been from the beginning.

But with a simple paragraph, written in Haeli's own hand, he would again have to come to terms with the disaster he often facetiously referred to as his "charmed life."

Although he had left the piece of lined notebook paper on the kitchen counter, he could still see the words as clearly as if they were hanging by a thread in front of him.

One statement pulsed in his mind.

I need to go away for a while. There are some things I need to do.

The sentence he should have fixated on was the one where she explicitly asked him not to try to find her. But that specific sentiment had been deleted from his memory the moment he decided to disregard the request.

What things do you have to do, Haeli? What is it that we can't do together?

The thought had occurred to him that there wasn't actually a *thing* at all. That the fictitious task had been invented to spare his feelings. The truth was, a week ago, Blake wasn't sure he possessed such a thing as feelings. Not the way he imagined normal people did. But his experience with Christa, Gwyn, and Lucy had caused him to reevaluate that notion. Allowing himself to be vulnerable was no easy transition. Still, the result was good even if the timing had turned out to be less than optimal.

Blake circled the perimeter of the subterranean room. He ran his fingers along the racks of processors mounted to the wall. He could feel the heat radiating from behind the blinking red and blue LED indicator lights.

In a way, the state-of-the-art computer equipment seemed a pathetic character. Built to churn complex code-breaking algorithms, the system was not unlike a greyhound kept in a cupboard. Its powerful legs atrophying with lack of use.

It had been some time since Blake had utilized the full capability of the system he had so meticulously built—if he had ever used its full capability at all.

Before his dust-up with the Cryptocurrency Evangelist Army, he had spent many hours a day in this room. Locating, exploiting, and cataloging vulnerabilities in supposedly secure networks. Maintaining classified software that he had built for the Central Intelligence Agency while he was still under their employ. Building software for clients as a freelance developer after retirement. But since then, he had done little of it.

This day would be no different. Except, while he had no intention of using the system to thwart a nefarious foreign government or to infiltrate a global communications network, he would be using it to find something much simpler and far more elusive. The truth.

Blake moved to the center of the room. He lowered himself into the seat of the Herman Miller chair with a sigh and spun himself toward the desk. With a press of a switch, the terminal came to life.

It was deceiving, really. The single station, situated in the center of the room, looked no different than one might find in any office. A few screens, a keyboard, a mouse. But it was merely an interface. An abstraction. Just as the buttons and levers of a fighter jet's cockpit enabled the pilot to unleash the beast's fury with the twitch of a muscle, it connected Blake's fingers to the awesome power of the system.

I need to go away for a while. There are some things I need to do.

At first glance, the note seemed a mystery. But in Blake's experience, there was no such thing as a mystery. Only an unsolved equation. Haeli left Blake's home and his life, that much was a given. But where was she going? Where was her trajectory taking her? If he were going to solve for x, he would first need to define y.

Of the list of traits he would have used to describe himself, the one he'd most recently embraced was pragmatism. It was a peculiar approach in his circles. Most preferred to skip the shovel and go straight to the dynamite. While the dynamite might be effective, it draws a lot of attention.

Blake withdrew his hands from the keyboard and pulled his phone from his pocket. He tapped the icon for the text messaging app and again on the thread entitled 'Haeli.' He brought up the 'info' tab. An image of a map flashed on the screen, then faded to gray. 'Location not found.'

It was worth a shot.

The callous message meant Haeli had either turned her phone off or switched off the ability for Blake to see her location. It also meant he would need to employ less conventional methods after all.

Back on the keyboard, Blake entered the command to list the tools and scripts he had installed. The green text scrolled over a black screen. The command was on the tip of his tongue but, for the sake of time, he welcomed a quick reminder. Three quarters of the way down, he found what he was looking for.

He typed.

CTST.

Talk about déjà vu.

During his time with the Agency, Blake had used this command line interface, or CLI, on a daily basis. With the forced cooperation of all United States based communication providers, federal agencies such as the CIA, NSA, and to a limited extent, the FBI, were provided access to real-time cell tower data. Blake had built the CLI to simplify the process of downloading and interpreting it.

The CTST tool, short for Cell Tower Signal Triangulation, took two parameters: The provider and the cellular phone number. The software gathered the raw data from any tower with which the cellular device was communicating and used it to derive a location. By measuring the time delay between the device and each tower, and the direction from which the signal was originating, or azimuth, the position of the device was triangulated using a basic mathematical formula. While its level of accuracy often fluctuated based on signal strength and other environmental factors, it would be accurate enough for his purposes.

Blake input Haeli's number. The blinking cursor froze for a moment, then spit out the result. Instead of a set of coordinates, as he had hoped, the software balked.

No signal detected.

The phone was off. And if she was serious about not wanting to be found, she had probably already discarded it in the Potomac. The words she wrote weren't just idle talk. No, she was taking steps to disappear.

Blake could have easily pulled her data from iCloud and obtained full backups of her device, but it wouldn't have done any good. She knew enough to turn the phone off before she ever left the house. What he needed was a totally different vector.

There was one other option. A script that Blake had not used since becoming a civilian. But if the previous options had been the shovel and the excavator, he would be reaching for the dynamite.

Although the public was probably not aware that their cellular provider was streaming their usage data to the federal government—unless they made it a habit of reading the thirty-seven pages of fine print—it was legally given and readily available. Its use was so commonplace that it carried little oversight. Access to the Transportation Security Administration database, on the other hand, was highly scrutinized.

Before committing to his new plan of attack, Blake ran a traceroute to be sure the proxies and tunnels were sufficiently obfuscating his Internet Protocol Address. Satisfied, he typed the name of the script and hit enter.

An 'Authorized Use' warning popped onto the screen. Below it, a prompt. He had half-expected the old script to have been obsolete in its method of gaining entry. But, just like that, he was in.

Fingers flying across the keys, Blake entered names and dates of birth for each of the aliases Griff had set up for Haeli when she arrived in Virginia.

Haeli Becher.

As expected, there was nothing.

Jessica Ruben.

Nada.

Cynthia Brook.

Nope.

Allison Gaudet.

Bingo!

There it was. As plain as day.

British Airways. IAD (Dulles-Washington) to TLV (Ben Gurion - Tel Aviv).

She had gone home.

It hit him in the gut. He told himself he understood. That he didn't blame her. Haeli had left behind everything and everyone she had ever known and traded it for him. It was too much to ask. Too much to expect.

As the pit in his stomach dissolved, a sense of relief replaced it. Not because she was gone, but because for once, he wasn't an impediment. She knew what she needed, and she acted.

With the kind of sincerity one can only have within the confines of their own thoughts, he wished her well. He wished her happiness. Still, he couldn't help but worry about her safety. She was supposed to be dead. And Blake had no doubt Levi Farr continued to harbor a burning desire for a second crack at her. By returning to Israel, she was flying dangerously close to the flame.

He reminded himself that she could take care of herself. More than anyone else he had ever met. She would make her way. A new life, loosely modeled after the old. A reimagining of an early version of herself, perhaps. It was what he had risked his life to make possible. As selfish as it felt, he hoped she remembered it that way.

Such regression wasn't an option for Blake. There was but one path for him. Forward. He was on the starting blocks again. Pointed in an arbitrary direction.

He pressed the glowing button. The monitors went dormant.

Ready. Set...

Sigh.

2

ONE WEEK AGO. PAVEL NIKITIN TIGHTENED HIS CORE, SHIFTED HIS weight, and drove his fist deep into Adam Goldmann's liver.

Goldmann wheezed and hunched over, as far as his restraints would allow. By now the pain was numbing. Despite Nikitin's fist carrying a disturbing amount of force—as if it were a concrete pendulum dropping from the highest rafter of the old warehouse building—Goldmann was content to receive the blows. It was what would come next that frightened him. He had no delusions that it would get worse. Much worse.

Pavel Nikitin was an artist. A master of administering pain. Goldmann had seen his work in the past. At the time, he felt pity for the poor soul in the chair. He remembered praying that he would never find himself on the receiving end. But he knew his time would come. No one can run forever.

Nikitin had honed his skills over a lifetime. Anyone who set eyes on him could see that his education came from personal experience. The scars on his face, arms, and hands were a roadmap through a brutal past. His large stature, square jaw, and piercing eyes may have been a prerequisite for someone in his profession, but there was one feature that set him apart—a mound of scar tissue where his left ear had once been.

It was his calling card. A main tenant of his folklore.

There were many stories about how Pavel Nikitin lost his ear. Passed around the seedy corners of the underworld, each iteration morphed into something further from the truth.

It was generally believed that Nikitin was born in the gulag. A product of rape, he was delivered in secret and kept hidden in sewage tunnels under the camp. It was there that the rats gnawed off his ear.

As he grew, he would emerge under the cover of darkness to prey on unsuspecting prisoners. Legend had it he would drag his victims underground and feed on their blood to acquire their strength.

Through the early nineteen-eighties in the Soviet Union, many families lost loved ones to the prison camps. Dozens of men and women disappeared, never to be heard from again. There was no explanation. No recourse. The Kremlin routinely denied that the Stalin era camps still existed, never mind acknowledging maleficence within them. For many, the idea of a soul-sucking demon child was as good an explanation as any.

While Nikitin reveled in the absurdity of his reputation, there was some truth to it. He was, in fact, born in the gulag. His mother, the wife of a mid-level mafia boss named Stan Nikitin, was imprisoned after her husband was killed for violating a postulate of the organization's code. Forbidden from marrying or having a family, the couple married in secret. The priest promptly turned them in.

The assassination of Nikitin's father fell to an ambitious, young KGB officer named Olezka Sokolov, who himself was rising through the ranks of the crime syndicate. After Nikitin was born, Sokolov took him in.

Separating from the KGB under less than amiable circumstances, Sokolov was forced underground. He devoted himself to the acquisition of power. And it wouldn't take long.

Through extreme brutality, Sokolov rose to the head of the organization. But he didn't stop there. To send a message to all who might oppose him, Sokolov murdered the heads of the ten most powerful criminal organizations. Not only in the USSR, but throughout the world. China. Columbia. The United States. It was a bold move that would make him one of the most feared men on the planet.

Sokolov had a knack for sending messages that were never dared forgotten. Nikitin knew this better than anyone.

As Nikitin matured, he became invaluable to Sokolov. An exceptional student driven by an insatiable bloodlust, Nikitin's own brutality surpassed even that of his guardian. It was the reason Sokolov took his ear. A lesson in humility, he called it, but Nikitin knew it was a warning.

The truth was, Sokolov's fear of challenge was unfounded. Nikitin was as loyal as they came. He lived by the thieves' law. He believed in it. Especially when it came to Sokolov.

But he didn't begrudge Sokolov his assertion of dominance. Just the opposite. Nikitin relished it. It was what spawned his own habit of collecting the ears of his victims. And the collection was extensive.

The practice wasn't rooted in some emotional hang-up. It was just fun. Sure, maybe the first time was motivated by a subliminal need to even the score. But it became a deliberate tactic to strike fear into those who would consider crossing them. Each time a body washed onto shore or was pulled from a shallow grave, the missing left ear would tell the world all they needed to know. Pavel was here. After all, every artist must sign his work.

Goldmann knew all of this. It was what fueled his fear. Death, he thought, was inevitable. Whether by the hand of Nikitin, Sokolov, or old age. But the thought of being mutilated, before or after, didn't sit well with him.

He didn't have a chance to dwell on it. As the plastic bag slipped over his head, Goldmann gasped, sucking the thin plastic film toward the back of his throat. His body convulsed and his vision began to blur.

He envisioned his death and the desecration of his body. It was different than he thought it would be. More welcoming.

Then Nikitin yanked the bag from his head.

Thick, delicious air filled Goldmann's lungs. The sensation consumed him, and he wondered if that was what it felt like to be born.

"What are you waiting for?" Goldmann panted. "Do it already."

Nikitin said nothing.

Since Goldmann was removed from the trunk and carried into the abandoned industrial building, Nikitin had not uttered a single word. There would be questions, but not by him.

Goldmann wasn't stupid. Far from it. His intellect was the reason he was able to elude Sokolov and his dog for the past two years. He knew why Nikitin was keeping him alive. Just as he knew who the approaching footsteps belonged to.

Sokolov had arrived.

Nikitin straightened his posture as the footsteps crescendoed and stopped behind Goldmann.

"I trust you've made our guest comfortable," Sokolov said.

"Very comfortable," Nikitin replied.

To Goldmann's ears, their gruff voices and thick Russian accents were almost identical. If Nikitin wasn't standing in Goldmann's line of sight, he would have sworn Nikitin was talking to himself.

Sokolov circled around Goldmann and peered down at him.

Goldmann met his gaze. They even look the same, he thought.

Although older and less grizzled, Sokolov had the same hulking stature, jagged jaw, and piercing gray eyes as his ward.

"I'm hurt," Sokolov said. "You never said goodbye."

Nikitin smiled, displaying a row of chipped teeth.

Sokolov leaned forward. "You should know, your family was very upset with you. Your own wife cursed you as she took her last breath."

"That's a lie," Goldmann said.

"Maybe, maybe not." Sokolov pulled several creased photographs from his pocket and held each to Goldmann's face, in succession. "Look at her face. Even separated from her body, you can see the anger. This anger was for you."

Goldmann swallowed hard and tried to fight the tears. The images of his dismembered wife and children were worse than he imagined. But he forced himself to look.

For two years he tried to prepare himself for the moment when he would come face to face with their deaths. All the while, resisting the urge to blame himself. He knew if he fled, Sokolov would kill them.

But he also knew that if he returned, Sokolov would kill them and him.

Sokolov tossed the photos on Goldmann's lap and grabbed his jaw, pressing his cheeks into his bottom teeth. "Now. Where are my diamonds?"

"I don't know," Goldmann said.

Sokolov let go and nodded to Nikitin, who swooped in with a wide hook to Goldmann's nose.

Blood exploded onto his face and lap, spattering the pictures.

"If you want to live, you will give me better answer than this," Sokolov said.

"You think I'm an idiot? I know you're going to kill me no matter what I say."

"Don't get me wrong mister Adam Goldmann, I will cut off your hands and your feet. You must suffer, yes? But I will make sure you live. All you have to do is tell me where are my diamonds."

"I told you," Goldmann said, "I don't know."

Sokolov shook his head and motioned to Nikitin once more.

Nikitin made a show of unsheathing a slender fillet knife and slowly walked behind Goldmann. With his left hand, Nikitin grabbed the top of Goldmann's ear and pulled outward.

"Wait, wait," Goldmann pleaded. "It's true, I was going to run off with the stones. Okay, I did run off with the stones. At least, I thought so. But when I opened the case, it was empty."

Sokolov laughed. "This is bullshit story." He shifted his gaze to Nikitin.

"No, no, wait!"

Nikitin brought the knife down with incredible speed. In a flash, Goldmann could feel the searing pain and the warm blood pooling on his shoulder and running down his left arm. Goldmann wailed.

"Sixty million dollars," Sokolov yelled. Droplets of saliva freckled Goldmann's face. "You will tell me where they are. Or you will know pain."

Nikitin reached over Goldmann and handed Sokolov the floppy slice of flesh and cartilage. Sokolov tossed it onto Goldmann's lap.

"I swear it." Goldmann shook his head vigorously to avoid passing out. "Someone switched out the case after I left Israel. I'm telling you the truth. I didn't have any contact with anyone except for my security detail. It must have been one of them."

"What are their names?" Sokolov asked.

"I don't know." Goldmann winced as the words left his mouth. He had come to learn that Sokolov was not fond of them.

"Take his other ear," Sokolov ordered.

Goldmann twisted in the chair. "Please— "

"And then it will be your eyes and then your balls," Sokolov growled. "We can do this all day, yes?"

"Look," Goldmann said. "I hired the team through Techyon. I don't remember all their names. One of them was a woman. Her name was Haeli. I don't know if that was her real name. That's all I remember. You've gotta believe me. You know I have no reason to lie."

"Shhhh," Sokolov put his finger to Goldmann's lips, then patted him on the head. "I know."

Sokolov walked around Goldmann. His even-tempo footsteps receded the way they came. Without a break in his stride, Goldmann could hear Sokolov call out from the distance.

"You may kill him now."

3

HAELI TOSSED HER KNAPSACK INTO THE BACKSEAT OF THE WHITE Mercedes sedan and climbed in after it.

"Marhaba," the driver said, "where do you like to go?"

Haeli glanced at the taxi license, displayed on the dashboard. *Yusuf ibn Ibrahim.*

"Yigal Alon Street, Tel Aviv," she said. "I don't know the address, but I'll show you where when we get close."

Of course, she did. She knew it well. But that was nobody's business but her own.

Yusuf nodded. "I can give you flat rate. Two hundred twenty. Is this good?"

Haeli did the math in her head. Two hundred and twenty Israeli Shekels would be about sixty-five dollars, maybe a little more.

The main highway, Route 1, was notoriously congested during the daytime hours. The trip could take thirty minutes to an hour.

Two twenty was probably a good deal. Not to mention, there was always room for negotiation. After all, only tourists accepted the first offer. But the money was of no concern. What she needed was flexibility.

"Just run the meter," she said.

L.T. RYAN

Yusuf smiled and pressed a button to start the meter running. He jerked the wheel, forcing the front end of the Mercedes between two other cabs waiting in line to exit the taxi stand.

Ben Gurion International Airport was as busy as Haeli had ever seen it. And she had seen it a lot. It was the gateway to countless missions and assignments. At the moment, however, there was only one mission on her mind.

"What's your name?" Yusuf asked.

Haeli had to think for a second. "Allison."

She had chosen to use the alias by a highly advanced, scientific method—it was the first passport she happened to pull out of her stash. In retrospect, she wished she had chosen a different one. She didn't like the name Allison Gaudet, though she wasn't sure why.

If she could have, she would have brought documentation for several different aliases. But getting caught with passports, licenses, birth certificates, and credit cards under multiple names would have been a huge red flag. Haeli was well acquainted with the security apparatus in Israel. It wasn't to be trifled with.

"You are visiting?" Yusuf asked.

"Yep. Just visiting," Haeli kept her answers curt. She didn't want to be rude, but she hoped the short answers would dissuade the man from asking any more questions. She was in no mood for small talk. Any conversation, no matter how trivial, would require more brain power than she was willing to devote. The backstory she had devised during the flight was still thin. It was something she would need to rectify before it became critical.

Yusuf merged onto Route 1. The traffic was not as heavy as she'd expected. But she knew that would change as they got closer to the city.

Haeli settled herself in for the ride and gazed out the window. Past the concrete barriers lining either side of the highway, there was only sky. In this area, none of the homes or structures along the flat landscape rose high enough to be visible over walls.

Ah, the walls.

Israel loved its walls. It was the land of gates and barriers and partitions. Most notably, the enormous one that delineated the border of the

West Bank, of course. But that wasn't all. In the city, residential properties often looked like fortresses, with high fences and heavy iron gates. Especially in wealthier sections. Parking lots, driveways, parks. All secured with concrete stanchions or spike strips or high-tech surveillance systems.

It was no wonder. The Tel Aviv district, like many other places in Israel, had been the target of terrorists for decades. Haeli remembered a time when rocket attacks, launched at the city from the Gaza Strip, just forty miles away, were a daily occurrence. Suicide bombers on buses, bars, and beaches. Just a normal Tuesday.

But the people of Israel were extraordinarily resilient. For most, the ever-present danger faded into the background of daily life. And it was no different for Haeli.

Since she was a young girl, she had never felt that her home was unsafe. But then again, she wasn't the average child.

Growing up in a paramilitary facility, she was shielded from the outside world for much of her youth. Shielded, but not sheltered. Her experience was more demanding than the outside world could have ever been. All of it had been about control. Controlling her fear. Controlling her body. Controlling her world.

By the time she was a teenager, she could kill a grown man with her bare hands. Not only in theory, but in practice. Lots of practice. With rigorous daily training and relentless evaluation, she would be forced to prove it over and over again. It didn't take long before she started to realize that the outside world should be more afraid of her than she was of it.

"There she is," Yusuf said.

In the distance, skyscrapers of varying heights bristled out of the horizon. The skyline of Tel Aviv and Ramat Gan was a comforting sight.

Since fleeing Israel more than a year ago, she had never felt like she fit in. Especially in the United States. But here, it was different. Here, she didn't feel like an imposter.

As the jagged skyline loomed larger, she found herself wishing she had spent more time appreciating the place. As an adult, she had been all business, rarely taking a moment to dip her toes into the Mediterranean or explore the rich history of the place.

Raised without religion, the significance of the holy sites never had the same draw they did to the rest of the population, Jews and Palestinians alike. But there was something to be said about the power of such antiquity, even from a secular point of view.

In different circumstances, she might have entertained a bit of soul searching. But not now. It wasn't that kind of homecoming.

"Get off here," Haeli said.

"Here?" Yusuf glanced over his shoulder, then back at the road. "It's better to—"

"I know. Just get off here."

Yusuf took the exit.

Haeli directed him to turn right onto Lehi Road. A green wire fence ran along the median, separating the eastbound and westbound lanes.

Fences and walls.

She directed him to take the next possible left and then rattled off a series of turn-by-turn directions that would snake them through narrow streets of the residential neighborhood.

Rows of small angular structures passed by her window. Each a variation of the last. A sea of cracked stucco and corrugated metal. It was almost imperceptible where one dwelling ended and the next began.

Had it always looked like this?

"You are not visiting," Yusuf said. "You are from here, yes?"

The surprise in Yusuf's voice amused her. She knew why he assumed she was a tourist. English had been her first and primary language. Her tutors had always been American, and her accent reflected it. Not that she couldn't blend in if she needed to. As part of her schooling, she was required to achieve fluency in several other languages, including Hebrew and Arabic.

"Let's just say I'm familiar with the area." She left it at that.

They were close now. Two blocks from her intended destination. She took a deep breath.

Along the right side of the road was a pair of multi-story apartment buildings. In the courtyard between them, something that stood out in Haeli's memory.

"Stop here."

Yusuf stopped the car as abruptly as she had blurted the command.

"This is good. How much do I owe you?"

"Two hundred thirty-two." Yusuf twisted his body to look at her. "See, flat rate is much better."

Haeli handed over two hundred forty shekels, grabbed her bag, and stepped out without responding. Her attention remained fixed on the courtyard. Yusuf pulled away.

Behind a wrought iron fence, the faded colors of the plastic slide and swings stood out against the sand. A flood of memories washed over her, and tears welled in her eyes.

Standing there on the sidewalk, staring at the vacant little playground, it was as if she were nine years old again.

She remembered how, every weekend, she would beg her father to take her for a walk.

"One last time," he would always say. Then they would walk to the market where he would buy her a sweet treat.

On every trip, they would pass by the playground. On the way there and on the way back. Every time, she would stop and ask if she could go in.

Maybe it was because it was such a foreign concept to her, or maybe it was an innate drive to play that exists in all children, but it called to her from beyond the fence. She could feel its draw, even now.

"This is private property. You don't belong there," he would say, as if reciting from a script. "Come. Let's get you home."

But this routine was not what triggered the emotional response. It was one particular memory, from one remarkable day.

Walking back from the market with a belly full of lemon wafers, Haeli stopped to look in on the playground. "Can I try it today?" she asked. Her father paused. She knew the answer. Then, the unexpected. He reached down, lifted her up, and lowered her on the other side of the fence.

"Come with me," she said. And then, something even more unexpected. Something that had never happened before or since. Her father, the venerable Doctor Benjamin Becher, hopped over the fence, took her hand, and jogged to the playground.

For twenty minutes, they played. Swinging. Hanging from the monkey bars. She even got him to go down the slide. And they laughed. Goodness, they laughed. It was the only time she could recall hearing him so much as snicker. Most importantly, it was the only time in her life that she could remember him treating her like a child.

She hadn't realized how impactful that afternoon had been on her. Even now she felt the urge to hop the fence and take a few swings. But there were important matters to attend to.

She pushed the past from her mind and moved toward the west. A few short minutes later, she had reached Yigal Alon Street.

There, right in front of her, was a massive building that sprawled for blocks. From the center of the squat compound was a soaring tower sheathed in tinted glass. At the top, six-foot-tall letters read: Techyon.

4

ONE DAY AGO. HAELI DRAGGED THE OVERSTUFFED SUITCASE BEHIND HER. The plastic wheels clattered as they ran along the textured concrete and skipped over the sidewalk's contraction joints. The unstable cadence slowed as she reached the bottom of the staircase.

Home sweet home.

Haeli looked up at Blake's townhouse. Not at any particular feature, but as a whole. As if she were seeing it for the first time.

Of course, that wasn't the case. For the past several months, she had stayed overnight on a regular basis. Walked up the front stairs more times than she could count. But this was different. This felt monumental. She figured the least she could do was offer an extra moment of introspection. If for no other reason than to feel she had done something to commemorate the occasion when she looked back on it.

Haeli smiled to herself. She pushed the retractable handle until it disappeared into the suitcase and hoisted the bag off the ground.

She bound up the stairs, punched in the code and made her grand entrance to an empty foyer.

"Honey, I'm home," she called out in her best Desi Arnaz.

She was aware Blake wasn't there to answer, but she couldn't help it. She was feeling playful, and she amused herself.

Haeli had no difficulty with that. Amusing herself was a skill she had mastered as a child. When she wasn't training or studying, she was confined to her room. She had no toys to speak of, other than a chest full of puzzles, which she had already solved. She'd occupy herself by acting out scenarios. Personal little plays, performed only for a small audience of reflective glass.

Looking back on it, the hours of role playing were the foundation for her ability to manipulate people and blend into any environment. As early as five years old, she would put on accents, experiment with different vocal intonations, and practice subtle physical mannerisms to differentiate the characters in her fanciful stories. Most importantly, she learned to control her emotions.

She could be the damsel in distress if it suited her. Cry at the drop of a hat, if needed. But she could also suppress all emotion. And it was this skill that proved most useful of all.

Haeli shut the door behind her and lugged the suitcase up the stairs to the second floor. She swung it onto Blake's bed and unzipped it.

The contents of the suitcase consisted of a few dozen items of clothing and a handful of beauty products. They represented the full inventory of her earthly possessions.

Living in a decommissioned CIA safe house had its benefits. Free rent. Basic furnishings. Quiet location. But it also had its inconveniences.

Fezz had cleared the temporary arrangement with his superiors, but it hadn't been run all the way up the flagpole. It meant Haeli had to be prepared to clear out at a moment's notice, should Fezz give her the word. It was for that reason she lived out of the bulky Samsonite suitcase.

For the past several months, she may well have been backcountry camping. She kept no food and left little trace of her presence. Whatever trash she generated—mostly consisting of takeout containers and plastic utensils—she immediately removed and deposited in dumpsters and garbage cans around the area. A moment's notice was all she would need.

But that was behind her now. She was setting down roots. Joining the ordinary world, if such a thing existed. And it made her happier than she imagined it would.

Cohabitation was sure to come with its challenges. Despite her small footprint, her former arrangement seemed disorganized in comparison to her new dwelling.

Blake was meticulous. There was no other word for it. Other than, perhaps, sick.

Everything had its place. If it didn't have a purpose, it didn't exist. Haeli feared the addition of her modest freight would threaten to send the entire system into disarray.

She opened the closet. There were two unused hangers, which no doubt had previously been occupied by two garments Blake had taken with him to Rhode Island.

Next, she tried the dresser, opening each drawer in succession, from top to bottom. The first, socks and underwear. The next, shirts. The third, pants. But the last—she could tell the last was empty as soon as she pulled it.

Only, as it turned out, it wasn't.

Lying in the otherwise unused drawer was a single business card. She didn't have to pick it up to know what it said.

Anja Kohler, Federal Bureau of Investigation.

The average person in her position would have removed the small piece of card stock and set about loading her clothes into the empty drawer. And she would have if the card had belonged to anyone else. But God only knew what kind of mausoleum she would be desecrating. Knowing Blake, she wouldn't have been surprised if he had set aside the drawer as some type of shrine. As if he were keeping it empty in case she returned.

As selfish as it felt, Haeli wanted nothing more than to push it aside. To push Anja aside. But she would rather Blake get there on his own when he was ready. And she had faith he would.

Haeli zipped the suitcase closed, dragged it onto the floor, and slid it into the closet.

Finish moving in. Check.

She sat on the edge of the bed and fell backward onto the plush comforter, arms outstretched. She could have closed her eyes for a few minutes, but the buzz from inside her pants pocket nudged her to reconsider.

There you are, Mick. Tell me you're on your way home.

Haeli sat up and fished the phone from her pocket.

There was a pending text message, but it wasn't from Blake. It was from a number she didn't recognize. She touched the notification and held the phone up to allow the facial recognition algorithm to do its thing. The text message appeared on the screen.

"Do I have your attention now?" it read.

Ugh.

Haeli tapped in her response. "Wrong number."

Before she could slip the phone back into her pocket, another message came. She considered ignoring it, but curiosity got the better of her. It wasn't as if she was in the middle of anything important.

She opened the text thread.

"The envelope, Haeli. Open it," it said.

Only a few people had her number. Whomever it was, they knew her name. Blake was the most obvious culprit. She had seen him place calls with a spoof number before. Was he back? Setting her up for a surprise? That would be just like him. The question was whether she should play along or call him out.

She couldn't help herself.

"Mick, I know it's you. What are you doing?" she typed.

There was no response.

Fine. I'll play along.

"What envelope?"

Still no response.

Apparently, she was supposed to work for it.

Haeli headed down the stairs to the foyer and checked the small table that sat by the front door. No envelope.

She opened the door, checked the stoop and inside the mailbox. Nothing.

"Blake?" she called out and listened for a response.

She remembered that she hadn't checked the basement. Was the vault door open? Blake was probably down there the whole time, laughing at her.

She headed for the kitchen.

As she reached the end of the hallway, she could already see the brown envelope sitting on the island countertop. She picked it up before heading over to the top of the staircase.

She peeked down at the vault door. Closed.

What are you up to, Mick?

Haeli giggled to herself. She had to admit, she was enjoying the suspense. There were limitless possibilities of what could have been inside the envelope. Tickets to a tropical getaway? Fezz, Khat, and Griff's retirement notices—that would be even better than the tropics. A love poem?

Okay, maybe there is a limit.

Pulling a stool from under the counter, she sat with her elbows resting on the granite. She unfastened the flap and dug into the envelope like a kid on Christmas morning.

A picture?

Haeli looked at the photograph. In it, Blake stood by a fence along the edge of a building, looking over his shoulder at the camera. In the background there was water and a long wooden dock. While she tried to hold on to her excitement, it was changing to confusion. This was Blake in Rhode Island, she assumed, but what was it supposed to mean?

Shoving her hand back into the envelope, she felt the gloss of another photograph. She pulled it out.

Jesus!

Her hands sprung open, and the photograph dropped to the counter.

This wasn't meant to be cute. And it certainly wasn't from Blake.

The picture of the mangled, severed head stared back at her. A pit grew in her stomach. Not because of the gruesomeness of the image, but because she recognized the face.

Haeli's thumbs flew across the screen of her phone. "Who is this?"

"I think you know," read the reply.

And she did. As soon as she saw it, she knew.

"Sokolov," she wrote.

Several messages came in rapid succession.

"I believe you have something of mine."

"I will give you two days to get me my diamonds."

"Text me when you have them. I will send you the address where you will bring them."

"If you fail to do so, the boyfriend dies."

"If you still fail to do so, you will die as well."

Haeli stared at the screen. No matter how hard she tried, she couldn't think of a response. She could tell him that she didn't have his diamonds, but it wouldn't matter. He *thought* she did. And if she knew anything about Sokolov, it was that he was anything but reasonable.

A feeling of rage surged inside of her. For the first time, she understood how Blake felt. She remembered what he had said about Anja and how his work had tainted everything he dared to love. He had expressed his concern that he would bring the same down on her. But now, it was the opposite. It was her that had put Blake in harm's way.

When she was alone, Haeli had accepted the risk. It was understood that every mission brought with it the chance of something going wrong. Something coming back on her, whether at the time or in the future. But it was no longer just her. And it was no longer acceptable.

She knew what had to be done.

Haeli shoved the pictures back into the envelope and moved around the island. She opened the drawer next to the stove and pulled out a pad of paper and a pen.

"Mick," she wrote, "Thank you for asking me to move in with you—"

5

Haeli leaned against the concrete column. Her feet ached and her eyes burned.

From her vantage point, she had a clear view of the guard station. She hoped the opposite wasn't true.

Hundreds of people had moved through the checkpoint over the past several hours. In and out. During that time, she had tried to not so much as blink for fear of missing her opportunity.

But the sun was hanging low in the sky and Haeli was beginning to wonder if this was a fool's errand.

As she lurked in the shadow of the Techyon tower, watching the steady flow of pedestrians passing by the gates on their way to wherever, a tingling sensation ran down her neck. Not from fear, but a sense of foreboding. Like the scene in a horror movie when the unsuspecting teenager is about to open the closet where the intruder is hiding, only to be distracted away at the last minute. It was the same with the oblivious public. Gliding past the Techyon gates like a fly buzzing around the leaves of a Venus flytrap.

Not that there was any danger to passersby. There wasn't. But heaven help anyone with a hair-brained scheme to breach the perimeter, uninvited.

To the casual observer, the Techyon Headquarters building would have looked like any other high-end corporate office complex. Guards, gates, and cameras were common security measures. Expected, even.

But beyond this deliberate facade was a level of security that exceeded most top-secret military installations.

Complex-wide facial recognition, automated airlock doors, gas, and other autonomous weapon systems would be a nasty surprise for anyone dumb enough to try to infiltrate. And then there were the anti-aircraft and anti-missile systems. Thanks to Techyon's own advancements in the field of artificial intelligence, the building itself had the capability of containing and eradicating a small army, if directed to do so.

Luckily, Haeli was not one in the unsuspecting crowd. She knew, even with her knowledge of the layout and inner workings of the security protocols, setting foot anywhere on the property would be a death sentence.

As much as it might have seemed so, Haeli didn't have a death wish. But even if she did, she wouldn't want to give Levi Farr the satisfaction. She had no doubt the founder and CEO of Techyon would love nothing more than to see her shredded to pieces.

It left her with one option. To wait.

After another fifteen minutes or so, she noticed a group of three people emerging from the glass doors at the base of the tower. Two women and one man, each carrying a different style bag. Their body language suggested they were engaged in lighthearted conversation.

As they reached the gate, Haeli could see one of the women smiling and laughing with the other. But it wasn't the women who garnered her attention. It was the arid, clean-cut man with jet black hair who accompanied them.

Even from a distance, she recognized him. His name was Michael Wan, and he was one of the reasons she was there.

As the group cleared the gate, Wan gave a small wave and the two women peeled off toward the south. Wan jogged across the street, straight toward Haeli.

Figures.

Haeli spun around and took up a brisk stride. She headed east for a few hundred feet, fighting the urge to look behind her, and ducked into the first storefront she came upon. It turned out to be a locksmith shop.

An obese man with a scruffy beard slouched behind a cluttered counter, fiddling with a lock cylinder. Based on the run-down state of the shop, Haeli assumed he was the owner and sole employee.

"Can I help you?" the man asked in Hebrew.

"Just looking," she answered in English.

"Ah. You prefer English. But you are Israeli, are you not?"

Haeli turned her back to him and ran her fingers over one of three carousel racks of keys that sat in the front window. She peered out at the street.

The man had dropped the cylinder, but still hadn't bothered to stand. "What are you looking for?"

For a moment, the seemingly nosy question got her dander up. But she realized he was only asking her what she needed. Without turning toward him, she offered an obligatory reply.

"A key."

"No problem," he said. "Give me the one you want to copy, and I'll tell you which ones you can choose from."

As the head and shoulders of Michael Wan streaked across the window, Haeli snapped her head around to face the store owner.

"That's okay." She moved to the door and cracked it open. "I changed my mind."

Haeli stepped onto the sidewalk and waited a few seconds to put a little more distance between herself and Wan. Then she followed.

She matched Wan's pace until he reached the corner and turned left. As soon as he was out of sight, she sprinted to the corner and peeked down the perpendicular street, managing to catch a glimpse just before he disappeared into a doorway.

The nature of his destination wasn't much of a mystery. The two small tables sitting on the sidewalk were a strong clue.

As she approached, the plain black and white sign confirmed her crack detective work.

Nahum Falafel.

Haeli's stomach groaned. She knew what it wanted. A Sabich. It had been too long since she had eaten her favorite food. Eggplant, hard boiled eggs, hummus, tahini, pita. The thought of it brought her back years and caused her to salivate.

But this was no time to get caught up with frivolous cravings. So-called comfort food would provide her none. What she needed was focus.

There was no way to know how long Wan would be. Was he eating in or just picking up? Was he meeting someone there?

She considered going inside, but then thought better of it.

This close to Techyon, the risk of being recognized was high. It was one thing to be on the street where she could flip her hair into her face and wander away from approaching pedestrians. But inside, Wan would be almost certain to make a scene. And a scene was exactly what she wanted to avoid.

To the left of the storefront was a narrow alley. Two sections of corrugated steel blocked its view from the street—one protruding from the falafel restaurant and the other from the adjacent building, a few feet behind the first.

Haeli slipped into the gap and snaked around the second panel.

The alley ran the length of the two buildings and was empty, apart from an array of garbage cans. The seclusion of the tight space brought a sense of relief. It was the first time since she arrived she didn't feel like she was being watched.

Backtracking around the inner panel, Haeli leaned her back against the building. From that angle, she could just see the sidewalk in front of Nahum Falafel's front door. It was a good tactical position, or as good as it was going to get.

Ugh. I need a cigarette.

Haeli didn't smoke. Never had. But in circumstances like this, having a pack of cigarettes on hand was a necessity.

A woman lurking in the entrance to an alley, for example, was likely to stand out. The same woman smoking a cigarette in the same alley— perfectly normal. The average person wouldn't have given it a second thought.

It was an artifact of the fight-or-flight response. Like all animals, the human brain was constantly making connections. Quantifying the level of danger based on how well the details of any circumstance fit with past experience. It was the reason many victims later say they knew something was wrong before they were victimized. But when the brain can justify something, it checks the box and moves on.

Of course, it was moot. She hadn't thought to pick up a pack ahead of time.

The sound of bells jingling signaled the door's movement. Haeli held her breath.

Two men emerged. Neither of them Wan.

They headed in Haeli's direction. She sprung forward, secreting herself behind the front corrugated panel. She waited until they passed, then returned to her original position.

As her back touched the building, the bells sounded off again. This time, it wasn't a false alarm.

Alone and carrying a white plastic bag, Wan stepped out, turned, and headed in her direction.

She slid back behind the panel and bent her knees.

Three, Two—

At the first glimpse of Wan's profile, she uncoiled, launching herself through the gap.

Wan's body lurched as she pressed her chest against his back and flung her right arm around his neck. As her forearm pressed into his throat, she brought her left hand to his chest and leaned her weight backward, pulling him toward the alley.

Instead of giving resistance, as she expected, Wan dropped the bag and threw himself backward, putting Haeli off balance. His momentum pushed them through the gap and into the corrugated steel with a clang.

Crushed between Wan's weight and the immovable panel, Haeli's grip loosened. Wan dipped, slipping his chin under her forearm. He spun around, snapping his elbow toward her face.

With her left palm, Haeli intercepted the blow and squeezed the meaty part of his arm, above the elbow. She drove the web of her right thumb and forefinger into Wan's throat and pushed. Wan stumbled and his back slammed into the side of the building.

Face to face, Haeli applied more pressure. Just long enough to see Wan's steely expression slacken. Not out of defeat, but out of realization.

"Haeli?" he wheezed.

She released her grip and smiled. "Nice to see you, too, Michael."

Wan peeled himself from the brick wall and rubbed his throat. "I thought you were dead?"

"I am." Haeli walked a few steps further into the alley.

Mirroring her movement, Wan's face still carried the look of disbelief—mouth slightly open, brow furrowed, eyeballs fluttering up and down. Haeli stood still, as if offering him an opportunity to take her in. For his mind to catch up.

"You're..." Wan swallowed, then reached out to touch Haeli's cheek. "You're alive."

Haeli realized she hadn't considered how the news of her death would have affected the people she left behind. When she fled Techyon —fled Israel, she understood the pain it would cause. But her death added another layer.

Not that leaving wasn't bad enough. Under the circumstances, she wished she could tell him that leaving was a hard decision. But that would be a lie. It wasn't that she didn't love him, or that she didn't care if she hurt him, but it was what needed to be done. She knew it, and at some level, so did he.

"What are you doing here?" he asked. "How are you here?"

"It's a long story. Which I'll tell you at some point, I promise. But right now, I have to ask you a question. Have you received any threats?"

"Threats? No. From who?"

Haeli pulled a folded photo from her pocket and handed it to Wan.

"God damn." His nose crinkled, and his top lip snarled at the gory image. "It's Goldmann."

"*Was* Goldmann."

"Sokolov," Wan said.

"Yep. I was given this lovely image because, apparently, he thinks we have his diamonds."

Wan folded the picture and handed it back to Haeli. He let out an unenthusiastic laugh. "Of course he does. Because Goldmann probably pointed the finger at us to avoid getting his head cut off. And how'd that work out for him?"

"About as well as it's going to work out for us now that Sokolov thinks we have them. He'll come for us. You know he will. All of us."

"This just keeps getting better, doesn't it? Goldmann steals the diamonds, almost gets us killed, and screws the whole operation. Now, this? We shouldn't have been involved in the first place."

"No, we shouldn't have," Haeli said. "But it wasn't our call."

"So, what do we do now?"

"I don't know yet. I just wanted to give you the heads up. Now, I need to find Chet and Little Ricky." The other two members of their team, Chet Ornal and Richard "Little Ricky" Bender had been reassigned before she left. She had no idea where in the world they could be. "Do you know where they are?"

Haeli pictured the faces of her two old friends. A fleeting sadness passed through her. She never got the opportunity to say goodbye to them, like she had with Wan. Even though she was only there to warn them, she found herself looking forward to the chance to make amends.

"Rick's in Germany, running training exercises. Chet's back at HQ, working on a smart weapons project. But I haven't seen him in a while. I can call them."

"Don't," Haeli said. "Sokolov contacted me on my cell, which means he's already monitoring it. Mine's off. You should do the same." Haeli reached into her bag and pulled out a phone. "Here, I've got an extra burner. Take it."

Wan nodded. He accepted the device, then produced his own cell phone to shut it off.

"My number's already programmed in there, it's the only contact," Haeli said. "I'll pick up another prepaid phone for Chet after this. Once

I figure out where I'm staying, I'll call you and let you know where I'll be."

"Don't be ridiculous. You've already got a place to stay. I've got two bedrooms and it's just me. It'll be safer."

"I don't know." Haeli noticed how Wan had perked up at his suggestion. "I'm not sure it's a good idea."

"Why?"

"You know why."

"Look, Sokolov contacted you, but not me. And I'm sure I would have heard about it already if Chet or Little Ricky had received anything. There's a good chance that you are the only one he's tracked down. Which means you'll be safe there. No hotel staff or surveillance cameras to worry about. Plus, just in case Sokolov's men do show up, it'd be better if we stuck together. At least we'd have a fighting chance."

Haeli groaned. "Fine." Sokolov had nothing to do with why she thought it might be a bad idea, but she decided to let it go. "I've got a few things I need to do. Text me your address and I'll come by a little later."

"Okay." Wan's eager fingers started typing. "Sending it now."

"While you're at it, text me Chet's address. I'll swing by to see if he's home."

"No way, Haeli. It's too risky. We'll go together."

"Michael, I'm not gonna—" Haeli closed her eyes and took a deep breath. "Never mind. You win." She motioned in the direction of the street. "Lead the way."

6

Two Years Ago. Haeli took the steps three at a time. At the top of the main staircase, Richard Bender stood waiting.

"What the hell is this about?" Bender said as Haeli reached the top. They walked.

"Don't know, but it's gotta be somethin' good," Haeli said. "Frank doesn't call a briefing with an hour's notice unless it's worth it."

"All I know is I'm supposed to go on leave in three days."

"That's right. The Greek goddess, right?"

"Her name's Maria. And it's Cyprus." Bender rolled his eyes. "But you know that."

Haeli chuckled. "Sorry, I forgot. It's been a whole twelve hours since you've mentioned her."

"I'm just saying. She's expecting me."

They reached the door to the conference room. Haeli squeezed Bender's shoulder.

"I'm sure you'll make your play-date. These things are fast and furious."

"I hope so." Bender flung the door open and motioned for Haeli to enter.

She took him up on his offer.

Inside, four people sat at the long boardroom table. On one side, her other team members, Michael Wan and Chet Ornal. On the other, the director of special operations, Frank Borstrom, and another man. Someone she hadn't met before.

"Thank you for your prompt response," Frank said. "Let me introduce a very special client. Mister Adam Goldmann."

Goldmann lifted himself from his chair, halfway between a sitting and standing position. He raised his hand in an indifferent wave.

Haeli had no idea who the man was or why he was there, but she was already put off by his mannerisms. Slightly overweight, with prominent bags under his eyes, he looked like a cocaine addict coming off a five-day bender. He had curly black hair, which he had tried to slick back with some kind of product. The top three buttons of his shirt were open, presumably to display the two gaudy gold chains that hung around his neck.

"Pleasure." Haeli took a seat next to Wan.

Goldmann sat.

Frank continued. "Mister Goldmann is in need of our assistance. I will let him fill you in. Please."

Goldman cleared his throat. "Thank you. Tomorrow, I will be traveling to Botswana to make a large purchase. I need you to ensure my security."

And?

Haeli waited for the rest of the story. Goldmann was clearly Israeli and, so it seemed, some type of businessman. The question was, what did that have to do with her and her team? She looked to Frank.

Frank took the hint. "Mister Goldmann is one of the premiere diamond dealers in Ramat Gan."

Goldmann smacked his lips.

Frank rephrased. "*The* premiere diamond dealer."

This was no surprise. Although technically in the city of Tel Aviv, Techyon headquarters sat in walking distance to the city line of Ramat Gan, the home of Israel's diamond exchange. One couldn't throw a rock without hitting a diamond dealer. But none of this explained why her team was there.

"To be clear," Frank said, "Mister Goldmann is going to be visiting the Kabo diamond mine in Botswana. He will be carrying an extremely large sum of cash and will be returning to Israel with a large quantity of diamonds. Simply put, your job is to make sure this happens without any issues."

"Are you serious?" Haeli asked.

Wan put his hand on Haeli's shoulder. She could feel him willing her to hold her tongue.

Frank ignored her. "Mister Goldmann has provided his itinerary, which has been included in your briefing notes. This is a one-night trip. In and out." Frank turned to Goldmann. "Mister Goldmann, per our protocol, you will refer to these four individuals by the following code names." He pointed at Haeli. "Principe." He looked back at his sheet, then pointed at Wan. "Celer." Then at Bender. "Fortis." And finally, at Ornal. "Acer."

Principe.

As code names go, it wasn't the worst. Every mission came with a new set of them. Animals, colors, days of the week. This time it seemed to be Latin or, at least something resembling Latin. As silly as it seemed, it was worth the effort. The names protected their identities and segmented one mission from the next. Any mention of the randomized monikers in later intelligence chatter would allow them to pinpoint the exact time frame and circumstances of the source.

Goldmann slumped and wiped his forearm across his forehead. Beads of sweat appeared as quickly as they were removed.

"I apologize if these names are a little much to remember," Frank said. "I've printed them out for you as a reference."

Goldmann stood up. "Principe, Celer, Fortis, and Acer. Fine. So are we all set for tomorrow?"

"Yes, of course. The team will pick you up at o' five-hundred."

"Good. Yes, very good. Thank you." Goldmann walked toward the door.

Frank stood and followed. "Let me show you out."

"Frank," Haeli said. "Can I talk to you?"

"Hold tight. I'll be back in a minute. Right this way Mister Goldmann." Frank opened the door and escorted Goldmann out. He shot a look at Haeli before closing the door behind him.

"This is bullshit," Haeli said.

"What did you do this time, Chet?" Wan said.

"What do you mean, 'what did I do?' I didn't do anything."

Wan slapped his hands on the table. "Well, somebody did. Why else are we being punished?"

"Why's it gotta be me?" Ornal asked. "Ask Little Ricky what he did."

"Hold on," Bender said. "There's gotta be more to this than they're letting on. Wait for Frank. I'm sure he's got a good reason."

Wan chimed in. "He's got a reason. But I bet it's not a good one."

"Was it just me or was anyone else skeeved out by that guy?" Haeli asked. "He seemed too nervous."

Ornal started to answer, but abandoned his comment when Frank appeared in the doorway.

"So?" Wan asked.

"So, what?" Frank shrugged.

"So, what the hell are we doing?" Haeli added. "Personal security detail? That's not what we do, Frank. This company has a whole division for security. We're a tactical team. This is special operations. Or did I miss something?"

"I know it's a change of pace," Frank said.

"Come on, Frank," Wan said. "It's babysitting duty."

"Look, this comes directly from Levi. He specifically ordered me to assign this to you."

"Is this guy a friend of his or something?" Bender asked.

Frank raised his voice. "I don't know! If you have a problem with it, take it up with Levi!"

The room fell silent.

"Look," Frank said. "I don't know what to tell you. It's beneath you, I get it. But it's an easy gig you can manage in your sleep. So, stop complaining and just get it done. Levi's happy. Everybody's happy. End of discussion. Go do your prep. I'll touch base when you get back."

Haeli stopped herself from throwing in the last word. After years of working for Frank Borstrom, they had established a friendly rapport. But it was best she didn't push her luck.

Frank left the room, and it again fell into silence.

After a moment, Wan picked up the bound packet off the table in front of him. He flipped the cover, leaned back in his chair, and turned to Haeli. "Principe. We're all ears."

7

ONE WEEK AGO. EVGENI BABIN DOWNSHIFTED AND SQUEEZED THE BRAKE levers, bringing the red and white Ducati Panigale to an abrupt stop, inches from the garage bay door.

He straddled the bike as he rooted around in the side pocket of his Kevlar jacket for the remote control. When he felt it in his hand, he pressed the top button without removing the plastic box from his pocket.

The door squealed and began rising. Like the curtain of an opera house, the retreating overhead door would unveil a true work of art.

It had taken Evgeni years to find and collect the over twenty motor-cycles he stored in the garage. And there was nothing he loved more than looking at them as a group. Ducatis, Indians, Triumphs, Harleys. Each special in their own right.

As an analyst, Babin found his day job stifling. Frankly, he found the whole of Israel stifling. Every morning, upon arriving at Techyon Headquarters, he would curse himself for showing up. After eight hours in a windowless room, staring at a computer screen, he would swear he wouldn't come back the next day.

So the cycle went, day after day. But his talent for recognizing patterns made him a perfect fit for the job. Plus, it wasn't like he was given a choice.

It was his hobby that brought whatever joy he had in his life. To anyone else, this place was an overcrowded storage shed. To him, it was Disneyland.

He held the clutch and twisted the throttle. Like a dose of medicine, the Ducati let out a melodic growl.

While Evgeni owned a few daily riders—a BMW 1250 RT, Suzuki GSX-R, and a Harley Davidson Sportster—some of the bikes in his collection he had only ridden once or twice for fear of marring them. The Ducati Panigale was one of them.

But it was a beautiful day and a special occasion. It was his thirty-fifth birthday. A jaunt on the one-hundred-sixty horsepower crotch-rocket was his birthday present to himself. That, and the new toy that was in transit from Germany.

As the Ducati's motor wound back down to a purr, Evgeni could hear the twang of the overhead chain. He skipped a breath as the bottom of the door passed his eyeline and a sea of gleaming chrome and brightly colored plastic seemed to spill out toward him. He smiled.

Then he saw something else. Something that wiped the smile right off his face.

Sitting in the saddle of a Harley Road King was Pavel Nikitin. And judging by the suppressor attached to the end of the pistol he was pointing at Evgeni, Nikitin wasn't there to extend happy birthday wishes.

Babin's first reaction was to run. So much so that his body threatened to act without his mind's consent. Luckily, he recovered his wits in time to rein in his muscles. If he were to run, he would never be able to stop running. Ever. Besides, he wasn't going to outrun a bullet. Even on a Ducati.

Pressing the kickstand down with his boot, Babin rocked the bike back and swung his leg over the saddle.

Stay calm.

"Pavel. Friend." He shut the bike off. "This is a surprise. Is something wrong?"

Nikitin shook his head. "Depends."

Evgeni took a few steps inside. He watched the muzzle of Nikitin's gun track his movements.

"Depends on what?"

Nikitin ran his free hand along the handlebars of the Road King. "On you."

"No, no, no." Evgeni wagged his finger. "I'm not killing anyone. I'm done. I paid my debt."

"Who told you this? Did I tell you this?"

"No. No one told me. But I've done everything you asked." Evgeni lowered his voice. "I murdered a man, Pavel. And I don't even know what he did to deserve it."

Nikitin laughed. "And you think this was payment of your debt? This is only a test. To prove your loyalty. Your debt is paid when he says it is."

"Then what? Did I do something wrong?"

"I need you to do something—"

Evgeni raised a hand as if he were going to interject.

"Don't worry. This is easy thing." Nikitin pulled out a folded piece of paper, pinched it between two fingers and held it out toward Evgeni. "Come, take it."

In a tentative dance between man and machines, Evgeni weaved through the motorcycles until he was close enough to reach the piece of paper. He retreated a few feet and unfolded it.

"Botswana? I don't understand. What are these dates?"

"We need to know names. Those who provide security for Adam Goldmann in Botswana on these days. That's all." Nikitin shrugged. "See? For you—easy."

"I can't." Evgeni's voice trembled. "I don't have access to these kinds of records. I don't even know where they're kept. And even if I did—if I got caught, they'd kill me."

"You would already be dead if not for us. Or did you forget who got you out of Russia—who avenged your father?"

"I didn't forget. It's just—why don't I get you something else?

There's a lot of good information I can give you. Tons of it. But what you ask, it's not possible."

"Everything is possible. It is possible for you to own all these motorcycles, yes? And tell me, how is this possible?"

Evgeni bowed his head. "Because of Mister Sokolov."

Nikitin grinned his jagged grin. "That is right. This means that all these things belong to him. You agree?"

There was no right answer to his question, and Evgeni knew it. As his response, he offered only a blank stare.

Holding the pistol level, Nikitin dismounted the bike, crouched, and lifted a plastic gas can off the floor by his feet. Without another word, he began pouring gasoline over the Harley Davidson. Then he moved on to the Triumph, which sat to its right.

"Wait. Please, don't."

Nikitin moved on to another motorcycle.

"All right, I'll do it!"

"What will you do?" Nikitin doused yet another.

"Stop it, please, Pavel," Evgeni pleaded. "I'll get you your names. Just don't burn them."

Nikitin tossed the can. It landed on its side and gasoline poured onto the floor.

Evgeni stood frozen as Nikitin worked his way over to him, the suppressor leading the way until it was pressed against Evgeni's forehead.

With his left hand, Nikitin pointed at the floor. Evgeni dropped to his knees.

"If you cannot get the records, you will find another way. One of them is called Haeli. Find out who she is and who she was working with. And do not forget, if you fail, they will all burn." Nikitin pressed the pistol further into his flesh. He leaned in and whispered, "And you will burn with them."

The pressure on Evgeni's forehead released, leaving a circular impression behind. He stayed on his knees, eyes lowered, as Nikitin walked toward the bay door.

From behind him, Evgeni heard the click of the door control, followed by the grinding of the casters as the door began to close. Then he heard another familiar sound. The chatter of the ignition and the Ducati's motor roaring to life.

Evgeni jumped to his feet and bolted toward the door. He ducked under it, just in time to watch the tail end of his beloved bike tearing out of the driveway.

8

Two Years Ago. Haeli tightened the valves. The flow of water dropped to a trickle, and then a slowing drip. She gathered her hair and wrung it out, then stepped out of the shower and onto the bathmat.

"Toss me a towel?" Haeli said.

Wearing only a pair of blue boxer briefs, Michael Wan was bent over the sink, working a toothbrush with vigor. Defined striations ran from his abdomen and along his side toward his bulging lats. Whatever Wan was or wasn't, Haeli knew one thing for sure—the man was as hot as hell.

He rinsed off the toothbrush, pulled a towel from the towel bar, and turned toward her. He hesitated.

Confined to the three-by-two terrycloth island, Haeli could feel his gaze lock onto her body. It excited her. She could feel her skin warming and tightening. As he drew closer, her legs trembled.

Grasping the towel at each end, Wan flipped it over her head and across her back. His smoldering gaze meeting hers. He pulled, squeezing her dripping wet body against his.

Then he kissed her. Or she kissed him. Either way, she lost herself in its depth and passion. Her body and mind throbbed in unison. Given another few seconds, she would have completely forgotten that there was somewhere they needed to be.

Haeli slid her hands upward and rested her palms on his swollen pecs. With a gentle push, she leaned her head back. Their lips parted.

"Ugh. We don't have time. We're gonna be late," she said.

"So, we'll be a little late." He leaned in and kissed her again.

For a moment, she indulged. Then she shoved him. This time, hard enough to cause him to take a step back and release one end of the towel.

Haeli snatched it from his hand and wrapped it around herself. "I don't do 'late.' And by the way, neither do you."

"You're so mean to me." Wan smiled.

"Hey, you're the reason I needed a second shower in the first place. I think you'll be all right. Now, get dressed."

Haeli walked into the bedroom and gathered her clothes from the floor. The same clothes she had picked out earlier and worn for about ten minutes.

She got dressed.

They weren't far from headquarters, but far enough that they'd have to drive to make it in time. It was the one thing she missed about living in the residence quarters. Then, she could roll out of bed and already be at work.

At first, she hadn't been eager to leave. Having grown up in the facility, it was comfortable to her. Even when she turned eighteen and started working for the company as a paid employee, she'd stayed for several more years. It was a perk unavailable to most—especially low-level operators. But because her father was who he was, she was made an exception.

As she reached her mid-twenties, a feeling of claustrophobia started setting in. She needed to get out on her own. To live her own life, if not her best life.

The apartment was nothing to look at. In fact, it was kind of a shithole. But it was hers and she was content there. So there she stayed.

Wan came into the room, picked up his pants, and set about

climbing into them. "What do we need a briefing for, anyway? I'm sure it's gonna be no different than the other two times."

"Who knows? Maybe he's changin' it up this time. Anyway, what are you complaining about? Frank was right, it's the easiest gig in the world and the bonuses are stupid good."

Wan shrugged. "That's what I don't get. Why are we getting paid so much extra to do next to nothing?"

"Just because nothing happened the last two times, or the last hundred times, doesn't mean it won't the next time. That's the danger with stuff like this. We can't get complacent."

"No, you're right. I just hope there's an end to it. Or are we gonna have to take these runs forever?"

"My guess is we'll be doing it until somethin' real goes down while we're away playing Kevin Costner. Watch how fast Frank changes his tune then." Haeli grabbed her bag and headed to the door. "I'll pull the car around. Meet me out front. And hurry up."

* * *

HAELI AND WAN STEPPED INTO THE EXPANSIVE LOBBY. AT THIS TIME OF morning, it was like Heathrow Airport. Dozens of people moved across the marble floor in intercepting patterns. All of them in their own heads, consumed with whatever temporarily dire tasks were atop their mental dockets.

Above, the overhanging corridors, separated from open air by glass-panel railings, teemed with employees of all walks. From lab technicians to executives. From operators to janitors.

At the top of the main staircase, leading to the second-floor reception atrium, Haeli could see Bender loitering.

They made their way to the steps.

"Little Ricky's gonna be all bent outta shape we're rollin' in hot." Haeli slapped Wan's backside. "I'll just blame it on you."

Wan chuckled.

As they reached the top step, they split apart, moving around either side of Bender. "Hey, Rick," Haeli said while she continued walking.

Bender caught up and fell in next to them. "Cutting it close, aren't we?"

"You know you don't have to wait for us. You can just go in," Haeli said.

"I know that."

"What?" Wan said. "You got someplace else to be? Another hot date with Aphrodite?"

"Her name's Maria. And no, doesn't look like it."

"Uh oh," Wan said, "trouble in paradise?"

They reached the double doors of the boardroom.

"She and I are done." Bender paused. "I think... I don't know."

"Shit. Sorry, man." Wan squeezed his neck.

"Can we do this later?" Haeli pushed between Wan and Bender, opened the door, and entered. The other two clamored in behind her.

What Haeli walked into was not what she expected.

What is this?

Ornal was already in the room. So was Goldmann. But Frank wasn't there. Instead, Levi Farr himself stood at the end of the table. The sober look on his face set off her internal alarm.

Standing behind Goldmann were two bearded men, one larger than the other and both wearing white button-down shirts with the sleeves rolled up to the elbow. Like Levi, neither of them looked happy to be there.

Haeli shot a look at Wan. She wondered if he had gotten the same vibe—like they had just barged into a funeral, waving streamers and blowing into the plastic noisemakers they hand out on New Year's Eve. Judging by the size of Wan's eyes, he had.

"Close the door," Levi said. "Take a seat."

Haeli pulled up a chair next to Ornal and across from Goldmann. Wan and Bender filed in next to her.

Levi sat. At the head of the table, he was a good ten feet away from anyone else. "You know Mister Goldmann. I'm guessing I don't have to tell you who our other guests are."

Mossad.

Israeli intelligence. She knew as soon as she laid eyes on them. What she didn't know was why they were there.

"Gentleman." Levi lifted his hand toward the two agents, palm up.

The larger of the two spoke.

"I am Ari. This is Gram. It is time you are all fully briefed into this mission."

Mission? What mission?

"As of zero three hundred hours this morning," Ari continued, "our friend, Adam Goldmann here, has graciously agreed to cooperate with the State of Israel. Apparently, he is rather put off by the idea of spending his life in prison."

Haeli looked at Goldmann. His usual nervous energy was missing. He remained inanimate with his eyes lowered toward the table. He was exhausted. Or relieved. Or both.

What was he involved in?

Haeli raised her hand, then spoke. "Did something happen that we weren't aware of?"

Ari nodded. "Safe to say. Let me give you the synopsis. Then we'll answer any questions you might have." He stepped away from Goldmann and began pacing in a tight pattern.

Gram stayed planted to the floor.

"Two months ago, we intercepted information that a well-known Israeli diamond dealer was working for the head of a Russian crime syndicate. A former KGB agent named Olezka Sokolov. Ever heard of him?"

Haeli shook her head. She looked to either side. Her teammates hadn't either.

"Sokolov is a major player in eastern Europe, but also throughout the world. He has powerful connections and is known to be extremely dangerous."

"Are you telling us Goldmann works for the Russian Mafia?" Wan asked.

Goldmann raised his head and glared at Wan. Haeli noticed the tears welling in his eyes. "Sokolov took my family. My wife. My children. He threatened to kill them if I didn't do what he said. I should never have let them travel to Turkey without me. And now—" Goldmann slammed his hands on the table. "What was I supposed to do?"

"Enough," Ari said. "This is true. His family was taken from their hotel room. Local assets have reason to believe the men involved were SVR—Russian Foreign Intelligence operatives. The information we've compiled suggests that in exchange for being allowed to operate his criminal enterprise, Sokolov has agreed to provide certain services. Things the Kremlin wishes to keep itself distanced from. That's where Goldmann comes in."

"It makes no sense," Ornal said, "why would the SVR need Goldmann to buy diamonds?"

"Because they're not buying diamonds," Ari replied. "They needed Goldmann, or someone like him, to make it look like the transactions were legitimate. He happened to be the lucky winner. When you were escorting him to Botswana, it wasn't cash in that briefcase. It was diamonds. Raw, uncut diamonds."

"Wait," Wan said. "We've been bringing diamonds *to* a diamond mine? In exchange for what?"

"Uranium." Haeli blurted. Her brain churned. Like a game of Sudoku, once a few pieces of the puzzle were filled in, the rest started falling into place. It all made sense now. "It isn't a diamond mine. It's just supposed to seem like one."

Ari smiled and pointed at Haeli.

"Of course." Wan's excitement surpassed Haeli's. "They sell off the raw diamonds as if they were a product of the mine. From the outside, everything looks legitimate. It's brilliant."

"What we didn't know, until yesterday, was how and where the uranium was being delivered. Our Russian assets hadn't heard anything, and all of the regular players were dark. We were at a loss, until—"

"You followed the money," Haeli said.

"Exactly. How do you not work for us already?" He turned to Gram. "How does she not work for us already?"

Haeli took it as an attempt at humor, though Ari hadn't so much as cracked a smile.

"Yes. We followed the money. Through Sokolov to Moscow. From Moscow to Tehran."

"You son of a bitch." Haeli stood up. Her face flushed with rage. She wanted nothing more than to climb over the table and beat Goldmann's face to a pulp.

Iran was the single biggest threat to Israel. Especially their nuclear weapons program. She was convinced that the moment Iran had the capability, they would try to wipe Israel off the map. And Goldmann, an Israeli, was helping them get there. Forget beating him. She could kill him.

Levi stood up. "Haeli! Sit down."

The use of her real name rang in her ears. She could see the acknowledgement on Goldmann's smug face. She despised him. Even more so now that he knew her name. But she managed to calm herself. With a deep breath, she lowered into her seat. "You knew the whole time?" She shifted her attention from the two Mossad agents to Levi. "And so did you."

"It's why I put your team on this," Levi said.

"Why didn't Sokolov put his own people on it?"

Goldmann started to speak, then paused and looked at Ari as if seeking his permission. Ari nodded and Goldman continued. "He told me he wanted me to do everything I would normally do, so it didn't look suspicious. The few times I've had to travel with a lot of cash, I hired someone through Techyon for security. So, that's what I did. I called you."

"When we intercepted the call, we contacted Levi." Ari said. "We agreed to wait and see how things played out. Your first two trips were under surveillance, but now that we know the uranium ends up in Iran, we no longer have time to waste. We have orders to put their operation down, permanently. Which, politically, will be a bit tricky. The Kabo mine is half-owned by Neo Molefi, who I believe you've met. The other half is owned by the corrupt Botswana government. You can understand how this complicates things a bit. We're going to need some solid proof before we can pull this off."

"So, what's the plan?" Ornal asked. It was proof that he was listening, after all.

"You're going to make the trip in exactly the same way you did before. As you know, Goldmann and Molefi meet privately, once he's safely at Kabo. This time he'll be wired with audio and video. He knows what he has to do, right Adam?"

Goldmann offered no reaction.

"In a perfect world, I'd love to get something more than just the transaction." Ari said.

Haeli leaned forward on her elbows. Compared to the last two trips, this one was shaping up to be a lot more interesting. "What do you have in mind?"

Ari smiled. "I'm glad you asked. Since the Kabo mine changed hands, the open pit has been abandoned in favor of a cave mining technique. Which means tunnels are dug under the deposits and the ore is extracted from underneath. The ore is loaded onto an underground rail that carries it to an adjacent facility for processing. If we could get pictures and video of the processing facility, it would be ideal. But it's likely not feasible. Like the mine, it's highly secure and you'll have no business there. The next best option is to somehow get access to one of the drawpoints.

"Drawpoints?" Bender asked.

"Yes. There are a few places where the ore is extracted and loaded onto the rail for transport. These areas are called drawpoints, and they move as deposits are depleted. Obviously, our satellites aren't of any use. If your team were able to access one of these areas and obtain a soil sample, documented by video, we would have the proof we need to put pressure on Botswana."

"Gentlemen," Levi said. "What you're asking of my people is extremely risky."

"I know, I know." Ari held his palms outward. "I'm not saying it will even be possible. But if you can create an opportunity to break away, undetected, it would go a long way to ensure our national security. And trust me, you will all be well compensated."

"We're in." Haeli said. "My team will get you what you need. Right?" Haeli looked to the others.

"Absolutely," Wan said. "Get us everything you have on Kabo. We'll find a way in."

Ari turned to Levi. The room fell into silence as all attention shifted toward the end of the table. Levi let out a loud exhale and then nodded.

"Excellent," Ari said. "You leave the day after tomorrow. We'll meet tomorrow afternoon to do a final walk through of the arrangements. Gram, anything to add?"

Gram glared at Ornal, then worked his way down the line.

"No."

9

Four Days Ago. "Where am I?" Chet Ornal squinted and turned his head toward the source of what little light was available. The blurred splotches resolved into a row of square windows along the roof line some thirty feet above. It was an old industrial building. What kind, he didn't know.

He felt the swelling in his lips. Tasted the blood in his mouth. His instinct was to touch his face. To read the story in the lumps and cuts like Braille. But his wrists snapped against the cuffs, fastened through the chair's back supports.

The balcony.

He remembered it now. The sound of glass breaking. The sense of disoriented panic.

Despite being awoken from a dead sleep, he had the wherewithal to roll over and open the bedside drawer. But it was too little, too late. Before he could grasp the pistol, the men had already descended on him.

Out of the corner of his eye, he saw movement. He twisted as quickly as his sore, stiff neck would allow. A man was approaching.

"Who are you? What do you want?"

Ornal could guess what he wanted. What they all wanted. Information.

Since joining the weapons program, he had been hypervigilant about this type of scenario. It was no secret that foreign adversaries would do anything to get their hands on the innovations he was now privy to. In fact, before transferring to the new job, he was required to retake training on resisting enhanced interrogation techniques. It was supposed to give him strategic options in the "unlikely case" something like this were to happen. He only hoped he had what it would take to endure whatever came next.

As the man came closer, and Ornal could see his features in more detail, his pulse quickened. Ornal had never met or seen or even heard of Pavel Nikitin, but it didn't matter. His scarred, busted face spoke volumes about the type of man he was, and the type of conversation this was going to be.

"Listen," Ornal said, "I know what you think, but you've got the wrong guy. I'm a grunt, man. I don't have access to secrets or anything like that."

"You would tell me if you did?" Nikitin asked.

He's Russian.

There was no mistaking the accent. But why were the Russians taking such drastic action? What did they already know about the program?

"Yes, yes, of course I would. Look at me. I'm chained up. The way I see it, I've got no other choice but to tell you whatever you want to know. But I guarantee, I don't know anything that would be of use to you."

Ornal winced. He knew he was laying it on too thick, too soon.

Nikitin laughed. "You are terrible liar. Good thing for you, I don't give shit about your work."

"You don't? What then?"

"My boss wants to talk to you about personal matter."

"Who's your boss?"

"You ask him yourself."

The click and scuff of each footfall echoed through the empty space. Ornal tried to look over his shoulder, but the limited range of motion in his neck prevented him from doing so. He wondered if it could be broken. Sprained, at the least.

From Ornal's left, the second man circled around and came into view.

Sokolov.

While he had never met Sokolov, he had seen dozens of pictures. And after what had happened two years prior, he wasn't likely to ever forget his face.

"Is this about Goldmann?" Ornal laughed. It amplified the pain in his chest and caused him to cough, which made it worse. "Come on, seriously? I don't know where he is if that's what you want to know."

"I know where he is." Sokolov said. "Every piece of him. What you're going to tell me is where my diamonds are."

"Your diamonds? How the hell am I supposed to know?"

Nikitin swooped in with a blow to Ornal's ribs. Ornal stomped his feet as he gasped for air through the pain.

"You do not hear me," Sokolov said. "From now on, every lie you tell, Pavel is going to cut off a piece of you."

Nikitin produced a blade from a sheath, fastened to his belt.

Ornal had initially felt a sense of relief and genuine amusement at the realization this was about something he had no knowledge of. Now, not as much.

Urgency returned to his demeanor. "Goldmann's the one who stole from you. He screwed us and took off with the case. I figured you already knew that."

Nikitin twitched. Sokolov held up his hand to keep his dog at bay. "You see Pavel, this is a clever guy. These are not lies. Mister Goldmann did steal my case. This is true. I will ask better question."

Sokolov took a step toward Nikitin and held his hand out. Nikitin placed the handle of the knife into Sokolov's palm. In one fluid motion, Sokolov spun around and drove the blade into Ornal's thigh. He twisted the handle as he punctuated each word. "Where are my fucking diamonds?"

Ornal cried out and squirmed against his restraints. As soon as he regained the ability to speak, the words gushed out in a rapid stream. "No one cared about your diamonds. We were there about the uranium. We were there to shut you down. I swear to God, I never saw them. I never even saw inside the case. Goldmann played us, just like he played you."

Sokolov let go of the knife and straightened his back. His eyes glazed over. Ornal hoped it was a sign of contemplation and not rage.

Nikitin grabbed the handle and ripped the blade free from Ornal's flesh. Ornal braced himself, but the pain wasn't as bad as he anticipated. It was more of a relief than anything else.

Nikitin disappeared around the back of the chair.

Ornal knew Sokolov didn't believe him. Sokolov was convinced Ornal knew where the diamonds were and wasn't going to accept anything less than a full confession. But Ornal had nothing to give him. Not even enough information to make something up.

There was no sense in denying it. Ornal was a dead man. But in the resignation, he was surprised to find that his biggest concern was not for himself, but for his team. He wished he could warn them. It saddened him to know the same fate was in store for them, and like him, they would never see it coming.

Escape was impossible. Handcuffed and injured, Ornal stood no chance against two men. Especially not these men. He could try to fight, but he couldn't win. Then again, he thought, what was the worst that could happen? He couldn't get *more* dead.

Ornal felt Nikitin's fingers clamp onto his ear. With all his might, he threw himself forward and into a standing position—the chair still attached at his back. He spun, sending the wooden legs careening into Sokolov's midsection. The legs splintered under the force. Sokolov didn't budge.

A smile flashed over Sokolov's face as he cocked back his fist and drove it into Ornal's nose. Ornal staggered backward and landed on the chair. The broken legs sent him to the concrete floor. The blood, pooling around his mouth and nose, bubbled as he groaned.

"Pavel, a moment." Sokolov said.

Pavel stepped over Ornal, and the two men walked away. Ornal watched their fuzzy forms recede as he lost consciousness.

* * *

"He does not know," Sokolov said.

"Possible," Nikitin replied. "Or he has not had enough pain."

"You are free to keep trying, but believe me, he will not have the answers we need."

"Should I bring another? The one who remains in Israel?"

"No, not yet." Sokolov ran the nail of his pinky between his two front teeth and then examined it. "We need pressure. These people are not who we thought they were. This one knows about the uranium. These are not hired muscle. No. These are spies. They will not be so easy to break. We need to find out what they care about it. I want to know everything about them. Who they are sleeping with, what family they have, what kind of pets they have. What are their secrets?"

"You want me to keep this one? Until we know more?"

"No. He is spent. I need you to go to the United States and handle the woman, Haeli. She is believed to be dead, yes? Someone makes themself disappear, they have done something they should not have done."

Nikitin thumped his chest with his fist. "I will handle her."

"We will take a different approach. I will give you instructions before you leave. For now, you can clean up this mess."

"With pleasure."

"And Pavel... Before you kill him, find out what he's been working on. It may be information I can sell."

Nikitin grinned his rotten grin. He withdrew his knife and set off to finish his work.

10

"You see them often?"

"No, not really," Wan said. "Since you left, it hasn't been the same. Everyone's moved on to different things. We do talk once in a while. Even got together four or five months ago. Little Ricky was dating this girl who does stand-up comedy. He asked if we wanted to come out and see her perform."

Haeli scanned the cars parked in front of the twelve-story apartment building. They were all empty. She did the same with the row of balconies running up the center of the building, staggered like the teeth of a giant concrete zipper. As far as she could tell, there weren't any eyes on them.

Haeli followed Wan toward the front entrance. "Was she any good?"

Wan grimaced. "No. Not at all."

Haeli laughed.

"But we had a good time. Got sloshed. You know, like old times."

She did know, and she missed it. The comradery. The antics. Despite all the hairy situations they had gotten themselves into, and out of, as a team, it was the goofy stuff that stood out in her memory. It was much like when she was with Blake and Griff and the others.

Wan pulled the heavy brass door and held it. "It's apartment 12B."

Haeli entered, surveying the interior. On the way over, she searched online real estate listings, finding two units for sale in the building. The listings provided pictures of the units' interiors. Each layout the mirror image of the other, but otherwise identical. It wasn't much, but she'd take whatever preparation she could get.

There were no pictures of the lobby, which she was surprised to find was less grand than one would assume, given the price tag. But while it was small and the ceilings were low, the light-colored tile and modern minimalist decor prevented it from being stuffy.

The only furnishings to speak of were a plush bench, perpendicular to the south wall on the left, and a white lacquered podium to the right. An older man with kind eyes and a sharp gray suit had departed the rear of the podium and was already descending on them. She assumed him to be the doorman.

"Can I help you?" the man asked in Hebrew.

Wan answered. And just as well—she was a little rusty and he was always better at speaking Hebrew, anyway. "We're just visiting a friend."

"May I have the name?"

"Chet Ornal. 12B."

"And your name?" The doorman moved to the front of the podium, reached over and picked up an acrylic clipboard.

Wan shot Haeli a look. Neither of them had expected the inquisition.

"We're not on the list," Wan said. "He's not expecting us."

Haeli chimed in. "We were in the area and figured we'd drop in and say hello."

"I will call up to Mister Ornal." Retreating behind his perch, the doorman lifted a receiver. "Who shall I say is asking?"

"Uh..." Wan stuttered. Haeli understood his reservation. Sokolov could be listening. Haeli was hoping to keep her little trip to the Middle East a secret for as long as possible. If he were to catch wind that she was there, she would lose any advantage her anonymity afforded her.

"Adam Goldmann," Wan said.

Haeli glared at Wan, her jaw locked in a dramatic clench and her eyes slightly squinted. The universal expression of disapproval, or so she intended it to be. Speaking that name was worse than giving their own. Wan's only response to her scowl was a shrug and a guilty grin.

"I'm sorry," the doorman said. "It doesn't appear that he is in at the moment. It seems your trip has been a waste."

"No, no. We were in the area—"

Wan took Haeli by the arm. "Thank you. Sorry for the trouble. We'll just give him a call later." Wan headed for the door with Haeli in tow.

Outside, Wan stopped, their backs toward the door.

"We've got to find another way in," he said to the buildings across the street.

"I don't think so," Haeli said. "I say we walk back in there, call the elevator, and go to the twelfth floor. He's a doorman. And he seems like a nice old man. What's he going to do to stop us?"

"He'll call the police, that's what he'll do."

"And by the time they get here, we'll be gone. You, me, and hopefully Chet, too."

"Fine. You go to the elevator, I'll distract him."

As they passed back through the door, Wan made a beeline for the podium. Haeli sauntered over to the elevators.

"We were thinking," Wan started, "if you wouldn't mind leaving a note for—"

The doorman looked over Wan's shoulder, keeping his attention fixed on Haeli. "You can't go up there." He circled around Wan.

Standing by the lit button between the two brass colored elevator doors, she weighed her options as she held her ground. She could either ignore him completely or come up with a polite way to say, "stay out of my way, I'm going up there whether you like it or not." Ignoring him would have been rude.

"We're sorry for the inconvenience. I promise it won't take long."

The doorman barreled toward her, but stopped a few feet short. He stomped his foot. "You are trespassing. You must leave now."

A chime signaled the arrival of the car.

This time, Haeli didn't bother with a response.

She slipped into the elevator before the doors had fully opened and pressed twelve. Wan squeezed by the doorman with an "excuse me," and joined Haeli.

Haeli could tell the man was at a loss for what to do next. He rocked back and forth as if he were contemplating leaping into the elevator.

As the doors shut him out, they heard him yell, "I'm calling the police."

"See," Wan said. "What did I say? He's calling the police."

"We'll be quick."

The doors opened on the twelfth and they followed the numbers in sequential order until they stood in front of the door to 12B. Haeli knocked and then joined Wan to pose for the peephole. There was no answer.

The elevator chimed and the second elevator doors opened. The doorman stepped into the hallway.

"Great," Wan said, under his breath.

The doorman called out after them. "He is not at home, I've told you. You must leave."

Haeli stepped forward to knock again. She felt something crunch under the sole of her foot. She squatted down to examine it.

Glass.

A small shard shimmered against the already gleaming polished stone floor. She saw another, and another. Getting low, face an inch from the floor, she looked down the hallway, toward the approaching doorman. She tilted her head side to side, catching the glint of a few more pieces, trailing away from the apartment.

"What is it?" Wan said.

"Someone tracked broken glass out of Chet's place," she said.

"What are you doing now?" The doorman appeared more frustrated than angry.

Haeli stood up. "Do you have a key for these units?"

"I do, but—"

"I need you to open this door, right now." Haeli put her hand out to thwart his inevitable protest. "Listen. Our friend may be in trouble. He may be hurt. Do you see this broken glass? Now, you can either open it, or we're going to kick it in, it's your choice. You've already called the police, right? If I'm lying to you, you can have us arrested."

The doorman's expression had changed from frustration to concern. Haeli assumed it was for Chet, but given the stern ultimatum, it could have just as easily been for himself. She had a sneaking suspicion he had not followed through on his threat to call the authorities. Either way, he relented and produced the master key.

As the doorman swung the door open and stepped out of the way, Haeli's heart sank. It was what she had feared. They were too late.

The aluminum frame of the sliding door leading to the balcony, was twisted and bent. Huge shards of broken glass littered the living room floor. The sound of traffic flooded in from the city below.

Haeli moved quickly into the single bedroom, with the faint hope that she would find him there. She didn't. What she found was a mess. Bedding strewn about. One chair flipped over and the other smashed into several pieces. Holes in the walls above piles of dusty debris. "There was a struggle."

Wan had moved into the bedroom and come up behind her. She startled as he put his hand on her back. "Bathroom's clear. I don't see any blood, do you?"

He was right. There was no blood. It meant that Ornal might have been taken alive.

"They must have dropped down from the roof to the balcony," Wan added.

Haeli looked over her shoulder to see the doorman standing just inside the bedroom. He was pale and silent.

"Did the police give you a time frame?" Haeli asked.

"I—I didn't call them."

Knew it.

"I need you to go downstairs and call them. Tell them there's been an incident and one of the tenants may have been kidnapped. Do you have cameras?"

"Outside and in the lobby, but they went out two days ago, and no one has come out to fix them yet."

Of course they did.

It was a given that Ornal's abductors would have disabled the cameras beforehand. Fortunately, the measure benefited her and Wan as much as it did Sokolov's men.

"Go, call them now. We'll stay here and wait for them. We need to be sure no one disturbs anything."

The doorman nodded and scurried off.

"Are we sure this is Sokolov?" Wan asked.

"Who else would it be?"

"I don't know. Wild party or something."

She gave him her best deadpan as she pushed past him.

From beyond the open apartment door, the elevator chimed, and the doors squeaked open and closed. "Come on." She moved into the hallway.

Wan followed her to the end of the hall and the two slipped into the stairwell.

In a few minutes, the doorman would return with the police. He would be frantic as he tried to explain to a suspicious audience that the man and woman were 'right here when I left.' His bewilderment promised to make it a comical episode.

Haeli and Wan would not be there to see it.

11

Two Days Ago. Yuri pulled the black SUV to the curb.

"This is good," Nikitin said.

A few feet away, past the cobblestone sidewalk and the strip of manicured lawn, the narrow opening to the alley was marked by two clusters of bulbous bushes.

The two men left the vehicle and mustered at the entrance.

Ahead, the pin straight asphalt strip was flanked on either side by salmon-colored cinderblock walls, which threatened to converge somewhere in the distance.

Yuri gripped the cell phone, holding it in front of him like a compass.

"You lead," Nikitin said.

Yuri brushed between the bushes, keeping his eye on the map as he walked.

Although each of the townhouses shared their exterior walls, melding them into one block-long building, the front-side facade was clearly marked to differentiate one address from the next. From the back, they all ran together.

They could have counted the doors and little wooden porches, but it would have required pulling themselves up the six-foot wall to catch a peek every twenty meters or so. Instead, the GPS would lead them to the right spot with little effort.

About half-way down the corridor, Yuri stopped and turned. He pointed at the wall.

"Right here."

Nikitin hooked his fingers over the top of the blocks and pulled. As he mantled, he straightened his arms and swung one leg over. "Clear." He swung the other leg and dropped.

Yuri followed suit with considerably less agility.

Nikitin meandered around the postage-sized yard, touching the backs of several chairs that encircled a portable fire pit. The cushions missing, the chairs were nothing more than a series of plastic strips strung between a metal frame. He lowered himself into one of them and kicked his feet onto the edge of the pit. "What are you waiting for?"

Yuri scuttled onto the deck and withdrew a leather pouch. He selected a couple of tools and went to work on the deadbolt.

It was the primary reason Nikitin brought Yuri. When it came to locks, he was the best. Even if he was useless for almost anything else.

But for this task, Yuri's shortcomings wouldn't come into play. Neither would Nikitin's own skill, for that matter.

They had been watching the Alexandria townhouse for the better part of two days. Nikitin was confident it was vacant. At least for the moment.

Nikitin had personally seen Haeli Becher come and go, ten minutes prior. And Tahk had reported that the owner, Blake Brier, was still in Rhode Island.

Tahk was a competent soldier and a trusted source. Nikitin took him at his word when he explained that Brier was running around a small island with a local cop, trying to find a missing girl—no matter how absurd it seemed. Nikitin also believed him when he swore he had nothing to do with the girl's disappearance. Given Tahk's proclivities, it wouldn't have been a stretch. Nor would it have been the first time.

But it was important that they all stuck to the script. Sokolov was clear that his instructions be carried out to the letter and Nikitin knew whatever his men did or didn't do was his responsibility. His ass was on the line, every bit as much as theirs.

"Got it!" Yuri swung the door open.

Nikitin rose and joined Yuri at the threshold. He turned his good ear toward the interior and waited.

"You won't hear anything," Yuri said. "Silent alarm. But trust me, we're good."

Yuri had disabled the phone lines at the box, knocking out the entire row of homes. It wasn't likely anyone would notice, even if anyone still had a working landline. But it was the cellphone jammer, nested between an array of car batteries in the hatch of the SUV, that would do the heavy lifting. It would prevent the alarm system from contacting the outside world. As well as every other device in a two-block radius.

Nikitin wasn't much concerned about the police. In his limited experience in the United States, the police had proven to be slow and uninterested when it came to routine calls. After a cursory check of the exterior, the call would be closed out and the police would move on to the next. Whether they were still inside or not.

What Nikitin was most concerned about was an audible alarm. Audible alarms tended to draw nosy neighbors, who quickly became dead neighbors. And *that* would be in direct contradiction to Sokolov's instructions. As long as all was quiet, all was well.

Nikitin stepped inside, traipsed through the kitchen and down the hall toward the front door. The panel on the wall flashed in a state of alarm.

Yuri poked around in the living room.

The reason for their visit was to deliver a message, but it provided another benefit. Intel.

Given the word, he and his men would take Haeli Becher. And while Nikitin would prefer to do it while she was walking from her car or while she was out for a run, an assault on the residence remained a good possibility.

Nikitin stood in the foyer, facing the front door. His muscles tensed as he imagined how he would defend the entranceway. There wasn't enough room on either side of the door to lie in wait. Any counterattack would have to come head on, or else be delayed until the intruder got further into the house.

To his left was a small table with a single drawer. Nikitin slid it open. It contained a ring of keys, a pad of paper, a couple of pens, and a tray full of loose change. Nothing in the way of weapons. He closed it and took a step back. Still, it nagged at him.

Reaching up under the table, he smiled as his fingers grazed the handle of the Glock. He slid it from its holster and tucked it in his waistband.

"So predictable." Nikitin said in Russian. He turned toward the living room. Yuri was no longer there.

Backtracking to the kitchen, Nikitin lifted his shirt and removed an envelope he had tucked into his belt at the small of his back. He placed the envelope on the countertop.

"Look what I found," Yuri said from somewhere outside of Nikitin's line of sight.

Nikitin followed the sound of his voice to the open staircase at the end of the kitchen. At the bottom, Yuri was examining a panel, mounted beside a vault door.

"This is something you don't see every day," Yuri said, "unless you live in a bank. Who are these people?"

For as much as they had tried to dig up on Haeli Becher and Blake Brier, something told Nikitin they hadn't yet scratched the surface. Whatever was inside that vault was of extreme importance to them. Which meant it was important to Sokolov.

"Can you open it?"

"The short answer? No. I mean, given some research, heavy equipment, and enough time, yes. But—"

"Forget it. I will handle it."

"You think you can get in?" Yuri started to chuckle, then caught himself. It was prudent. Nikitin tended to have an adverse reaction to deprecating humor.

"No. But you and I both know who can."

Yuri's facial expression expanded and contracted. From confusion to realization, back to confusion. "And they're going to just give us the code?"

Nikitin's mouth twisted into a snarled grin. "You only have to know how to ask."

12

"Mick! Mick! Mick!" Fezz, Khat, and Griff pounded the high-top table. The rowdy welcome hardly roused the few patrons who sat at the bar with their eyes glued to the Washington Nationals game.

The joint's owner and default bartender, Arty, flipped a towel over his shoulder and gave a silent wave as Blake crunched through the substrate of smashed peanut shells to join his friends.

A boneyard of empty pints and shot glasses filled the center of the round table.

"Jesus Christ," Blake said. "Still got that drinking problem, eh, Fezz?"

Fezz stood. "Watch yourself little man. I can drink just fine."

Blake laughed. "Come'ere, ya big dumb animal."

They embraced with a few hardy pats on the back.

Fezz was one of the few people Blake knew who could refer to him as a "little man" and get no argument. At six-foot-three and a lean two-hundred-thirty pounds, Blake was as physically imposing as the next guy—unless the next guy was Fezz. By all accounts, the man was a bonafide freak of nature.

Blake slid onto the vacant stool and gave a fist bump to Khat and then Griff.

"Thanks for the notice," Blake said.

"You're welcome." Khat stood on the stool's cross supports. "Arty. Shot and a beer for Mick."

"Look at baby-face over here," Griff said. "You didn't have to clean up for us."

Every year when the warm weather hit, Blake would get the urge to shave off his beard. Once in a while, he'd act on the impulse. That morning was one of those times.

Blake stroked his smooth chin. "It was getting to be a pain in the ass. Just be happy you haven't hit puberty yet, Griff."

Griff flicked him an affectionate bird.

"Seriously though—" Fezz belched. "Glad you made it. Not the same without ya."

Fifteen minutes prior, Blake was leaving an appointment at Coldwell Banker when he received the drunken invite. With slowed speech, Fezz had ordered him to join them. Blake didn't need to ask what the occasion was. While the four-hundred square foot dive bar wasn't a regular haunt, it was a tradition. A superstition, really. And their presence there meant only one thing. They were shipping out.

"You want in on the pool, Mick?" Khat asked.

"Twenty bucks," Griff added. "Pony up, hotshot."

Blake rolled his eyes. "Let me guess, the ring?"

"You know it." Khat bristled with excitement. "I understand if you don't want to. I wouldn't go against me either."

Fezz bellowed. "My money's on anyone else but you."

It was like time never passed. Blake thought back to the last time he sat at that table as part of the team, preparing for his final mission— although he hadn't known at the time it would be his last. He recalled having the same conversation, centered around the same dumb bar game.

A ring, hanging from a string, and a hook on the wall. The premise was simple. Stand behind the line, swing the ring, and land it on the hook. It was pointless and trivial, but when bragging rights were on the line, the ragtag group could make anything into the Battle of the Bulge.

"I'll pass," Blake said. "Doesn't feel right taking your money. You being civil servants and all."

Khat stood up. "Okay, okay. You're scared. It's all right. Eye-hand coordination's not what it used to be. We get it." He retrieved the ring from the hook, brought it behind the line, and pulled until the string was taut. "Let me show you how it's done."

"This is your turn," Fezz said. "Don't be trying to sneak in any practice runs."

"Only need one." Khat closed one eye and rocked the ring forward and back, keeping tension on the line. Then he released.

The ring swung in an arc, missing the hook completely.

"Ohhhh, you suck." Griff laughed.

Everyone did—except for Khat. He slunk back to his seat.

Arty dropped off a pint of light beer and a dark, amber-colored shot. "Not as easy as it looks, is it?"

"Not for big-mouth over here," Fezz said.

Arty hadn't asked what Blake wanted to drink. Blake decided it was best not to ask what he decided to pour. He threw back the shot and chased it with a gulp of beer.

Jack Daniels and... Miller light.

It wasn't as highbrow as what he had become accustomed to. But it hit the spot.

When in Rome.

Fezz slapped Blake on the back. "There ya go, Mick. Five more and you've almost caught up. Arty, another round."

Blake spun his stool toward the bar. "Not for me, Arty. I'm just stoppin' in for one. Places to be."

"Where you gotta be?" Khat said. "Hot date? Heard you're an eligible bachelor again. That explains the shave."

An awkward silence lingered between Fezz and Griff.

Khat smiled and shrugged. "What? Too soon?"

"No. You're right," Blake said. "I'm a free man."

"I don't understand it." Fezz gulped the last of his beer. "After all of that, she just walks out? Still can't wrap my head around it."

"You and me both," Blake said. "Not to be a sap, but before I left, I thought we had a break-through. You know, like we stepped it up to the next level or something. I spent so much time resisting it, I missed it. Instead of just enjoying what we had while it lasted. I—" He shook his head and exhaled. "I don't even know what I'm talking about."

"Man, you *are* in a bad way," Fezz said. "Now you definitely have to stay and drink with us."

"That's why I don't get attached to 'em," Griff said. "No honey's catching me in that trap. No way."

Fezz chuckled. "Famous last words."

Khat forced a puff of air through his teeth. "Forget about you. I'm gonna miss her. It's not gonna be the same without her."

"Look at you gettin' sentimental," Griff said. "She didn't even like you."

"She liked me more than you."

Blake brought his hand to his forehead with a slap. "Can we just drop it? I don't want to talk about Haeli. What's going on with you guys? I mean, you're *here*, right?"

"You know the drill," Fezz said. "Another day, another set of bad actors."

Griff got up and grabbed the ring Khat left dangling. "I might as well get my turn over with."

"Don't suppose you can say where you're headed?" Blake already knew the answer. As close as they were, he would never expect them to divulge classified information unless there was a legitimate need for Blake to know. And curiosity didn't count.

"Watch the news in a day or two," Fezz said.

It was enough said. Wherever they were going, it involved a high-level target. The fact that they were pulling the trigger meant there was a credible and imminent threat to national security. In a way, Blake was glad he didn't know.

Clink. The brass ring skimmed the hook and swung back.

"Who sucks now?" Khat poked.

"Got closer than you." Griff took his spot at the table just as Arty arrived with another round—minus one.

"You forgot Mick," Fezz said.

"He's the boss." Arty unloaded the tray.

"If you don't want to talk about Haeli," Griff said, "how 'bout you tell us what the hell happened in Rhode Island."

Blake took a deep breath. "Long story. Basically, I impersonated an FBI agent for a week, almost got myself killed, and somehow got out of there without being arrested. You know, the usual."

"Oh yeah," Fezz said, "really long story."

Griff laughed mid-sip. He tilted the glass level as beer dribbled down his chin. At that, even Blake had to laugh out loud.

"The funny thing was, I was there to help Anja's sister and her family. Kinda ended up being the other way around."

"But you found the girl?" Khat asked.

"Found the girl and a little bit of closure."

"Well, then." Fezz nodded and lifted his glass. "To closure."

"Screw that," Khat said. "To kickin' ass."

Blake decided he could get behind either. He lifted his glass, then finished what was left of the pint.

Fezz hopped off the stool and headed over to the dangling ring. "Someone's gotta show y'all up."

Blake stood, reached into his pocket, and threw two twenty-dollar bills on the table. "That's it for me. Listen, you guys watch your backs. Any of you gets killed, you're gonna answer to me."

Khat and Griff shuffled around the table for a handshake and gruff hug.

"Sure you can't hang for a bit?" Griff asked.

"I've got a couple things I need to do. We'll catch up when you get back." Blake walked behind Fezz who already had the ring in hand and was lining up for his shot. He reached up and squeezed Fezz's monstrous trapezoid. "See ya later, Brotha."

Fezz turned. With the ring in his left hand, he offered a handshake, then bumped his shoulder into Blake's. "Be good."

Blake smiled, pried the ring from Fezz's hand, and let it swing.

By the time the pendulum completed its arc and the ring came to rest on the metal hook, Blake was already through the door.

13

Two Years Ago. Adam Goldmann fiddled with the third button from the top on his Armani dress shirt. With several strands of conductive thread, the miniature button camera and microphone were connected to a chip, sewn into the hem of his shirttail.

"Don't touch it." From the passenger seat, Haeli craned her neck to check on Goldmann, who sat in the middle of the second row, pinned between Ornal to his left, and Bender to his right.

Since they left the hotel, there was something off about Goldmann. Besides sweating and fidgeting, he was uncharacteristically quiet. Haeli worried the pressure of being wired was getting into his head.

"Get a grip, Goldmann," Haeli said.

Wan glanced back from the driver's seat and then returned his attention to the road. "Relax. Nothing changes. We're all doing exactly what we always do. No need to overthink it."

Goldmann let go of the button and dropped his hand onto the stainless-steel case, which rested on his lap.

Wan was right. Nothing had changed. They used the same hotel. The same armored SUV. The same stainless-steel case, handcuffed to Goldmann's left wrist.

Plus, Goldmann had the easy job. He was to do exactly what Sokolov had ordered him to do. Deliver the diamonds.

For Haeli, it wouldn't be as simple.

In the two days that had passed since they'd learned of Sokolov's scheme, they had brainstormed about scenarios which would allow them an opportunity to break away from Goldmann and get access to one of the mine's drawpoints. Even in the best case, they knew that it would be too risky for more than one of them to attempt it.

As team leader, Haeli felt a strong responsibility for the wellbeing of her men. It was why she volunteered to attempt the reconnaissance on her own.

When they were on site during the previous two trips, they saw several workers coming and going. Each of them wore the same orange coveralls and once-white hard hats. Haeli's entire plan revolved around her ability to recover a set of the equipment from an unsuspecting, and recently unconscious, worker. Over ambitious, maybe. But it was the best they could come up with under the circumstances.

Even if she could manage the disguise, she knew she would still stand out. To date, she hadn't seen any female workers, and certainly none with her light olive complexion. But it would be far better than sneaking around wearing black tactical gear and a drop holster.

Wan slowed and turned off the main road onto the hard-packed sand. Ahead, beyond the shimmering mirage, was the village of Boitshwarelo. Home to several thousand Batswana, the small oasis was an eclectic collection of grass roof huts, concrete hovels painted with colorful murals, and rickety wooden structures. A blip in the vast desert, Boithshwarelo's only notoriety came from being the de facto gateway to the Kabo mine.

From the opposite edge of the village, they would access a narrow, paved road that served as the mine's only vehicular access. For forty kilometers, the access road would cut through the sea of Kalahari sand and deposit them at the enormous compound.

Haeli and the rest of the team had studied the maps and satellite imagery and were satisfied they had a working knowledge of its layout.

Just inside the gate was the main office where their previous visits had terminated. But beyond the one-story building were several square kilometers of infrastructure. Wastewater pools, tank farms, power generation facilities, heavy equipment maintenance yards, and of course, the pit itself. All of it protected by security fencing, barbed wire, and armed guards.

The processing plant sat three kilometers to the east and could only be reached by an internal access road and rail system, also fully enclosed within the secure perimeter.

While Israeli intelligence displayed confidence in their identification of the four tunnel access locations, the underground layout largely remained a mystery. Once below, Haeli would be at the mercy of her own common sense and powers of deduction.

"Come on!" Wan leaned into the brake pedal and slapped the steering wheel with both hands.

An old gray pickup truck, carrying six sun-beaten shirtless men, had turned into the roadway with no apparent regard for the SUV.

Based on the number of men, Haeli wondered if they were heading to the mine. One thing was for sure. Wherever they were going, they were in no hurry to get there.

"Take it easy," Haeli said. "We're still ahead of schedule."

She looked out the passenger side window. A group of women meandered along the strip of sand that had been designated as a road by the tire tracks left by previous traffic. Each balanced a different style of plastic bucket on the crowns of their heads. They had bare feet which, like everything else in the country, were coated with sand. The women smiled and laughed amongst themselves.

Throughout her travels, Haeli had always been fascinated by the daily lives of people who lived and thrived in the most inhospitable places. She wondered where the women were heading and what the rest of the day held in store for them.

"Imagine living here," Haeli said.

"No. I can't." Wan grimaced.

The question prompted Bender to break his hour-long vow of silence. "Is there any part of this country that isn't desert?"

"Would you rather be in Iraq?" Ornal leaned forward to look past Goldmann.

"Okay, I'll give you that one." Bender sank back into meditation mode.

As they approached the crumbling pavement of the trip's final leg, the pickup truck swerved to the side and stopped. The six men in the bed, and the two in the cab, stared as they passed. Wan punched the accelerator, leaving a cloud of dust as a parting gift.

The tires changed pitch as they left the sand and began buzzing along the solid road. Haeli ducked to get a view of the pickup through the passenger side mirror. She kept her attention on the truck until it started to fade from view. It hadn't moved. Nor had any of the men disembarked, as far as she could tell.

There was little conversation as they sped along the desert floor. Haeli considered it a good sign. No second guessing. No rehashing. They were ready to get it over with.

By the time they reached the gate, it seemed as if only five minutes had passed since they left the village behind. The clock on the dashboard had elapsed thirty.

Wan rolled down both driver's side windows as he approached the guard booth. The single occupant, a bald man with charcoal colored skin, wore green camouflage fatigues. Its irony wasn't lost on Haeli. There wasn't anything green from there to Gaborone.

The guard didn't speak or modify his slack expression in any way. He pressed a button, and the gate began to rattle open.

Wan pulled in, swung in a half circle, and stopped in front of the building. The others waited for Wan to shut off the engine and crack his door before following his lead. Like synchronized swimmers in a dry run, the four stepped out from the air-conditioned cabin into the blazing sun. They stood posted by the vehicle as Goldmann climbed out.

Three more men had appeared from inside the building. They stood on the excess portion of the building's concrete slab, just outside the door.

On his own volition, Goldmann made his way over. The team flanked him. One on either side. Two at his rear.

One of the soldiers held the door. "Come in, Mister Goldmann. Mister Molefi will join you shortly." He enunciated the English words, forcing them through his accent.

The men didn't explain that the team was not welcome to join. They didn't have to. The order of operations had already been well established.

Goldmann entered with two of the men. The third pulled a pack of cigarettes from his thigh pocket, drew one out, and shoved it between his lips.

Haeli wandered over to the SUV and leaned against the front fender. Wan, Ornal, and Bender crowded around her.

Peeking around Bender at the idle soldier, Haeli felt nothing but nagging annoyance.

Hurry up.

If this visit had been anything like the others, it would be twenty or thirty minutes before Neo Molefi would arrive for the meeting. Haeli had no doubt his chronic tardiness was intentional. It was a message. "My time is more valuable than yours."

Either way, between the time Goldmann would have to wait and the time he and Molefi would need to conduct their business, Haeli would only have a half hour to do what she needed to do. A half hour, at the most. Every drag the man took was another percentage point subtracted from the probability of a favorable outcome.

Haeli moved so that Bender was between her and the smoking man. She whispered to the group. "I don't think this is going to happen. I'm gonna run out of time."

"Give it a minute," Ornal whispered, without looking at her.

Haeli took meditative breaths as the man sucked the cigarette down to the filter. Then he pulled out the pack, lipped a fresh cancer-stick, and used the burning ember of the previous one to light it.

* * *

GOLDMANN TOOK HIS SEAT ACROSS THE PRESSBOARD DESK FROM MOLEFI'S empty high-backed chair. The two soldiers backed out and shut the door behind them.

To the left of the desk was a second door, through which Molefi would make his grand entrance—whenever he got around to it.

There was a time when Goldmann would have felt the need to assert his own dominance. He had, after all, worked a lifetime to achieve the level of status he had become accustomed to. He was the best in his field. Or, at least, the most successful.

But he no longer felt like the same man. His family taken from him, his future uncertain, he had been manipulated on all sides, and it had taken its toll. He was broken. And there was nothing anyone could do to put him back together.

It was the reason he made this decision. A last-ditch effort to take control. As it was, he was a lost cause. But another man, a new man, unencumbered by Adam Goldmann's predicament, stood a chance at survival.

Mossad had stripped him of his ability to make his own choices, just as much as Sokolov had. But he had reclaimed that power. He had chosen this moment. The hour of his rebirth.

Expecting Molefi to be a while, he was surprised to hear Molefi's voice booming from behind the rear door after only a minute or two. Molefi spoke in a language Goldmann didn't understand, but it sounded like Molefi was delivering an ass-chewing to whoever he was talking to.

As the doorknob turned, Goldmann reached up and yanked the third button down, popping it free. Four copper strands peeked through the empty buttonhole. Goldmann squeezed the button in his fist and stood.

"Mister Goldmann, good to see you. Please, take a seat." Molefi closed the door.

Goldmann remained standing. "Listen to me closely. The deal is off. We have been compromised."

"What do you mean compromised?"

"My security detail is working with the Israelis. Mossad. We are all in danger. You must act quickly. They know about the uranium. They know about our deal."

"How?" Molefi moved in a circle, to the door, toward Goldmann, and back to the door. "Why would you bring them here?"

"I had to warn you."

"Warn me? You—" Molefi raised his hands like he was about to lunge at Goldmann's throat. Then he dropped his arms to his sides. His chest rose and fell. "Stay here."

Molefi moved around Goldmann and opened the door. The two soldiers who had escorted him, remained posted on the other side. As Molefi slammed the door closed, Goldmann could hear him say "Where are they?"

Goldmann walked around the desk and slid open the top drawer. He rummaged around until he located the handcuff key he remembered Molefi keeping there. Leaving the case handcuffed to his left wrist, he dropped the key into his shirt pocket and headed for the rear door.

* * *

HAELI GLARED AS THE SECOND CIGARETTE WANED DOWN TO WITHIN A drag or two of the filter. If he lit another, any chance of sneaking away would be blown. She watched and waited.

The door flew open and the other two soldiers burst out, the barrels of their sub-machine guns pointed at Haeli and her crew. Taken by surprise himself, the smoking man tossed the cigarette and raised his own weapon. His attention remained fixed on his comrades as if waiting for further instruction.

Haeli stepped forward as Ornal and Bender slowly worked their way around the front of the SUV, toward the driver's side. Wan held his position near the front grill.

"Hold on guys. Take it easy." Haeli raised her hands in front of her. "What seems to be the problem?"

14

WAN JOINED HAELI AT THE FRONT DOOR. "THE BACK LOOKS NORMAL."

Haeli motioned to the camera mounted above the door frame. "These record right?"

"Of course, what would be the point if they didn't?"

"Just checking," Haeli said. "I say we clear the inside, then look at the cameras to make sure no one's been lurking around."

"That's fine. But I guarantee no one's in there. These locks weren't cheap. Nothing's broken or been tampered with. Still buttoned up tight. We're good."

Wan produced his key and unlocked the deadbolt.

Haeli scanned the street. Nothing.

Wan poked his head inside, then moved all the way in.

Haeli followed behind him.

The kitchen, dining area, and living room occupied one open space. Between the kitchen and the living room was a short hallway with a door on the right and a door straight ahead. Bedroom and bathroom, she assumed.

Between the kitchen and the dining area was a counter with three high stools. Wan moved around the counter and carefully opened one of the drawers. He withdrew a Beretta 9mm pistol and crept toward the hallway.

Haeli walked close behind, only pausing for a moment to slide a knife from the block on the back counter.

Wan pushed the first door with his foot and stepped in, gun first.

Haeli stood by the door and watched Wan clearing the bedroom as she kept her eye on the bathroom door at the same time.

When Wan was done with the closet, he returned with a second pistol in his left hand. A Jericho 941.

"Here, take this," Wan whispered.

Haeli took the weapon and checked that it was loaded. Wan returned to the bedroom, knelt on the floor, and threw back the bedspread to expose the underside of the bed.

If there was anyone hiding in the apartment, the bathroom was the only place left they could be. Haeli moved to the bathroom door. Holding the pistol at head height, she pushed the door open with the knuckles of her left hand.

Empty.

She kept her sights on the shower curtain while she approached. Using the flat side of the knife blade, she shoved the curtain to the side.

"Bathroom's clear."

Wan met her in the hallway. "Yeah, bedroom's all good too. Told ya it was fine." He walked to the front door and latched the deadbolt.

Haeli flipped the gun around, muzzle pointing down, and held the handle toward Wan. "Here."

"You hold on to that for now."

"Thanks." Haeli tucked it in her waistband, then pulled the strap of her bag over her head. She placed the bag on the counter. "So this is your new place, huh? Not what I expected."

"Why's that?"

"I don't know. Seems kinda stark. Where's your guitar? And that ugly Matisse print you loved so much? I mean, where's all your stuff?"

Wan smiled. "At home."

"You said this was your home."

"No, I said it was my apartment. And it is. I just don't live here."

"Who does?"

"No one, Haeli. I keep this place in case I need to lay low. It's completely under the radar. It's not in my real name. I get no mail here. No one knows about it."

"Wow. Paranoid much?"

"Considering there might now be a psycho trying to hunt us down, I don't think so. You're not paranoid if they're really out to get you, right? Isn't that what they say?"

"You do have a point." Haeli chuckled.

"Good news is, we can stay here until we figure out what to do about Chet. What *are* we gonna do about Chet?"

Haeli sighed. "I don't know. He could be anywhere. If he isn't dead already. We've gotta put a stop to this. There has to be a way to prove to Sokolov we don't have his diamonds."

"Maybe we contact Sokolov and make a deal with him. If he tells us where he found Goldmann, we can retrace his steps and figure out what he did with the diamonds. Sokolov gets them back, lets Chet go, and leaves us the hell alone."

"That's ridiculous. Sokolov isn't going to make a deal. And if it were that easy, don't you think Sokolov would have already done the same? He's got more reach than we do, even with your Techyon connections."

"That's it." Wan clapped his hands together. "We have to take this to Levi. He'll—"

"No. Absolutely not. Levi cannot know I was here. No one at Techyon can know I was here. Understand?"

"But—"

"Michael. No one. You have to promise me."

Wan's shoulders dropped. "Ugh. Fine. What is it with you? First, we hear you and your father are dead. Then you show up out of the blue, very much alive, but you won't go near Techyon. What happened? And what about Doctor Becher? Is he—"

"He's dead." She cleared the lump in her throat. It rose again.

"I'm sorry, Haeli." Wan put his hand on her shoulder, then pulled her close and wrapped his arms around her. "I know how much you loved him."

Haeli buried her face in Wan's chest and fought back the tears.

"I don't know what happened, but I'm glad you're back. It's going to be all right. We'll get through this." Wan leaned back and put his finger under Haeli's chin. He tilted her head upward and looked her in the eye. "Trust me. Okay?"

Haeli smiled and nodded.

Wan leaned in and pressed his lips to hers.

For a moment, it all came rushing back. Everything they had once shared. Before she knew what she really was. Before she knew what Techyon was.

Haeli pulled away. "I can't."

Wan touched her cheek. "It's okay, I understand."

"No, you don't understand. Things have changed. I'm not who you thought I was. I'm not who I thought I was. You and I, that was a different life. I have a new life now."

"That's not true. You're the same Haeli I've always known. I can see it. I get why you felt like you had to leave. But you don't have to stay gone. You and I, we can get a second chance. If you don't want to stay here, I can come with you."

"That's not it, Michael. There's someone else. Don't you get it? I'm in love with someone else."

Wan's chest deflated, and his shoulders dropped. His face contorted and then slackened. "Oh."

"I'm sorry, Michael. I've moved on."

"Yeah, I thought I did too. But seeing you—"

"I know." This time it was Haeli who reached out to touch him. "It's not that I don't care about you. Or that I didn't love what we had together. But that's in the past. Please don't be mad."

"I'm not mad, Haeli. Embarrassed, maybe. But not mad."

"Come on." Haeli smiled. "Michael Wan doesn't get embarrassed."

Wan laughed. "That's true."

"I am happy to see you again. But Sokolov is the reason I'm here. For you and Chet and Little Ricky. God, Little Ricky. He doesn't even know any of this is happening."

"He's lucky he's out of the country."

"I wouldn't be so sure. Don't you remember the briefings? Sokolov's organization is heavily rooted in Germany. Most of Europe. Jesus, pretty much everywhere. Rick's no safer there than here. Probably less so. We need to get to him."

"I agree. I'll put in for a few days of vacation and we'll go find him. We can leave tomorrow."

"We could start driving tonight," Haeli said.

"Driving? Are you crazy? How do you propose we get through Syria on our own? I don't know about you, but my passport still says Israel. No, we'll fly."

"If we fly, we'll be unarmed. We can't take the chance. How about by boat?"

"Haeli, think about what you're saying. It's five days to Italy on the freighter. It's not an option. I'll make some calls. I can get us a couple of weapons. Maybe even have someone meet us near the airport."

"All right. See what you can do." Haeli dropped her eyes to the floor. An awkward silence lingered. "Hey, you mind if I take a shower?"

"Of course not, please, help yourself to anything."

Haeli picked up her bag off the counter and walked toward the bathroom. She stopped to look at Wan. "Thank you."

"For what?"

"Everything I've never thanked you for."

Wan smiled. "You want a shower beer? I'm having one."

"No. Thanks. Later, maybe." Haeli flicked on the light and closed the bathroom door behind her. She pulled her shirt over her head, gathered her hair away from her face, and looked in the mirror. She felt as tired as she looked.

Haeli was no stranger to leaping in headfirst with nothing but a flimsy plan, if any plan at all. But she couldn't see the endgame here. They would go to Germany. And then what?

She wished Blake were there. She should have told him. He would have known what to do next.

Reaching into her bag, she pulled out her toothbrush, a t-shirt, and a clean pair of underwear. She turned on the water in the shower and unclasped her bra, letting it fall to the floor.

"Haeli!" Wan banged on the door.

"Not gonna happen," Haeli said.

"No. You have to see this. Open the door, Haeli."

Haeli sighed, covered her bare breasts with her forearm, then unlocked the door and threw it open. "What?"

In his left hand, Wan held an envelope. In his right, a photograph. He held the photograph toward Haeli. "It was stuck to the fridge."

The image of Adam Goldmann's head stared back at her. The same picture she had received in Virginia.

"We've gotta go. Now."

15

Two Years Ago. The three soldiers fanned out and inched closer, keeping their shaky weapons on their targets. One of them spoke.

"You don't move."

The team froze.

Through the door appeared another man. He had lighter, coffee-colored skin and wore a short-sleeved button-down shirt which featured large, wet stains around the armpits.

"Molefi?" Haeli asked.

"You ask as if you don't know." Molefi stepped off the landing into the sand. "There is no need for games. Mister Goldmann already told me who you are. You have made a big, big mistake coming here."

Haeli glanced at Wan. The telepathic message was clear. Goldmann had betrayed them. The plan had changed.

"Take their guns," Molefi said.

Two of the soldiers looked to the smoking man, who reluctantly slung his sub-machine gun to his side and approached Haeli.

Haeli glanced at the sky. Somewhere beyond the few wispy clouds was a high-altitude drone, its telescopic lenses capturing the unfolding scene below. But none of that would do them any good at the moment.

If they were going to stay alive, they would need to act first. Goldmann was a lost cause. Now, survival was all that mattered.

With hands still raised in the air, Haeli moved back to the front edge of the SUV and turned around, offering her back to the approaching man.

She felt the tugging on her thigh as he tried to free the pistol from the drop holster.

"It's locked in." She pivoted a quarter turn, blading herself to the man and presenting him with her right hip. Without moving her arms, she pointed her finger downward. "You have to press the release."

Her body position was intentional. Shielded by the fumbling soldier, the other two would not have a clean shot—at least, not without the risk of killing their own man. It was the best opportunity she was going to get, and she intended to capitalize on it.

As he leaned in again, pulling the pistol with his right hand while using his left to manipulate the release, Haeli snatched the handle of the sub-machine, still slung over his shoulder. She flipped it upside down and pulled the trigger with her pinky finger.

With her face buried in the soldier's chest, Haeli swung the weapon from side to side, blindly spraying a barrage of bullets toward Molefi and his other two men.

Wan, Ornal, and Bender dove behind the armored SUV as the soldiers managed to return fire.

The instant Haeli felt the magazine run dry, she snapped back and kicked the smoker in the abdomen. The force propelled her backward, sending her careening through the air, toward the front driver's side corner of the vehicle.

Before her shoulder blades contacted the ground, she had already pressed the thumb release and rocked her pistol free from the holster. She fired two shots, striking the soldier in the chest.

As Haeli rolled behind the front tire, the angry zip of the sub-machine guns rang out again. Bullets clanked along the broad side of the SUV.

Boom. Bender's forty-five barked two feet from Haeli's head. It left behind a dull ringing in Haeli's left ear and a pile of bloody, green camouflage beside the now empty guard booth.

"Got him," Bender said.

Haeli dropped to a prone position and shimmied a few inches from the tire, until she had a clear view under the vehicle. From her vantage point, she could see one of the two remaining soldiers trying to hoist Molefi's limp body to its feet. His gun dangled freely as he bent over.

Molefi's sweat-stained button-down was saturated with blood. The soldier didn't seem to know it yet, but Molefi was dead.

After a brief silence, the growl of a sub-machine gun resumed, and more bullets battered the side of the SUV and ricocheted off the acrylic windows.

Haeli had no visual on the soldier who was shooting, but she had a shot at the bottom half of the one who was trying to render aid to his dead boss.

Haeli lined up the sights of her Glock with the soldier's left knee and squeezed off a round. His knee exploded and his leg buckled forward. As his body crashed to the sand and his head came into view, she squeezed once more.

"One left." She slid out from under the SUV. "Who's got a visual on him?"

"He ducked inside," Wan said. "Forget him. Get in."

The two driver's side doors were wide open. Ornal had already climbed into the front passenger seat. Bender was hoisting himself into the back.

Haeli wanted nothing more than to finish off the last guy. And then Goldmann, for good measure. But she knew Wan was right. At some point, there would be more of them. A lot more. They needed to get out fast. Out of Boitshwarelo. Out of Botswana.

Wan waited for Haeli to get in before jumping into the driver's seat and starting the engine. Haeli pulled her door closed as Wan gunned the accelerator. The SUV fishtailed until its nose lined up with the closed chain link gate. They sped straight toward it.

"Hold on," Wan said as they crashed through. The frame rocked and pieces of metal scrapped along the windshield and roof.

Wan jammed the brakes and threw it in reverse.

"What are you doing?" Ornal yelled.

Clearing the busted gate, Wan slammed the brakes again. "Take the tires."

Just outside the rear passenger window was a Land Rover, parked behind the guard booth. Haeli knew what Wan was getting at. There was at least one left, if not more. The last thing they needed was someone giving chase.

Bender rolled down his window halfway, pulled his forty-five, and fired twice. The two front tires blew out and the front end drooped.

Another flurry of bullets clacked against the rear window of the SUV. Haeli turned to see the third soldier leaning out of the doorway, emptying another magazine in their direction.

Wan mashed the accelerator. The tires chirped as they hit the paved road and gained traction. The speedometer rose quickly and settled at a hundred and seventy-seven kilometers per hour.

Haeli knelt on the back seat, facing the rear. For nearly fourteen minutes she watched, but there was no one.

Not behind them.

"Heads up," Wan said.

"This isn't good," Ornal shifted in his seat.

Ahead, where the road ended and the village began, the old gray pickup truck sat sideways across the road. A line of eight men sprawled out to either side. Even from some distance, Haeli could see the men were armed.

Wan let off the accelerator. "Damn. You were right. We should have taken out that last guy."

"No," Bender said. "These guys were already set up. They were waiting for us to get back. They must be trying to roll us. It's the diamonds they're after."

"Doesn't make me feel any better," Ornal said.

Their speed bled off but Wan kept the vehicle rolling toward the roadblock.

"Wait. Is that what I think it is?" Haeli extended her arm between Wan and Ornal and pointed.

One of the men was climbing into the bed of the truck. There, mounted to a tripod, was a large gun. Now close enough to even make out the men's facial features, Haeli was pretty sure they all knew exactly what they were looking at.

"No way," Wan said. "A Browning?"

The World War II Era Browning M2 heavy machine gun posed a specific problem and they all knew it. Its fifty caliber rounds were likely to slice right through the SUV's armor.

Wan pulled his seatbelt and clipped it in. "Put 'em on. And hang on tight."

The SUV lurched as the motor surged and the speedometer jumped, once again.

Haeli grabbed for her seatbelt. The momentum pushed her back into her seat.

Wan lined up with the rear end of the pickup and pinned the pedal to the floor.

The SUV closed the gap in a matter of seconds.

As Haeli clipped her seatbelt, she saw the man in the bed swing the barrel of the big Browning toward them. She closed her eyes and braced for impact.

16

BLAKE GRASPED THE TWO ONE-HUNDRED-POUND DUMBBELLS AND YANKED them free of the rack. He walked them to the bench and sat, dropping the weight to the floor by his feet.

His pocket buzzed. He peeked at the screen.

Harrison.

Abandoning his station, Blake moved to the mats in the corner of the gym, laid out as part of a warm-up area. He sat on a large, inflated rubber ball and answered the call.

"Harrison. To what do I owe the pleasure?"

"What? A guy can't check in now and then?"

"I don't know, can he?" Blake continued the question game.

"Okay. Okay. I have a favor to ask. A question really."

"Shoot."

"My office is working a fraud case. Sort of high profile. A question came up and I thought you might be the guy to ask."

"You know I'll help if I can. What is it?"

"Well, I was wondering, is there any way to find out if a particular suspect had opened any bank accounts? Domestic or off-shore."

"Not legally," Blake said.

Harrison lowered his voice. "That's not what I asked."

"Ah. Of course. Tell ya what, you send me the guy's information and I'll look into it."

"You're the best. You know I hate to ask. How've ya been?"

"I'm hangin' in there."

"I checked in on Christa. Lucy seems to be doing well."

"Yeah, she's a resilient girl."

"Spoke with Chief Fuller, too. More stuff coming out about Robert Foster. Crazy story. This job gets weirder every day. Now that you've got a taste of it, you oughta sign up for real."

Blake chuckled. "I'm a little old for joining the FBI. Plus, I never liked you guys anyway. All those rules."

"Can't argue with that. But you did a hell of a good job. Talking to Christa's neighbors, you're a local legend around there now."

"You know I didn't do anything. My whole contribution was having a hard skull and making good bait. Not exactly superhero status."

"Na. It's about putting the pieces together. Ruling out the dead ends. Getting everyone pointed in the right direction. You can't single hand-edly save the world every time."

"I'm not looking to save the world, period. Christa and Gwyn had it right. It's time to slow it down and focus on what's important. Ya know I contacted a realtor about selling my place?"

"Really?"

"Well, I've been checking out my options, anyway. There's nothing holding me here anymore. Not really. I was thinking of maybe renting a place up in Newport. Enjoying some of that New England salt air."

"Why don't you pay a visit during the winter before you make that decision. Winter's a whole different animal. But if you're set on it, I can keep my eyes open. Ask around."

"Thanks, Harrison. Go ahead and send me that info. I'll take a look when I get home."

"Will do. You take care of yourself."

"You too."

Blake hung up.

Harrison turned out to be a solid guy. Blake had grown to trust him. To consider him a friend. He wondered how Harrison would feel about joining him and the others, should he ever get the business off the ground. He and Hopkins both. Given the unique service they could all provide as a group, they'd fetch a premium. And once they got up and running, there would be plenty of money to go around. More than enough to make it worth their while.

Blake had called his contact, Whitby, hoping to call in a favor. Given what happened in the Himalayas, he figured Whitby owed him one. And he didn't ask for much. Just enough of an investment to get them started and to entice Fezz, Khat, and Griff away from their pensions. Unfortunately, Whitby declined. As it turned out, saving someone's life didn't go as far as it used to.

Struck by the realization that he was still balancing on an exercise ball, daydreaming about something that wasn't likely to ever happen, he bounced himself into a standing position, put his phone back in his pocket, and set off to resume his next four sets of personal punishment.

17

Two Years Ago. "How's the wrist?" Levi asked.

Haeli banged the plaster cast on the table. "I could do some damage with this thing."

"I bet you could. How about you, Chet? All of you. How are you feeling?"

Chet nodded.

"Pretty damn good, now that we're back," Bender said.

Wan raised his matching wrist cast. "I second that."

Haeli concurred. They had all suffered injuries. But concussions and broken bones notwithstanding, they had all come through surprisingly well. Due in large part to Michael's quick thinking and determination.

With a broken nose and orbital, and a fractured wrist, Wan continued driving as fast as the crumpled SUV would take them. He managed to get them far enough south, before the SUV ran out of gas, to trek the remaining distance to South Africa on foot.

Granted, it had taken several days, and they were forced to ration a twelve-ounce bottle of water between them. But it was better than any of the alternatives.

Truth be told, if they had not been intercepted by the extraction team when they were, they would have died. At least Mossad had gotten something right.

"Well, I appreciate you all coming," Levi said. "There's ample video so I don't expect the debrief to take long."

The phone at the end of the table beeped. Levi walked over and picked it up. "That's fine. Send him in."

A moment later, Ari walked into the conference room and without a word, sat across from Haeli and her team. Sans sidekick, Ari wore a blue blazer, with the top two buttons of his shirt open. He adjusted his cuffs and laid his forearms on the table. "Tell me, why in God's name did you let Goldmann get away?"

The team shared confused looks. If Haeli didn't know any better, she'd say Mossad was less appreciative than they ought to be.

"Is that a trick question?" Bender looked around the room as if waiting for someone to fill him in on the joke.

"You have botched this thing beyond repair," Ari said. "Not only did you fail to obtain any evidence, you killed a conspirator and potentially the main witness. Not only did you lose our asset, you let him get away with over a hundred and sixty million shekels worth of diamonds. You accomplished nothing. Less than nothing."

"Hold on a minute," Bender said. "You're the one who trusted Goldmann and forced us into this situation. We were nearly killed for your inability to manage him. He sold us out. But then again, you know as well as we do he never should have been there in the first place. He was a loose cannon and you knew it."

The overhead lights shone off Ari's forehead. His scarlet hue made him look like he was about to burst into flames.

"Everyone take a breath," Levi said. "You wanted to debrief. Let's debrief. Start with what happened in the room? Between Molefi and Goldmann?"

Ari sat back in his chair and exhaled. "We don't know. We lost the feed before Molefi arrived. The next thing we knew, Molefi's outside and this woman is mowing him down."

"We were made," Haeli said. "Goldmann ratted us out. Molefi told us so. Right before he told his soldiers to disarm us. They were working together. Against you. We were as good as dead if we hadn't taken action."

"And by you killing Molefi, Goldmann was able to waltz out of there. Who's working for who?"

"That's enough," Levi said. "I get you're upset about your operation. But I will not stand by while you accuse my people of somehow being complicit in Goldmann's escape. Haeli did what she had to do to save her life and the lives of her team. She has more loyalty in her little finger than your whole organization put together."

Ari stood up. "It's not wise to cross us, Farr. This whole farce of a business you've got going on, it's because we allow it."

"Let me tell you something." Levi crossed the room until he stood face to face with the irate Mossad officer. "I know a lot of people much higher up the food chain than you. If you want to play that game, let's see who can cause more damage to who. Your ass is on the line for this, there's no way around that, but if you so much as lift a finger to try to take down my agents with you, I will feed you to the beast myself. If you like your job, I'd suggest you leave now."

Ari didn't respond. He turned and stormed out of the room, slamming the door behind him.

"Thank you," Haeli said.

Levi walked to the door. "No problem. I mean it, you did a hell of a job out there. Now go get some rest. There will be no more meetings about this." Levi exited the room.

"You heard the man," Ornal said. "Let's go get some rest."

"If by rest, you mean 'the bar,' I'm in." Bender said.

The group stood up and meandered out the double doors to the second-floor hallway, overlooking the lobby.

"You comin'?" Ornal asked.

"You two go ahead," Wan said. "We'll catch up."

"You don't know where we're goin'"

"Funny," Wan said. "We'll meet you there."

They were going to Suramare, a rooftop bar overlooking the White City section of Tel Aviv. Haeli knew it as well as Wan did. Not because it was a usual haunt, but because out there in the desert, they made plans to go there when they got back. It was Ornal's idea, whether he remembered it or not. At the time, none of them were sure they'd actually get the chance to go anywhere, ever again.

"You okay?" Wan said. "You seem a little, I don't know, affected. It was hairy out there. If you wanna talk about it—"

"It's not the mission. I mean yeah, it was a disaster, but I'm good with that. It's just..."

Wan waited for Haeli to finish her sentence.

"It's my father."

"Your father?"

"I've been thinking. What kind of life is this?"

"Look, things go bad sometimes, but it's not always like that."

"That's not what I mean." Haeli gathered her thoughts. "What if you could take a break? See what else is out there for you. Would you? If you could."

"No. I've seen what else is out there. So have you. That's why we do what we do. And we're good at it."

"I know," Haeli said. "Forget it. I'm just tired. You go ahead. Let me go freshen up and I'll join you guys in a couple." She kissed him. "Bye."

"See you later, then."

As Wan walked away, Haeli felt the urge to call out to him. To thank him for saving their lives. For everything he had done for her. But it was too late. He was gone. And she wasn't sure she would ever see him again.

18

HAELI RACKED THE SLIDE AND LET IT SPRING BACK INTO PLACE. "CAN'T believe you got all this." Haeli tucked the pistol into the small of her back and reached back into the duffle. She pulled out an extended magazine, already loaded with 9mm rounds.

"I told ya he'd come through," Wan said.

"So you did." Haeli hoisted the bag off the floor and tossed it into the back seat. "How far?"

"GPS says ten minutes."

"Great."

Aside from the pit stop to meet Wan's contact, they had made good time on the road. Haeli wished the same could be said for the rest of the journey.

The only flight they could get on such short notice was a red eye on Blue Air, which left Tel Aviv at 1:30 AM. Unfortunately, a long layover in Bucharest turned a sub-five-hour direct plane ride into a sixteen-hour trip.

Although she had hoped to get to Bender sooner, at least they were out of Israel. It should, if nothing else, buy them some time.

Haeli had been skeptical about the idea of flying but, with a duffle bag full of guns in hand, she was happy Wan won the argument.

That's not to say the trip wasn't without its difficulties. Customs was a little dicey. And the lack of communication with Wan was unnerving.

To limit the possibility of raising any red flags, she and Wan had to book separately, sit separately, and avoid any contact in the airports. Haeli was traveling under a false name. Wan was traveling under his own. It was a wonder to her that a man who took enough precaution to maintain a secret apartment didn't own a fake passport. As well as she knew him, there were some things she could never figure out.

"How are we gonna get in touch with him when we get there?" Haeli asked.

"We're gonna walk in the front door. What have we got to lose? If Sokolov's men are already watching Rick, then what does it matter? It's not like we'd be leading them to him."

"Not sure I follow the logic, but I'm on board. We don't have time to waste by trying to be stealthy."

"What, you don't want to follow him to a take-away place and drag him into an alley?"

"Na." Haeli laughed. "That's no fun. It's been done already."

"Cute. So, are you ever going to tell me what happened to you? Why everyone thought you were dead?"

"You know what? Yes. When this is over, I will tell you everything. But I've gotta warn you, it's a long story, and you're not gonna believe a word of it."

"We've got five minutes before we get there."

"Yeah, not enough time. Not by a long shot. Trust me though, I'll tell you. I owe it to you."

Wan looked at Haeli sideways.

Haeli smiled. "I promise."

Wan seemed to settle on the fact that he wasn't going to pry anything else out of her at that moment. He focused his attention between the road and his phone's screen.

After a few minutes, they saw the sign for the "Techyon Training and Development Center."

From the road, the building, or buildings, were not visible. The driveway disappeared into the heavily wooded area.

Haeli had never been to this facility, nor any number of Techyon-owned properties scattered throughout the globe. She had been trained entirely in-house and worked exclusively out of headquarters. Not that it would have mattered. This facility, like the Frankfurt satellite office, was only five years old anyway.

Wan turned down the driveway and snaked through the forest. It was still early dusk, but the heavy growth darkened the path and caused the automatic headlights to turn on.

"Look at this place," Wan said.

"I don't see anything but trees."

"My point exactly."

The path lightened and the edge of a building came into view. As it grew into a whole building, the parking lot also became visible. A handful of cars remained in the lot.

"Heads up," Haeli said, "we've got someone moving."

A large statured man wearing a red polo shirt and black cargo pants was walking across the parking lot toward the grouping of cars.

"Not someone." Wan chuckled. "*The* someone."

Wan picked up the speed, then turned into the row of parking spaces. He opened his window and hollered, "Little Ricky, fancy meeting you here."

Bender turned and squinted, as if he couldn't place the face so far out of context.

"Mike?" Bender moved closer. "What the hell are you doin' here?"

"Not just me, I brought you a surprise."

Haeli leaned over Wan's lap. She waved. "Hi Rick."

"Haeli? It can't be!"

Wan put the car in park and stepped out, leaving the motor running. Haeli got out of the passenger side, ran around the car, and threw her arms around Bender.

"Holy crap," Bender said. "You're supposed to be dead."

"So people keep telling me," Haeli said.

"What are you two doing in Germany?"

"I'd like to say we came for a visit, but it's a little more unpleasant than that," Wan said. "Something's happened. We would have called but we didn't want to blow up your spot if he wasn't already on to you."

"Who?"

"Sokolov," Haeli said.

"Sokolov? What about him? Something to do with Botswana?"

"We'll fill you in on all the details," Haeli said, "but the long and the short of it is that Sokolov found Goldmann and Goldmann pointed the finger at us. Now Sokolov thinks we have his diamonds and he's giving us an ultimatum. We have reason to believe he has Chet. We needed to get to you before he did."

"That makes no sense," Bender said. "How does he know who we are? Goldmann didn't even know our names. Not to mention the fact that Goldmann escaped with the diamonds still handcuffed to his wrist."

"Well, Goldmann's dead, I can tell you that much," Wan said. "And maybe Chet too."

"No."

"We don't know that for sure," Haeli said. "But we could use your help, Rick. We've gotta get somewhere safe where we can regroup and figure out how we can put an end to this. Or to Sokolov."

"We can go to my place," Bender said.

"No good," Wan said, "they tracked Haeli down in the U.S. and they found my apartment. My other apartment."

"Seriously, they found the penthouse?"

"The penthouse?" Haeli asked.

"Yeah, Mike keeps a separate apartment, so when he picks up a chick at the bar he doesn't have to take her back to his house. That way she can't find him when he doesn't call her back. We call it the penthouse."

Ugh. Figures.

Wan shot Bender a disapproving look. "That's not important. The point is we need to be untraceable. To buy ourselves some time."

Haeli opened the rear door of the rented sedan and put one foot on the frame. She turned back to Bender. "Hop in the front. We'll leave your car and take this. It's under my name. Which, of course, isn't my name."

Bender's gaze twitched. It moved past Haeli and toward the wooded driveway.

Haeli turned to see a pair of headlights cutting through the darkness under the tunnel of trees.

"One of yours?" Wan asked.

"Everyone should be leaving for the night. Don't know who this could be."

The deep blue BMW stopped, a quarter of a football pitch away. A tall, slender man with either a bald head or tightly cropped hair and a dark shiny suit stepped out of the passenger side of the vehicle. The man took two steps toward them, then stopped. Three other men got out of the car and started moving to join the first.

It was difficult to tell for sure, but it appeared to Haeli as if the man had a deformity. As if he was missing an ear, or else the dimensions of his head were disproportionate.

"This isn't good," Wan said.

"No. It's not." Haeli reached into the back seat and slid the duffle back onto the ground. She pulled the pistol from her waistband and held it at the low ready, using the car to conceal the weapon.

"Is that Sokolov?" Bender asked.

"I don't think so," Haeli pushed the front driver's side door all the way open and called out over the roof. "Can we help you with something?"

The man in the front turned his head as if saying something to his companions. Although Haeli couldn't hear what he said, the gist of it became obvious. The three men swung their arms out from behind them, each displaying a matching H&K MP5 submachine gun.

"Get down!" Haeli yelled.

Bender and Wan dove to the ground as bullets blew out the windows of the sedan. A few 9mm rounds passed through the skin of the car on both sides but managed to miss all three of them. Other rounds were absorbed by the seat upholstery, or door panels. A cloud of foam particles filled the passenger compartment.

The gunfire ceased.

"Not the woman!" Haeli heard the man yell. His accent was Russian. This wasn't Sokolov, but it was most definitely one of his men.

Haeli reached inside the vehicle and shifted it into drive. "Grab the bag."

As the car started to roll, Wan scooped up the bag and dug into it.

The three crouched as they moved, keeping pace with the car as it inched closer and closer to the wood line at the end of the lot. Wan passed a pistol to Bender then pulled out another for himself.

Haeli popped up over the top of the car and fired a few blind rounds down-range. Before ducking low again, she caught a glimpse of the men. They were closer and continuing to advance.

"We're going to have to make a break for the woods," Haeli said.

"You go first. I'll cover you," Wan said.

"No. Did you hear what he said? 'Not the woman.' I can buy you both a few seconds to get into the trees. I'll be right behind you." Haeli looked to her left. In another few feet, the front tires would hit the curb separating the grassy apron from the lot. From there it would be only twenty feet to the wood line. "As soon as the car stops, run."

"Haeli Becher," the Russian man said. "You come with us and your friends will live."

"Give me another." Haeli held out her left hand.

Wan pulled another pistol from the bag and slapped the grip into her palm. "It's loaded. They all are."

The sedan rocked back and forth as it hit the curb.

"Now." Haeli popped up and with both hands began firing. She moved from behind cover and twisted her body, firing to her side as she ran for the wood line. Before she dove into the brush and rolled behind a tree, she could see one of the men clutching his side and dropping to his knees. "I got one."

"Where's Rick?" Wan pressed his back against an adjacent tree trunk.

Haeli peeked out toward the sedan. Bender was lying in the grass. Motionless. "Rick!"

Still no movement.

"He's down," Haeli said.

"No!" Wan twisted to get a look. "I'm going to get him. Lay down some cover fire, I'll drag him in." He tossed the bag toward Haeli.

"They're too close," Haeli said. "You won't make it. I'll go."

"I love you, Haeli. Don't forget that." Wan stood up and barreled through the brush and out onto the grass, firing rapidly.

"Michael, don't!" Haeli spun out from around the tree and fired both pistols. She saw another of the men go down as the tall Russian dove behind the trunk of the sedan.

The rest seemed to happen in slow motion. One painful millisecond at a time. The slides of her pistols locking back. The spray of blood jetting out from Wan's back. The path his body took as it careened toward the ground and came to rest, a few feet from Bender.

Haeli dropped her hands to her sides and let the two empty pistols slide out of her fingers and onto the ground. In her mind she was screaming at the top of her lungs, but the words came as no more than a whimper. "No, Michael, No."

For a brief second, Haeli wished she could walk out onto the patch of grass, lay down with Wan and Bender, and die. But the motion of the approaching men snapped her out of her temporary psychosis. Her innate drive for survival took over. Fight or Flight. Only, she wouldn't have to choose. She would opt for both.

She grabbed the handles of the duffle bag, and of her rage and hate, and darted further into the woods.

19

HAELI LIFTED HER HEAD AND PEERED OVER THE ROTTING TREE. HER CHEST rose and fell rapidly. Each inhale vacuumed fungi spores into her nostrils. The odor of damp mold and mushrooms overwhelmed her sense of smell.

She hadn't gone far before finding the fallen tree and the depression between it and a cluster of low-lying vegetation. She had hoped her pursuers would have figured she kept moving, trudging deeper into the woods. It might have given her the opportunity to backtrack and escape to part of the Techyon property. But that hadn't been the case.

The men milled about, pinning her in. As any remaining light fizzled out, and the forest dipped into an inky blackness, more vehicles had arrived. More men with flashlights. Combing the forest floor.

It wasn't necessarily a bad thing. The waving lights allowed Haeli to keep tabs on each of their positions. To count their numbers.

Before long, she would be forced to move. But not yet. Not until it was necessary.

Haeli thought she saw two more flashlights flickering, further in the distance. She realized it was the headlights of a vehicle.

Great. More of them.

Haeli cursed herself for not studying the map. In fact, she had no idea how deep the woods went or what was beyond them. She knew nothing about the area.

It occurred to her that her smart phone was in her pocket. Turned off since she left Virginia, it probably still had battery life. If she could get a signal, she could use the mapping app to find her way out of there.

The problem was the light from the screen would be a dead giveaway. She would have to move. She'd have to risk it.

After a few moments, three more lights grew closer. These were definitely flashlights. Over the past hour, their numbers had grown from two to six, and now nine. She wondered how many more there would be.

One of the lights moved away from the line and appeared to be growing brighter than the others. It was moving toward her. One light, one man, moving in her direction.

She squeezed the handle of the pistol in her right hand. If she were forced to use it, the rest of the men would immediately descend upon her. But if she was spotted, she might have no choice.

The light stopped moving, about fifty feet to her east. Then the light blinked out.

Haeli's eyes had adjusted to the darkness, and she thought she could make out the silhouette of a man. He appeared to be standing with his feet spread apart and his arms at his sides.

What is he doing?

The answer came as his voice broke through the relative silence.

"Haeli."

The Russian accent. The same man from the lot.

"Do you know who I am?"

No, it wasn't the same man. Similar, yes. But this man had a smoother tone. His English was less broken. The fact that he seemed to believe she should know him was proof enough.

Sokolov.

"Why don't you come out, Haeli. There is little hope. You cannot hide forever."

Haeli held her breath.

"No? Okay. Do you know what I am holding in my hand?"

He paused.

"No, of course not. I will tell you. It is my mobile. Why do you care, you ask? You care because right now, at this moment, my men are waiting for my call. Waiting outside your boyfriend's home in Virginia, USA."

Haeli fought the urge to spring out of her hiding place and charge at him, right then and there.

"All I have to do is give the word and Blake Brier is a dead man. And this will be your fault, no? When all you have to do is give me what is mine. So you will come out now, Haeli Becher. You will tell me what I want to know."

Reaching into her left pocket, she felt the contour of the burner flip-phone. Trying to avoid even the slightest noise, she carefully shifted her weight, transferred the pistol to her left hand, and reached into her right pocket. She drew out her personal smartphone and pressed the screen to her chest. Her thumb found the power button and squeezed.

"You leave me no choice," Sokolov said.

Haeli could see the faint glow of his screen as it lit the underside of his chin.

She was out of time. With her left hand, she slid the pistol into the small of her back.

Now or never.

Haeli sprang to her feet and bolted, releasing the phone from her chest and putting it to her ear. "Call Blake," she said, holding the voice activation button.

A flurry of voices, yelling in Russian, crescendoed behind her. The rustling of boots crashing through the underbrush registered in her subconscious.

Her legs burned as she weaved and ducked trees and fallen limbs.

Then, he answered.

"Mick. I'm sorry. I'm sorry to bring you into this. You have to run. Now, Mick. Right now!"

She hung up the phone, shoved it down the front of her pants and into the crotch. She cut right for twenty or thirty feet and dove into the brush.

As she caught her breath, she could feel a sharp pain radiating from the inside of her left forearm. She reached down and pulled the sharp end of a thick, splintered branch from her flesh.

The cluster of flashlights slowed and broke apart, fanning out in all directions.

She touched her arm. It was slick with blood, but the wound felt superficial. She grasped the jagged branch. Felt the weight of it. If she had landed a different way, she might have been impaled. The natural spear could have easily punctured her abdomen or lungs.

It gave her an idea.

She was done being hunted.

Now, it was her turn.

20

BLAKE PULLED THE PHONE FROM HIS EAR AND LOOKED AT THE SCREEN. IT had disconnected.

A chill ran down his spine. There was fear in Haeli's voice. Not just for him, but for herself. She was in trouble. And, if he didn't act fast, he would be too.

Blake darted to the front windows and cracked the blinds. Just enough to allow him to peek through. He scanned the street. Cars lined the curb, as usual. But it was impossible to know if any of them didn't belong.

Rounding the corner from the living room to the foyer, Blake drove his hand under the half-table and felt for the handle of the Glock. He found nothing but an empty holster.

Haeli. What did you do?

Below the table sat the pair of gym shoes Blake kicked off when he arrived home a few hours earlier. He slipped them on and headed toward the kitchen.

Haeli's message hadn't contained much information. He knew there was a threat, but the nature of it remained a mystery. Someone was coming for him. But who? And why? He couldn't begin to guess.

Was it Levi? The police? Did it have to do with the scene they caused at the Venetian in Las Vegas? Someone else from his past?

And how would Haeli know? Wasn't she in Israel?

He wouldn't have time to answer these questions. "Get out, now," she had said. Whatever was coming, it was coming soon. Very soon.

At the bottom of the stairs, Blake punched in the code, pushed through the vault door, and headed straight for the closet. He opened the door, stuck his finger into the latch receptacle, and flicked the tab.

He closed the door, twisted the knob, and pulled. This time, the entire frame swung open, revealing the shelter behind.

Fingers attacking the safe's keypad, he swung open the heavy door and pulled out one of the pistols. A Glock 43, already seated in an in-the-pants holster. He jammed the holster between his hip and his gym shorts. It sagged against the drawstring. He tightened it the best he could.

On top of the safe was a black knapsack. Blake snatched it and pinched the two unzipped sections to prevent it from flopping around. After loading several boxes of ammunition into the bag, he zipped it halfway and slung it over his shoulder.

The room had been built for this very contingency. He could close the vault door, shut himself into the shelter, and wait it out. There was a cot, a latrine, and enough food and water to last for months. Underground, behind a hidden passageway, and not documented on any plan or public document, the bunker would never be found. Especially if one didn't know to look.

But there was a problem. Haeli was in trouble. And if he were to have any chance of finding her in time, he couldn't be pinned in.

No, he needed to get out. It was time to abandon ship.

Blake moved back to the computer lab and pushed the closet frame until it clicked. He grabbed a laptop and charger from the shelf, dropped the bag off his shoulder, and stuffed the electronics inside. He zipped it closed and slipped both arms into the straps.

As he approached the vault door, he paused.

Just inside the room, mounted to the wall, was a large red button. Blake lifted his hand and rested his palm on it.

The likelihood that anyone would be able to breach the vault door was almost nil. But could he risk it? In the wrong hands, the classified information and software contained within the dozens of solid-state drives could have catastrophic consequences. Not to mention his own exposure.

By pressing the button, he would be setting a process in motion to wipe all of it. Strip it down to bare bones. His life's work would be gone in a blink. Everything except the collection of tools he had installed on the laptop.

Blake closed his eyes and pressed.

The entire room seemed to come alive. Fans wound up. Lights blinked from every corner of the room. Racks of servers, all working at full capacity toward one task. Self-annihilation.

There was no time to mourn. He forced the vault door closed and engaged the actuators. The cylinders slid into place.

At the top of the stairs, Blake could see the back door beyond the kitchen. He listened for movement elsewhere in the house. It was quiet.

Back at the front living room window, he peeked through the blinds once again. Now, there was no guessing. Three men were getting out of a black Mercedes sedan, double parked beside Blake's Dodge Challenger. The driver stayed in the car.

One of the men looked up at the window, as if locking eyes with Blake through the slit in the blinds.

Blake bolted to the back door, scooping up his wallet off the counter on the way.

Phone, Wallet, Laptop, Gun.

Everything he could possibly need.

He emerged into the garden, without bothering to shut the door behind him, and sprinted at the cinderblock wall.

Off his last stride, Blake leapt, planting his hands along the top edge and vaulting himself over the wall.

The moment his feet touched the alley, a new predicament presented itself. He had landed smack dab between two men. Two formidable—yet surprised—looking men. Each holding a pistol equipped with a suppressor.

Blake's legs, already coiled from the landing, drove his full weight toward the man on his left. He drove his palm into the man's face, like a giant, angry squid. He pushed, driving the man's head into the cinder block wall on the other side of the narrow alley.

In one continuous motion, Blake drove his knee into the man's stomach, causing him to double over.

Leaning his chest over the man's back, Blake gripped the left-handed man's arm and slid both hands downward, forcing the arm straight until he reached the pistol.

Out of the corner of his eye, Blake could see the other man leveling his own pistol.

Blake slid the index finger of his left hand inside the trigger guard, on top of his attacker's finger. He hooked his calf around the man's legs and rocked backwards.

As the two tipped over, but before hitting the ground, Blake squeezed the man's finger on the trigger. The round hit the second man at center mass. Blake squeezed again, striking him in the neck, and dropping him to the ground.

Now on his back with the first assailant on top of him, Blake wrapped his legs around him, reached over with his right hand, and grabbed the slide. Holding tension, Blake twisted the gun until the barrel lined up with what he approximated to be the man's nose.

Blake tried to press the trigger. This time the man resisted. His own trigger finger pushing against Blake's with a strength conjured out of pure survival.

For several seconds they struggled, locked in a pretzel tableau—the man staring into the barrel of his own gun.

Blake strained his neck forward and gnashed his teeth into the man's ear.

The man let out a yelp.

With jaw clenched, Blake snapped his head back and pulled the trigger.

A dulled report rang out from the suppressor. The man's muscles turned to jelly.

Blake rolled to the side, dumping the limp body.

Then he ran.

21

Haeli crouched low. She placed her foot down, shifting her weight with incremental pressure. The tip of the spear poked out into the darkness.

The slow, methodical process started over. Step. Shift. Little by little. Taking care not to rustle any dead leaves or snap any dry twigs underfoot.

The last ten minutes had been spent working her way back in amongst the men. Staying within the cover of the dense undergrowth. She would soon be in position to pick them off, one by one.

But it was Sokolov she wanted. All it would take was one well-placed blow.

And she was close. Twenty, maybe thirty more feet away. She moved. Another step closer to the shadowy outline of the monster.

"Take her alive," she heard Sokolov say. "Whatever it takes."

Then he turned and retreated the way he came.

Haeli froze and watched the silhouette fade into the background. He was leaving. No, he was escaping.

Nothing could be done to save her friends now. They were all dead. Nor was there anything else she could do to help Blake. He was on his own.

But did the facts resolve her of her responsibility? In her mind, they only served to solidify it.

Maybe Blake had time to escape. Maybe she would, too. But it wouldn't matter. Sokolov would keep coming. Anywhere she went, however careful she was, he would find her. He would find *them*.

Haeli's mind reeled. She knew if she let the moment pass, she might not get another. But even if she was successful in taking out Sokolov, it likely meant a death sentence.

It was a risk she'd have to take.

Gripping the makeshift spear with all her might, Haeli clenched her teeth, bent her knees, and pounced.

The wiry brush scraped and tore at her skin as she ran headlong toward the retreating figure. She raised the spear, hands spread apart.

Wham. The muscular body of a man crashed against her like a swinging bag of rocks. The world flipped upside down. By the time she got her bearings, she was flat on her back and the man was on top of her.

A punch landed, deep into her ribs. She wheezed.

Another landed, lower, in the abdomen.

Haeli reached up and clawed the man's lips, then nose. He tipped his head to protect his eyes. She dug her nails into whatever skin she could get a hold of.

He leaned on her, one hand mushing her face, the other pressing on her chest. He called out in Russian. The others chattered in response.

Her cheek pinned to the dirt, she had no view outside of the man's sweaty, sausage fingers.

When she landed, the sharp branch was knocked loose. But it was somewhere nearby. Haeli searched the ground by feel, raking her arm back and forth as if carving a snow angel.

By the volume of their voices, the other men were only seconds away from joining the party.

She felt the pricking point against her probing knuckles.

The spear.

Sliding her hand six inches behind the point, she burrowed four fingers under it and lifted. Her other hand ran upward, over the man's brow and onto the top of his head. She grasped a thin tuft of hair.

Using her tactile control of the man's head as a guide, she drove the spear toward what she hoped was his throat.

For a split second the point met resistance, then sank in with a pop.

The meaty palm released. The man fell backward, his attention consumed with the horrific wound.

With her back still toward the ground, Haeli used her hands and feet to propel herself backward in an awkward, frantic crab walk.

The men converged. The beams of their flashlights flittered all around her.

She flipped to her knees, dug her feet into the soft ground, and pushed off with her hands to bring herself upright.

But it was too late. They encircled her. All of them, except Sokolov.

There was no use trying to reach for the pistol she had tucked in the small of her back. She could already feel that it had fallen out. When she was tackled, she assumed.

She had no weapons. No options. No chance of rescue.

Unless...

As a last-ditch effort, or as she hoped it would appear, she reached into her pocket, pulled out the flip phone, cracked it open, and started dialing random digits. The hope was that if they confiscated her phone, the one they watched her try to use to call for help, it might not occur to them she would have another. Tucked into the crotch of her pants.

They would eventually find it, yes. But every moment the smart-phone broadcasted her location was another breadcrumb in the trail. She had called Blake with the phone, so he would know it was powered on. And, if he was alive, he would do what he does.

The men shouted commands.

Haeli dropped back to her knees and tossed the flip-phone to the ground. She raised her hands and through rapid breaths, she said, "ты победила, ты победила—You win, you win."

22

BLAKE RACED ALONG THE SIDEWALK.

To the pedestrians, he blended in with the other joggers. Mothers pushing strollers, couples holding hands. None of them gave Blake a second look as he blazed by them.

When he started running, he had no destination. Far away from where he started was good enough for him. But as he zig-zagged through Old Town, he found himself in the vicinity of a place he knew he could go. Where he'd be able to stop for at least long enough to regroup and come up with a plan.

The men who attacked him didn't look familiar. They didn't appear to be well regimented men, like Levi produced. Brutal, yes. Stone cold killers, most definitely. But not military.

Blake left the sidewalk and cut through the park. Children played, people laid on blankets, reading books and sunning themselves. Blake kept moving, hopping a low stone wall, and crossing the parallel street.

Two more blocks.

He looked over his shoulder. Into the park. Down the street. There was no way they would be able to follow him. Not unless they were tracking his phone.

Damn. The phone.

Blake stopped, took his phone out, and powered it down. He looked around again. No black Mercedes. No grizzled looking thugs. Well, none that seemed to have any interest in him.

Resuming a jog, the sign, mounted above the Sumatra coffee shop storefront, caught his eye. He had visited the coffee shop on a few occasions. Iced Triple Old School Americano. Delicious. But the drink wasn't the only thing that stood out to him about the place. The interior was narrow but long. And there was an entrance on both sides—this block, and the block behind it.

He headed for the shop.

Before reaching the glass door, he slowed and composed himself. Sauntering in, he looked up at the menu board as he moved past the counter and toward the far side of the store. The four patrons and three employees didn't seem to notice him. He slipped through the opposite door and back onto the street. As soon as his sneakers hit the sidewalk, he was off again and into a full run.

If someone had been following, the diversion through the coffee shop might have bought him some distance. Hopefully, it was enough of a distraction to allow him to traverse the final block unobserved. If he could get off the street before they got eyes on him, he'd be home free.

As he turned the corner, he found himself under the tattered green awning that marked the entrance to Arty's. He rushed inside.

Arty was leaning on the customer side of the empty bar, staring up at the TV. He turned to acknowledge his incoming patron.

"Whoa, you guys back already?" Arty asked.

Blake caught his breath. "No. I didn't go anywhere. Odd man out."

Arty wasn't exactly read in. But the team had been going there long enough for him to get the gist of the situation. They'd come in, get boozed up, and yammer about going off to kick some ass. Then they'd disappear for a week or two. It didn't take a PhD to figure out what they did for a living. Especially not in that town. Guys like them were almost always military—ish. They sure as hell weren't politicians.

"Where is everyone?" Blake picked out a table against the wall and sat.

At almost four o'clock in the afternoon, the place would normally be seeing some decent activity.

"Slow day," Arty said. "Bobby and Phil just left. Second wave will be filterin' in soon, don't you worry."

On cue, a man wearing a backward Phillies baseball cap walked in and headed straight for the bar.

"Hey Chuck," Arty turned back to Blake. "See, what'd I tell ya? What can I get ya?"

"A water's fine."

"A water? Don't know what that is. Is that like a Bud Light?"

Blake chuckled. "Fine, whatever you wanna bring me. I've just gotta do something quick for work."

"Knock yourself out." Arty headed toward the bar. "Chuck, I thought I told you not to wear that shit in here."

Blake pulled the laptop from his bag and set it on the table.

"Arty, what's the WIFI password?"

"Password. With a capital P."

Of course it is.

Blake punched it in.

First things first. If he was going to figure out what was going on with Haeli, he would first have to find out where she was.

Luckily, he knew her cloud password, which meant it would be a trivial task to pinpoint her location.

He navigated to the cloud web portal, punched in Haeli's email and password, and clicked on the icon of the map.

The global view shifted and zoomed itself in, dropping a graphical push pin in the center of the screen.

Germany?

It was getting stranger by the minute. As far as Blake knew, Haeli didn't have any family or even work ties to Germany. She had booked a flight to Israel. That made sense. But how did she end up in Europe?

He zoomed out slightly.

Eberbach.

Or, rather, just outside it.

It was an unusual location. A small town, east of Heidelberg. Essentially in the middle of nowhere.

Blake was familiar with the area from his time in Stuttgart. He had never been to Eberbach, but he'd been around the general area. An hour and a half north of Stuttgart and south of Frankfurt, the area was old and picturesque. Not the kind of place Haeli normally gravitated to.

The thought popped into his head that he should just call her back. Maybe she would be in a position to pick up. But what seemed like an obvious solution was quickly squashed when he pulled his phone out and remembered he shut it off. And for good reason.

What he needed was to get closer. If she was in trouble, he wasn't going to be any good to her there. Four thousand miles away, he wasn't exactly poised for a quick response.

That much would be an easy fix. A few clicks in the browser and *voila*.

Lufthansa. Direct flight from Dulles to Frankfurt, eight hours and twenty minutes, leaving at 9:05 PM. If there was an available seat, it would put him in-country in thirteen hours. Accounting for the time zone offset, rental car and customs delays, and travel time to the Eberbach area, he could be to Haeli by 2:00 PM.

Blake clicked through the prompts, entering the required information.

Done.

A one-way ticket to Frankfurt, Germany. He would have added the digital boarding pass to his phone's wallet but, under the circumstances, he'd have to check in at the ticket counter—the old-fashioned way.

Having secured a ticket, Blake felt as though a small amount of weight had been lifted off him. But it was unwarranted. There were still so many questions.

He thought back to the sound of Haeli's voice on the phone. Frightened. Out of breath. She was running from something. Was that why she left? Running from something?

There was one way he might find out.

Of the forensic tools he had installed on the laptop, the most relevant was a piece of software that could parse phone backup files. Given proper credentials, the software would download device backup archives from a user's cloud account and parse the data into human readable form.

Blake located the software and ran it. The graphical user interface appeared, prompting for the cloud credentials. He entered Haeli's information. A list of available backups popped up. He chose the newest, which, based on the date and time stamp, appeared to have started when she turned her phone on to call him, twenty minutes prior.

The download completed quickly, and a progress bar showed that parsing had begun. Now, he would wait.

"One water." Arty dropped the pint glass on the table, sloshing the liquid over the end of the glass. "On the house."

Blake laughed. "Thanks, Arty."

If Arty was put off by Blake taking up space and not adding anything in the way of revenue, he didn't show it.

On the screen, the progress bar jumped from half to full, then disappeared. A menu appeared. Phone calls, text messages, photos, videos, and a dozen other categories.

Text Messages. Sort by timestamp. Newest to Oldest.

He started to read.

His stomach dropped as if the textual content had reached out and punched him in the gut. It provided some answers, but even more questions. Who was this Sokolov? What diamonds?

One message jumped out. "If you fail to do so, the boyfriend dies," it said.

It was the answer to the question that had burned his mind since he'd returned from Rhode Island.

Blake didn't know who Sokolov was, but he would bet the farm the guys who just paid him a visit did. He would go to Germany, but it was starting to become clear that he might be in over his head. Sokolov was a Russian name. But he had reach in the US? In Germany? How many people did this guy have at his disposal?

All the training and experience aside, Blake was only one man. He needed help. But with Fezz, Khat, and Griff off the grid, he knew he wasn't going to get it.

The best he could do was use the travel time to gather as much information as he could on this Sokolov. The rest he'd figure out when he got there.

Blake closed the laptop and stuffed it into his bag. He peeled a fifty from his billfold and tucked it under the untouched glass of water.

"See ya later, Arty."

"Right-o." He gave a wave.

It was ironic. It was tradition for him and the team to come to Arty's before every mission. And now, as if directed by some cosmic force, there he was again.

23

HAELI'S EYES DROOPED, AND HER HEAD BOBBED.

The leather belt snapped across her jawline again. "No sleeping."

She snapped her head upright and opened her eyes wide.

Since she left Virginia, she had not slept a wink. Not on the trip to Tel Aviv. Not on the trip to Frankfurt. It wasn't that she didn't have the opportunity, but she had been so charged up by the circumstances, it wasn't in the cards. Instead, she had stared out the window of the plane and run through scenarios, over and over. Scenarios that would never come to pass. Now, she wished she had forced herself, if only for a few minutes.

Her exhaustion was taking its toll. If her estimates were correct, she'd been tied to the chair for somewhere between fifteen and twenty hours. Which meant she had gone over three days without sleep. She would start to lose touch with reality soon. And her captors knew it.

Beaten, psychologically tormented, and deprived of any food or water, she was fading fast. But she had made a pact with herself to not give up. To not let them break her spirit. The moment she relinquished that, it was over.

Her mind was still clear enough to realize that she would be in it for the long haul. One day was only the tip of the iceberg. No one had asked her a single question yet. They hadn't demanded anything.

On top of it, Sokolov had yet to show his face since she was captured.

As the men bound her and carried her from the woods to the car, she had gotten a glimpse of him. But then he was gone.

While she was being moved, the men had made no attempt at blindfolding her. Even still, she couldn't begin to guess where she was. She knew it was a couple hours or so drive. There were mountains. A lot of trees. And something that looked like the ruins of a castle, early in the journey. But none of that helped her get her bearings. She just wasn't familiar enough with the country for any of it to matter.

Once they arrived at wherever she was, the men stripped her of her clothing and tied her to the chair. Tasked with guarding her, the men came and went in shifts. The latest two bumbling blockheads were a treat. Obviously ordered to keep her awake, one had taken to whipping her with his leather belt. The other preferred the backhand.

At least they were gentlemen enough to leave her in her bra and underwear. So far, there hadn't been any indication that they planned to sexually assault her. In fact, they seemed quite content with plain ol', run-of-the-mill, aggravated assault.

Well, that wasn't entirely true. There was the one man who exposed himself and seemed to have gotten a kick out of slapping Haeli in the face with his manhood. He and the others had gotten a good laugh out of it. She wondered how much he would have been laughing if she could have gotten her teeth around him. And she had tried. Oh, she had tried.

Her current two babysitters were all business. They diligently carried out whatever little responsibility they were given.

Haeli looked around the room for the umpteenth time. Hoping to see something that could help her turn the tables, should she ever find herself free from her restraints. But there was nothing. Nothing except bare cement and the bright florescent fixtures which flooded the windowless room with perpetual daylight. And of course, the metal door through which the newest Russian nitwit just appeared.

"Numbers." The new man pointed to the phone in his hand. Her phone. "What are numbers?"

Haeli tilted her head back and giggled to herself.

They left the phone on. Idiots.

When they first arrived, they had dumped her onto the floor. One of the men stepped on her chest while another yanked her pants by the ankles. As he ripped them free, her phone was sent skittering across the concrete. Haeli not only assumed that it was damaged, but that they would have immediately powered it off. Neither seemed to be the case.

It gave her hope. If Blake was out there, it would only be a matter of time before he or someone would come looking for her. She was at least happy to tell herself that.

"I don't remember," Haeli said.

With his left hand he held the screen a few inches from her face. With his right, he sparked an electronic stun gun. The crackle echoed off the bare walls. The display didn't come with a verbal command, but its message was clear. No passcode? Zap, zap.

Haeli shrugged and shook her head.

Then, as promised, came the pain. The business end of the device jabbed into her side and the electrical arc sent pain shooting through her neck and down her legs. Her body tensed. Her abdominals rippled. And then it stopped.

"Numbers." He tapped the screen with two fingers.

Haeli caught her breath, then groaned. "Sorry. I forget."

It came again. Same spot.

Her muscles locked and her back arched. This time, it stopped as quickly as it started. Not because the man was done, but because of the order that came from over his shoulder.

"Enough."

Sokolov. It's about time.

"Leave," Sokolov said.

The man with the stun gun spoke in Russian. Sokolov answered. Haeli understood most of it. Sokolov assured him they would get the passcode from her, in time.

As the man was leaving, Sokolov barked another instruction in Russian. Demanding another chair.

The man left the door open as he went to retrieve it. In the adjacent room, Haeli could see wood-paneled walls and the edge of a metal filing cabinet. Besides letting in the pungent aroma of cigar smoke and rotting fruit, the open door let in the sounds of the outside world. The swish of brake chambers as compressed air was released. The shudder of a diesel engine. Then another, and possibly a third. Haeli wondered if she was at a warehouse of some kind. A distribution center or a trucking company.

Sokolov didn't speak again until the chair was delivered and he had made himself comfortable. He sat a few feet away, facing her.

"Now, let us talk, yes?"

The door slammed shut behind Sokolov, sealing out the context of the distant surroundings.

Haeli shifted and tried to ignore the pain in her back and jaw and ribs and just about everywhere else. She blinked herself as awake as she could manage. Keeping her wits about her would be critical.

"I think we've said everything there is to say, don't you think? You want your diamonds, and I have no idea where they are. Doesn't that about sum it up?"

Sokolov let out a deliberate laugh. "Where are my manners? Would you like some water?"

Haeli didn't answer.

Sokolov nodded to the man with the belt. He hustled into the adjacent room.

Wood paneling. Rumbling diesel. Another whiff of the putrid odor.

"You are a very beautiful girl. I think you are smart, too, yes? Tell me, do you know how long a person can live without food?" He paused for an answer that was never coming. "No? Three weeks. Without sleep, who knows? Let us call it an experiment. For science if you like."

The other man returned, wheeling a metal stand with a bag of clear fluid hanging from it. He brought it behind Haeli's chair.

"This is, what do you call it?" Sokolov pointed to the crook of his arm. "The needle."

"An I.V.," Haeli said.

"Yes. And do not worry it is only—uh—salt."

"Saline. Yeah, wasn't worried."

In truth, she had been. Still was. God only knew what they were planning to inject her with. Sodium Pentothal? LSD? Her arms tied behind her, she couldn't see the needle being inserted. But she felt the man's clammy hand clamped around her elbow. And then the pinch.

"Without this, you will die much too quickly. So, we do this. There are very many wonderful things planned for you."

"I can barely wait." Haeli knew that her mouth was instigating things her body wanted nothing to do with. But she couldn't help herself. This was a battle of will, more than wit, and she needed him to know that hers was still intact.

"Of course, you can tell me what I want to know right now, and you go home to your boyfriend Blake Brier and I will not be forced to kill you and him. This is win-win situation, yes?"

Haeli wanted to cry. Blake was alive. Sokolov's words had all but confirmed it. She had been able to warn him in time.

"He'll find you, you know." Haeli laughed. A low, evil laugh, against a broad grin. Spittle mixed with the blood dried on her lips and trickled from the corner of her mouth. "He'll make you pay."

"It is true. He is a slippery guy. But do not mistake, he will die. And he will know it was you that brought it on him. But!" He held his index finger upward. "But. The good news is, now you can still save him."

"Let—ahem." She tried to clear the dry, scratchy lump at the back of her throat. "Let me ask you something. Why are you so sure I know anything about your diamonds? Because that weasel said so? Think about it. If Goldmann hadn't planned on fleeing, if he only fled because things went south and someone else got ahold of the diamonds, how would he have the money needed to disappear and stay hidden for so long?"

"A desperate person can surprise you. He was not a stupid man. Very resourceful. But he was a very bad liar. You ask me how I am so sure?" Sokolov leaned in. "Because I know people. I can see into their souls. Like I can see into yours."

"Yeah? How's it look?"

The wrinkles around his eyes deepened.

"Like fifty million dollars' worth of diamonds."

24

NIKITIN PACED, BOUNCING BETWEEN THE STACKS OF DISCARDED TIRES LIKE a pinball that had been launched and then abandoned. Listlessly knocking its way downward, toward inevitable failure.

"Wait here," Sokolov had said, before storming off to confront their captive. Twenty minutes, an hour, ten. It didn't matter. When Sokolov returned, he would be there. Exactly where he was instructed to be.

Nikitin looked around. He had never been afraid of dying. It was an impending eventuality. For him, just as it was for everyone else on the planet. And while he'd always figured it would be delivered to him by a bullet, he hadn't given much thought about where it might happen. The crumbling, defunct loading dock ramp seemed as good a place as any. Fitting, really.

As the breeze kicked up, pieces of litter scurried about. A flattened paper cup. A flimsy plastic bag which wrapped itself around Nikitin's ankle and latched on, even as he tried to kick it free.

The scent of rain was in the air, but the sun continued to peek through the clouds. Its rays snuck through the gap between the building and the encroaching wood line. It warmed his skin.

A few feet away, young tree limbs reached out over the thicket. With each gust, they waved. Beckoning him.

But he wouldn't be going anywhere.

Pain. Death. These things were easy. Admitting to Sokolov that he failed was the hard part. Harder than he imagined it would be. In all the years, he had never needed to utter the words.

Others, yes. But not him.

Nikitin had stood witness to what happened to the men who returned with only excuses. He himself had been the instrument of Sokolov's vengeance on more than a few occasions.

But unlike them, he had no excuses to offer. He had chosen the men. Charged them with carrying out Sokolov's instructions. Made the decision to leave the United States before the job was done to be by Sokolov's side. The blame fell squarely on his shoulders. Along with the shame.

There would be no struggle. No resistance.

Nikitin had no doubt that Sokolov knew he was no match for him. The same way a tiger handler knows he would be at the mercy of the beast should it choose to turn on him. It was a truth that was never dared spoken. Not by him, not by Sokolov, not by anyone.

But it made no difference. Nikitin's loyalty was all that he had. And he intended to take it with him.

His only regret was that he would go out a disappointment. No longer trusted enough to be on the other side of the thick concrete wall. On the inside with Sokolov. But if he were being honest with himself, it wasn't only his exclusion that ate at him. He had set his heart on something. A trinket, really. One pretty little ear. A delicate specimen worthy of the distinction of being the final trophy in his collection.

As the raindrops finally began to thwap against the rubber tires and ping off the metal roof, Nikitin's mind settled.

He waited.

* * *

"Pavel. What are you doing out here?" Sokolov threw up his arms.

"You told me to—"

"Come with me. We're going to take a drive to the woods."

Nikitin fell to his knees and bowed his head. "Do it here. Right now. I am ready."

A droplet streamed from his hair, still drenched from the passing shower. It rolled over his brow and caught in his eyelashes before dripping onto his cheek. Incapable of emotion, it was as close to shedding a tear as he was ever going to come.

"Ready? For what? Get up. I need you to help with something."

"But are you not going to kill me?"

"Kill you? Why would I do that? You are much too valuable to me, Pavel."

"I have failed."

Sokolov came close and put his hand on Nikitin's head. "You never fail, Pavel. It is your best quality. Stop being dramatic, it does not suit you."

"But, Brier."

"It is a very big screw up, yes. But it is not yours."

"It was my men. My responsibility."

"My men," Sokolov snapped. "And they will be dealt with. Anyway, the boyfriend does not matter. Dead, alive, either way. As long as she thinks he is alive, we have leverage."

Nikitin stood up and faced Sokolov. "You do not want them to finish job?"

"I do." Sokolov paused. "But what if we make a little change? Have them find Brier and take him alive. Yes, then she will have to make her choice. She will have to be witness to her decision."

"I will go back to United States. I will do it myself."

"No, there is no time. Victor and the others will handle it. They are already there. And I need you here. If she does not talk, we may need your—how do the Jews say?—'brand of persuasion?' And if she does talk, well then, you can have her anyway.

"Thank you." Nikitin sighed, releasing the remaining tension in his muscles he hadn't realized was there.

Sokolov's trust seemed firmly intact. And he might just get his trophy after all.

"Tell me, did you find any family?" Sokolov put his hand on

Nikitin's back in a subtle signal they were going to walk. Nikitin responded, keeping Sokolov's pace as they rounded the corner of the building and emerged into the empty lot.

"No. Her mother and father are dead. I do not believe that she has any other family."

"This is a shame. But no matter. We have her friends."

"Her friends?"

"The recently dead ones, Pavel. The ones you just killed. The ones we are going to pick up. Haeli Becher looked very lonely to me. I think it is time we set up a little reunion."

25

BLAKE LEANED TOWARD THE PASSENGER SEAT AND ADJUSTED THE LAPTOP so the screen would be visible at a glance. On the map, the icon showing Haeli's position hadn't changed since he boarded the plane in Washington D.C.

When he left Arty's, the map showed Haeli's location to be in a wooded area on the outskirts of Eberbach. The satellite view showed a building nearby, but the address was not readily available. There were no street level images and, even if there were, the building looked to be set too far back from the road for it to matter. It took some digging to determine that the building belonged to Brighton Holdings Inc, a wholly owned subsidiary of Techyon.

The discovery served to substantiate what Blake already assumed. Whatever was going on, Techyon or, more specifically, Levi Farr was likely behind it.

While at Dulles, he checked again to find that the signal had moved about eighty-five miles to the east. If the GPS was accurate, Haeli, or at least her phone, was at another facility in Dietenhofen, near Klein-haslach. Unlike the Techyon property, no digging was necessary. The mapping software reported the address and business name. "Hofmann Müllabfuhr GmbH." A waste management company.

As far as Blake could find, it wasn't owned by Techyon, Brighton, or any other subsidiary. It was a true mystery.

But when boiled down, there were only three viable options. One, Haeli was, in fact, at this place. For what reason, he couldn't begin to guess. Two, Haeli tossed her phone into the trash and it ended up on a truck headed to the waste facility. Or three, Haeli was in transit and it only looked like she was stationary at the location because the GPS hadn't updated.

After breaking down these options, one by one, he decided scenario number one was the soundest. Partly based on his questionable logic, and partly because he wanted it to be true. Needed it to be. If he had any chance of finding her.

Besides, the other possibilities wouldn't hold up to scrutiny.

If she had tossed her phone in the trash, it would have had to be somewhere local. The facility was a two and a half-hour drive from her initial ping. But if it were reasonable to believe she was in Dietenhofen when she'd discarded it, it would be just as reasonable to believe she was where the map said she was.

As far as option three, it was dispelled when he landed in Frankfurt. Before exiting the terminal, Blake utilized one of the power outlets, installed in the armrests of the seats at the gate, to charge his dead laptop battery for a half hour. It was precious time wasted, but there was a plethora of information from Haeli's phone backup that might prove useful in the near future.

He had spent most of that thirty minutes staring at the map. The indicator had remained firmly planted, exactly where it had been when he left.

There was a fourth option, or a variation of the third. He'd call it three-B. If Haeli was in transit and ran out of battery or turned the phone off while at or near the waste management facility, there was a possibility that the map simply continued reporting her last known location instead of showing nothing at all. Since he wasn't able to find the answer in the technical documentation, he was unsure if such a thing could occur, and if so, for how long.

The bottom line was, there was only one actionable choice. Haeli was there. She had to be.

Now, as he pushed the sluggish rental car as fast as it would go without flying apart, he was almost there as well.

The lack of a speed limit on A6 had come in handy—the beauty of the autobahn. He would have disregarded it anyway, but it was nice to know that he wouldn't have to worry about catching the eye of the police, on top of everything else.

Already having passed through Ansbach, he was nearing Kleinhaslach. From there, it would be just one more road before he reached his destination.

Judging from the satellite view, the final road cut through farmland before reaching a forested area. It was a clear catching feature. Once he saw trees, it would be time to start looking for the building.

As he followed the map, he compared what was outside his window to the overhead view. It was just as he envisioned. Farmland to either side. The trees in the distance.

He slowed as he got close. The building came into view.

The structure was a square block with a small, empty parking lot in front. One story with a flat roof, it bore none of the old-world architecture of the nearby village.

Blake pulled to the side of the road and studied the screen. Though not visible from the road, there were multiple buildings on the property. Blake counted five separate structures, two of them exceptionally large. There was what appeared to be a line of boxes. Pits separated by a partition. In the image, there were eight trucks. Two in the driveway that spanned from Blake's location to the road at the opposite side of the property, six in an open area between the two largest buildings.

The complex appeared to be a transfer station and a truck depot. The buildings likely housed maintenance garages, maybe some kind of recycling center, and there would have to be offices, he guessed.

But the layout and use of the various structures was of little importance. What mattered was the one small, boxy, customer-facing building in the front. It was where the Haeli's orange location indicator resided.

Now that he was there, he was confident she was there as well. It was like he could feel her presence, as ridiculous as that seemed.

The next step was coming up with a plan.

There were cameras on the building, so they would see him coming. But would it even matter? The small lot suggested that customers must show up from time to time. Who was to say he wasn't one of them? Assuming his German wasn't too rusty. Why not just waltz in the front door? Being unarmed, a soft approach was really the only option, anyway. Plus, as far as he knew, Haeli could have everything well under control.

Blake put the car in drive and started to pull out. A green and yellow garbage truck approached from behind. Blake pulled back to the side of the road and waited.

The truck passed him, turned into the driveway, and disappeared deep into the complex.

Though there were subtle differences, the truck was not unlike one might see on the streets of any town in the U.S. Essentially a rolling trash compactor.

In a way, he missed living there, in Germany. Maybe because it represented a time in his life when things were less complicated. Maybe the culture just suited him. Either way, it brought a strong sense of nostalgia and longing.

He pulled out, swung into the driveway, and took a hard left into the empty lot. Pulling into the first space, facing the front door, he practiced what he would say in German. Just an average citizen who needed to dispose of some trash.

With Techyon involved, something told him that the notion would prove all too true.

26

"THIS IS WHAT IT'S LIKE INSIDE AN EGG," HAELI MUMBLED. "WE'RE ALL inside it. It's how we stay warm."

The men were still there, somewhere in her peripheral vision. Weren't they? They were laughing at her. But there was nothing funny about their predicament. One wrong move and they would be swallowed by the vacuum of space.

Haeli squinted. The intricate code, embedded in the web of thin cracks that ran throughout the walls and concrete floor, had faded before she could fully decode them. They blurred to a milky gray soup.

She knew they saw it, too. Out there. Maybe that was their plan. To feed her to it.

But they were in for a surprise. Even now, her fingers dug at the knot. They never stopped moving. Even though her arms had grown to ten feet long, her hands continued their work. Haeli told them to give up. But they wouldn't listen. Even still, she was grateful for their effort.

Her head bobbed and her eyelids fell.

Crack.

The heavy hand twisted her head and snapped her into the present. A moment of clarity washed over her. She was still in the room, tied to the chair. There were two men with her. They had drugged her. But she had made more progress on the knots, behind her back.

She knew this all along, didn't she?

The rush of reality was like a drug in itself. A strange reverse high. She struggled to hold onto it, but it was no use. It was a tease. A ploy to get her to stop flapping her wings. To tire out so that she would plummet into the fissure.

Her fingers clawed. Why did they insist on doing that?

"No sleeping." The voice echoed from deep below. It bubbled up through the water.

Then, there was a crash. Louder than anything she had ever heard. She covered her ears with her wings.

A portal opened in the bright sphere of light. A deep black hole. And they were coming through. They had found a way to infiltrate.

It was like a door. Yes, exactly like a door. And the two-headed monsters were moving right through it.

"Drop him there," one said. "Prop him up the best you can."

They looked so much like humans. But that wasn't possible. The two had seemed to rip themselves in half. As if shedding their skin, they dropped their disguises to the floor, revealing their true forms.

But they looked more human now, not less. It was another ploy. Haeli was keen, and she noticed that one of them hadn't fully completed the transformation. He was missing an ear.

She giggled.

Amateurs.

This wasn't the first time she'd seen them, was it? They had come to her in a dream, perhaps.

"You're wasting your time, I don't believe in you," Haeli said.

One of them spoke. His mouth moved to make a show of it, but the sound didn't match. It was a telltale sign. That, and the fact that the sound moved through her like she wasn't even there.

"Pull it. The dose is too high. Let her level out for a while."

"Don't pull it," Haeli said. "If you pull it, the whole thing will unravel. Then, how will we hold it up?"

"See what I mean?"

Haeli wondered what language they were speaking. *See what I mean?* Were these real words? Or did they make them up? Maybe it was a code. To tell the others it was time to strike. They had started closing in. Trying to sneak up on her. They wanted her hands. Long ago, her hands had worked hard at untangling their tails. Those hands could fight them off, but not these. These had gone limp. Completely motionless. She felt the others begin to gnaw on her arm. They bit into the crux of her elbow with their pointy fangs.

"Good. Put it back in if she starts making sense. We will be back in a couple of hours. Call if she says anything about the diamonds."

The two figures receded through the portal. It shrunk and blipped out of existence.

"You forgot your skin." Haeli yelled. But it was too late, they were gone.

At first, Haeli thought she might be able to reach the grotesque body suits if her arms were free. Try them on, or at least see how they work. But she realized her arms had retracted and would no longer be long enough to reach.

It hadn't dissuaded her hands in the least. They had resumed their work. Toiling away at their senseless task. For a moment, she felt a connection to them. Like she was able to influence them. To make them do her bidding.

But she had grown tired. So tired.

She closed her eyes and marveled at the colors inside her eyelids. The bright light, just a little duller, now carried hues of orange and yellow with hints of blue and purple.

Crack. "No sleeping."

Her eyes snapped open. She glared at the man.

Where had he come from? Had he always been there? Had they moved her while she was sleeping? Was this the room she remembered from her childhood? When the Russians locked her away. When they killed her friends?

No, that was only a dream. She was happy they were there with her. Michael and Little Ricky. They would laugh when she told them about it.

"Hi, guys. I'm so glad you came with me," Haeli said.

"Of course," Wan replied. "I'd do anything for you, you know that."

"I know. But I'm sure you've got better things to do."

Bender was his sarcastic self. "I know I do. Where are we anyway?"

Haeli looked around. "We're in the room."

"Oh." Bender nodded, knowingly. "And who are they?"

Haeli stared at the two men, who had huddled together, a few feet from the door. Who were they? Indeed.

"Are they the ones who killed us?" Bender asked.

Haeli laughed. "No. That's ridiculous."

"How do you know?" Wan wondered.

Haeli considered the question. How did she know? But a bigger, more anxious question popped into her mind. "Did someone kill you?"

"Yes."

"Was it my fault?"

Wan and Bender didn't answer. But their shifted gaze told her all she needed to know. She remembered now why she was there. She was to avenge them. It was the reason she had rubbed her fingers raw, working them into the gaps in the knots.

She could feel the slack. The looseness of the binding. She was close to freeing herself.

"Psst. Ricky," Haeli whispered. "I have a secret to tell you."

"Don't Haeli." He rolled his eyes toward the two men. "Not in front of them."

"Why?"

Wan spoke through barely parted lips. "They're holding you captive, Haeli. Do you understand? You've gotta snap out of it."

"Yeah, Haeli. You've gotta remember what really happened. We were killed. You were captured. We're not really here. I mean, we're here, but we're not talking to you."

Haeli hated when Bender stated the obvious, as if he was the only one who understood anything. "I know, Ricky. What do you think I am?"

"Then you know you've got to get out of here."

Haeli looked at the men. Ricky was right. They could be the ones responsible. She felt hatred for them. She wanted to smash their smug, snickering faces in. One of them looked at her through the back of his head.

"What are you looking at?" Haeli goaded.

They both glanced at her and then turned away, dismissively. One leaned in close as if whispering in the other's ear. Haeli could hear the murmuring but couldn't make out the words. She took advantage of their inattention.

Slipping one hand from the restraints, she flashed her free hand toward Wan and Bender. The surprise on their faces was priceless.

Before slipping her hand back into place, she pressed her index finger to her lips and winked.

27

BLAKE SMILED AND APPROACHED THE COUNTER. HE HAD LEFT HIS SUIT jacket in the car and rolled up the sleeves of his dress shirt to appear more casual. It didn't exactly scream blue-collar, but as Fezz would say, it was what it was.

"Hallo. Wie gehts?"

A man with blond hair and covered in tattoos, looked him up and down. "American?"

So much for that.

"Used to be, yeah. That obvious, huh?"

"Uh huh." The man looked back down at his phone screen. "What do you need?" His English was perfect, but he had a thick German accent.

"Just looking for some info." Blake leaned over to catch a glimpse at what the man was looking at. "Netflix, eh? Babylon Berlin. Great show."

At first, Blake thought the guy was holding Haeli's phone. But it was a different model all together.

"What kind of info?" He asked.

"Oh, yeah. I'm moving and I've got some junk I need to get rid of. Some broken exercise equipment, a couple pieces of furniture, stuff like that."

Without taking his eyes off the screen, the man peeled a sheet of paper off a stack and handed it to Blake. "We take bulk items by weight. Metal, wood, plastic. Prices are listed."

"Danke." Blake slid the paper along the countertop and then pretended to peruse its contents.

Behind the counter and through the open door, Blake could see two men in the next room. One was holding a phone, the other was standing next to him, looking on. They spoke in Russian.

"Hey, maybe those guys back there wouldn't mind coming out and helping me unload."

The man looked up and shot Blake an annoyed look. He leaned in his chair as if looking in the back room, even though he wasn't in a position to see the men inside. "They don't work here. And that's not how it works. Pull to the back, someone will direct you where to dump it."

"Right," Blake said. "Okay. Just one other quick question. Did you see a woman about this tall, dark hair, really attractive?"

"Look around. What do you think?"

"Yeah, kinda figured. You don't mind if I ask your friends, do ya?" Blake started to move around the counter toward the back room.

"Halt. You can't go back there." The man punctuated his protest by holding up his hand. He even took enough initiative to get off his chair and stand in the doorway after Blake had passed through.

"Gentlemen, sorry to bother you. I can see you're busy." Blake took a quick look around the room. To the right there was a desk with several monitors. Each showed a grid of four images. Video feeds from surveillance cameras around the property, he assumed.

It was nothing one wouldn't expect to find. Except for one thing. There, on one quarter of one screen, was an image of Haeli, sitting in a chair in the middle of the room with several other people around her. By her posture, it looked as though she was bound.

Blake's heart sank. Rage filled the void in his chest.

He turned his anger toward the Russians, just in time to see one of the two men lifting his shirt and reaching for the handle of a pistol, tucked in his waistband.

Blake lashed out, striking him in the face with an elbow.

As the second man drew his weapon, Blake came down with a hammer fist, swiping the gun from his hand before he could fully raise it. It went flying across the room and landed near the corner.

The first man recovered and again tried to reach for his waist. Blake drove his heel into the man's ankle. Without waiting for him to register the pain, Blake hooked his right arm under the man's right armpit and moved as if he were going to circle around him. Blake's momentum forced the arm back and upward, allowing him to reach in with his left and pluck the pistol out of the man's pants.

Before the second man could even think about intervening, Blake had already fired two shots into the first man's side, just under his armpit. The placement would ensure that the projectile would penetrate the lungs and heart. A sure-fire way to take the fight out of him.

As the dying man slumped to the ground, Blake fired twice more, dropping the second man where he stood.

Then he swung the sights toward the doorway. The tattooed man stood frozen. His arms flew up like they were spring loaded.

"Walk over here and get on the ground."

He complied.

"Lay on your stomach and interlace your fingers behind your head. If you move, I will shoot you, understand?"

"Ja. Ja, Ja," he stammered.

"What's your name."

"Reiner."

"Okay Reiner. Don't do anything stupid and you'll be fine."

Blake held the pistol toward Reiner but directed his attention to the screens. He tried to make sense of what he was looking at. Two men stood together. They didn't appear to be talking. Two other men were on the floor in front of Haeli. One was sitting, slumped over his knees, and one was lying on his side. It appeared that these men were unconscious, but Haeli's mouth was moving as if she were talking to them.

"Is there audio?"

Forehead pressed to the floor, Reiner answered with no hesitation. "Ja. You have to click it. Just click the one you want to hear."

Blake grabbed the mouse and clicked the image of Haeli. The audio blared.

"—and now you're stuck in here with me," Haeli said. "I should've done more. Why didn't you run? You told me you were going to run."

What the hell?

It was Haeli, but it hardly sounded like her. It was as if she were possessed. Blake searched the screen for more controls. There were none. He right clicked Haeli's image. A pop-up menu appeared.

Full screen.

With the larger view, it was clear that the two men on the floor were not moving at all. The one on his side had his arm raised slightly off the ground. It would be almost impossible to keep perfectly still under such prolonged strain. Unless he was a yoga master, Blake was pretty sure the guy was in rigor mortis. It led to a lot of questions. Three major ones, off the top of his head. Why was Haeli there? Who were the men? And why was she talking to a couple of corpses?

"Where is this video from?" When he didn't get an answer, he realized why. "Sit up. Sit up and look at the screens."

With his hands locked behind his head, Reiner rolled and then bent at the waist, straining to get a look.

Blake pointed. "This one. Where's it from?"

"Building five. It's at the back of the lot. It's the old sorting center. But they built a new one. That building's empty. I think they're planning to knock it down."

"And who are these men?" Blake motioned to the closest Russian. The pool of blood had creeped from under him and across the floor, almost reaching Reiner's feet.

"They work for the owner. That's all I know."

"What's the owner's name."

"I don't know. He's a Russian guy."

"You don't know who you work for?"

"I work for Wolf. He runs the place. The Russians? When they're here, I just stay out of their way. Everyone does."

Blake considered pushing, but he didn't have time to keep going around in circles with the guy. Instead, he pointed at the floor.

Reiner got the message and laid back down on his belly.

"How do I get to building five?"

"Straight down, last one on the left."

If he were going to get her out of there, he'd need to know what he'd be up against. He clicked for the menu and returned to grid mode.

Assuming all four feeds on Haeli's monitor were from the same building, it looked like there were only four men in total, not including the dead ones. Two with Haeli and two others in a different room. This second space looked like an office. There were two bare desks and a few filing cabinets. Unlike the large, garage-like area Haeli was in, this one was small, had carpet, and the walls were made of wood paneling.

Blake clicked on the image to bring up the audio. The two men were speaking in Russian. They talked fast, but Blake was able to translate most of it.

Both had similar features. Scarred faces, crooked noses, angular jaws, buzz cut hair. They were stereotypical Russian mobster types, for sure. One of them did most of the talking while the other simply nodded, his lips pursed like he had just smelled something awful.

"If we leave now, we can be back in two hours. Three at the most. If she hasn't changed her mind by then and Victor hasn't found Brier, you can start cutting pieces off of her."

Found Brier? Cut pieces off her?

He could have put his fist through the screen.

Blake waited a moment to see if the two were leaving. The two exterior cameras, arranged on the same monitor, showed two vehicles. One black, one white, both Mercedes. As the two men left the frame on camera two, they appeared on camera three, walking to the black Mercedes and getting in.

"Reiner, do you have any handcuffs or flex cuffs? Zip ties maybe? Something I can secure you with?" Blake walked toward the corner, picked up the second pistol and stuck it in his belt line, opposite the other.

"No, nothing," Reiner said.

"That's too bad. If I can't secure you, I'm gonna have to shoot you."

"Top drawer. There's zip ties in the top drawer."

Blake chuckled.

He pulled zip ties from the drawer and fastened Reiner's hands and feet. When he was done, he checked the monitor. The black Mercedes was gone.

Blake smiled.

Two guns. Two bad guys.

He liked those odds.

28

HAELI BIT HER LIP. INSIDE, SHE WAS CRYING. SOBBING. WEEPING. Screaming.

Outside, she was still.

It had been several minutes since she regained her capacity to think clearly. Or at least since she became aware of it on an analytical level.

She mourned for the two men laying lifeless at her feet. Two of the kindest and strongest people she had ever known.

Now, the curtain was drawn back on their fragility. Flesh and bone, impervious to nothing.

And she was no different. All the genetic enhancement in the world couldn't change that fact.

A lifetime of training. Of service. Of struggle. Could all be wiped away on a whim. A trailer hitched to a misguided and unnecessary crusade.

Alas, her sweet, brutal friends. They were there with her, but not because they were physically present. Their mottled, bloating shells retained no relation to the men who once inhabited them. It was because of their bond. A bond that had been forged, not in fire, but in the simmering pan. Not in death, but on the very precipice of it. They had lived on that ledge for as long as she had known them.

Michael, Ricky, Chet. They were all there. Infusing her with a new vigor, as if donating the memory of their vitality to the cause. She, the hand. The instrument of their collective wrath. She stored it. Fostered it.

She looked at Wan's puffy face with loving eyes. Once upon a time, they had been inseparable. She had loved him. Still did. Her connection with Blake didn't change that, only put it in perspective. She and Michael didn't belong together, not in that way. But it didn't diminish her feelings for him.

With Blake there was passion and longing and volatility. It was selfish, like she needed him more than he needed her. She craved him and at times, hated him for it. She cared for Michael in a different way. A selfless, unconditional love unencumbered by passion.

"I'm sorry Michael," she said. "I'm sorry I couldn't be who you wanted me to be. This isn't your fault. It's mine. It's all mine. Please, Ricky, Michael, please forgive me."

She spoke to them now, not out of drug induced psychosis, but out of necessity. The men who watched over her would expect it. And if she didn't deliver, there would no doubt be another dose of—whatever they had given her.

What had they given her? LSD, Peyote, Psilocybin? She was no expert, but it was her understanding that the effects of these chemicals lasted many hours after exposure. But she had started coming down quickly. Then again, her sense of time at this point could hardly be considered reliable.

Before she had blasted off to another planet, she considered making up a story. A wild goose chase, attached to a trail of conditions that would buy her time. But that was before. Before she had slipped herself free of her restraints. Now she had the upper hand. They just didn't know it yet.

Sokolov's level of depravity was astonishing. He had brought the corpses to unnerve her. Guilt her. Break her. But it had the opposite effect. Without them, she might have felt beaten and alone. Instead, she was empowered.

But if she was going to succeed, she needed the men to be

distracted. Separated. She was weak, and so, so tired. It was the reason she had been biding her time, waiting for her moment. A shift change. A bathroom break. Something. But these men were firmly rooted to their posts and likely would be for some time.

She looked to Bender and Wan. She spoke to them again, but this time, only in her thoughts.

Any ideas?

And just like that, with the question, came her answer. She would speak to them. Speak *through* them.

"Come on Rick, I can do this, I can hold out."

She scoffed. Rolled her eyes.

"If I tell him where they are, he'll kill you. He'll know we stole them. I don't want you to die, Ricky."

Her voice wobbled. Out of the corner of her eye, she could see the two guards reacting. Their full attention, now hanging on every word.

"I'll do it Rick, I will. I never wanted the diamonds in the first place. I told you they were nothing but trouble."

She bowed her head as if listening. Nodded.

"Yes. I'm ready. I can't do this anymore. I'll tell him. I'll tell him, now."

Haeli straightened her back and stared out into the distance.

The men conferred with muted excitement. Like schoolgirls gossiping while the teacher's back was turned. One of them hurried through the door, leaving the other with his proud smile.

However long it would take the absent man to fetch Sokolov, it wouldn't be long enough.

Haeli slid her hand from the restraint and used it to free the other. She grasped the back of the chair and stood, bringing it a few inches off the ground. She stared the remaining man down.

"I'm invisible!"

"Sit down." He charged toward her.

Haeli stood her ground.

"Sit down, or I'll sit you down." He put one hand on each of her shoulders and pushed. The legs of the chair clicked back to the floor. Haeli was seated.

The man stood facing her. His body a few inches from Haeli's face. The holstered pistol a few inches more.

"You can see me?" Haeli asked. "Are you invisible, too?"

The man blew air through his teeth and shook his head. He turned to return to his position.

It was the perfect sequence of events. Exactly as she had planned. He had given up his distance. Given her his back. And now she would capitalize on it.

Haeli leapt forward, throwing her arms around his neck, and clamping her legs around his waist.

The man flailed, trying to shed her. She squeezed tighter.

He clawed at her thigh. She could feel the bulge of the pistol digging into her flesh. Crossing her feet, she drew her knees in, locking him out from any access to the weapon.

On her forearm, she could feel the pulsing of his carotid artery. It hammered away, increasing in speed and intensity. His muscles tensed. Panic was setting in.

Haeli could feel her own strength waning. She took rapid, shallow breaths.

The man staggered and spun, twisting and contouring like a bucking bronco. He skittered backward, smashing Haeli into the unforgiving wall. Stumbling forward, he set up for a second run. She braced herself.

Smash.

The blow knocked the wind out of her. The pain so intense, she feared he may have fractured her spine.

Still, she squeezed. Summoning every last morsel of energy in her tired and broken body, she clamped down as if her life depended on it. Because it did.

He slowed. Stumbled. Buckled.

Haeli rode him to the ground. Using her legs as leverage, she arched her back and grunted through clenched teeth.

Outside her own body, she wouldn't have recognized herself. A rabid animal, panting and foaming. Blinded by rage.

The stone-hard mass of muscle between her legs began to soften.

He convulsed.

And then, he was out. Limp and useless.

With barely enough strength to roll the man over, she scooched herself out from under him. She worked her way to her feet and in a near delirious haze, stumbled toward the rear door.

Please be open.

She turned the handle. Sunlight streamed through the gap.

It felt like freedom. But it wasn't. Not yet. She would have to run. She would have to endure whatever came next. And they wouldn't be far behind her.

A throbbing sensation still lingering on her inner thigh.

Her mind was slow. Each thought a deliberate culling of her remaining faculties.

The gun. Take the gun.

As she turned back, the door behind the sleeping man opened, revealing his stunned partner.

They locked eyes. Both frozen in an action-reaction gambit. Once again, it came down to the familiar fight or flight. Such was the story of her life.

He blinked. She bolted.

Into the open air she sprinted. Over gravel and unkempt grass. Ahead, there was a road. Pitted and potholed. It led somewhere. Somewhere away from there.

She looked over her shoulder. The man was gaining on her.

Legs burning, breath failing, she knew she wasn't going to make it. She had given everything she had. For Michael. For Ricky. For Chet and for Blake. Nothing left on the table. But it wasn't enough.

As she reached the edge of the roadway and stepped onto the aging asphalt, her legs slowed. Like a car that had run out of gas, she coasted toward the inevitable.

29

BLAKE PLACED ONE OF THE PISTOLS ON THE PASSENGER SEAT FOR EASE OF access. He threw the car in reverse, cut the wheel, and punched the gas. While still moving backwards, he slammed it back in drive.

The little motor jolted and grabbed the gears. Blake mashed the pedal, sending the bucket of bolts around the corner and onto the access road.

A garbage truck, coming from the interior of the complex, squealed. Its driver broke hard and laid on the horn. Blake fish-tailed clear of the truck's front bumper and took off like a toy car that had been wound up and released.

Building five. Last one on the left.

As the first building whizzed by, Blake looked ahead. On the right was an open area, lined with dumpsters. Behind it, a building with disproportionate garage doors. To the left, two more smaller structures.

But it was what was in the middle that caught his eye and lured him into action. The petite frame of a woman, half-naked, running like she had fallen but had yet to hit the ground.

Behind her, a muscular man gave chase. He was close. There was no time for contemplation.

Blake almost lifted off his seat as he stood on the accelerator. He bore down on them.

Three... Two... One...

The moment he hit the point of no return, when no amount of braking would prevent a crash, he laid on the horn.

Haeli's head snapped around as she dove into the tall grass at the edge of the road.

Her pursuer didn't.

It was a fatal mistake.

The bumper made contact with his legs, crushing them into floppy ropes that dangled below him as he lifted off toward the windshield. The spidered glass a parting gift on his way over the roof and back to the roadway.

Blake skidded to a stop and jumped out to assess the threat. The bloody pile didn't present one. And never would.

"Are you all right?" Blake darted to Haeli's side and touched her, gingerly.

"Mick. You made it." She smiled and giggled. The way she did when she had one too many cocktails.

"We've gotta go. Come on, I'll help you." Blake put his arm under hers and pulled her to her feet. Then led her toward the passenger side of the car.

"When we get home, can I take a nap?"

Blake chuckled. "You can sleep for a week if you want."

Holding her with one arm, he opened the door and tried to help her in. She resisted.

With two fingers, she touched his lips. Then leaned in and replaced her touch with a kiss.

Every second wasted could have meant the difference between life and death.

Yep. Totally worth it.

"Mmm." She put her hand over his mouth and giggled. "Sorry. I haven't brushed my teeth."

She was in rare form, for sure.

Blake reached over her and moved the laptop and pistol off the seat. Haeli lowered herself in and he shut the door.

On his way around the front of the car, he surveyed the damage. Besides the spider-webbed window, the hood was dented, the front grill was mangled, and the bumper was tilted. Otherwise, it had fared well.

The problem was not the damage. It was the blood and hair that accompanied it. Odds were, it was going to draw some attention. Which meant the first order of business was getting rid of it.

Blake hopped into the driver's side.

"Never a dull moment, eh?" He looked in the rearview mirror, shifted into gear, and started toward the rear exit. "I guess I've got some catching up to do." He turned onto the main road. "Might as well start from the beginning."

He turned to her.

"Haeli?"

She was fast asleep.

30

BLAKE'S SHOES AND SOCKS SAT PERCHED ON A BOULDER, OVERLOOKING THE
Danube River. Not the mighty Danube of Budapest or even Vienna.
Here, it was but a stream.

This hadn't been the intended destination. In fact, there hadn't been
one at all. After driving two-and-a-half hours in a mostly south or
southeast direction, zigzagging through back roads to avoid any inad-
vertent predictability, it was where they ended up.

The open patch of forest seemed like a good place to pause. It
wasn't far from the road, but it was private enough. And he wanted to
conserve their remaining fuel.

Once Haeli woke, they would discuss the next steps. Choose a destination. But for now, he would let her sleep. And he would use the time
for something productive.

With his sharkskin slacks hiked up to his knees, Blake waded bare-
foot in the river. He dragged the Brooks Brothers dress shirt back and
forth, allowing the current to wash away any blood or bits of flesh. He
balled it up, wrung it out, then dipped it again before plodding back up
the embankment to the car.

He slopped the pile of fabric onto the windshield and scrubbed, raking it across every snagging fracture. The water, tinged with red, ran into the wiper channel and found its way to the earth.

It wouldn't remove the traces of DNA—that would require specialized chemicals. Blake's actions weren't rooted in science so much as common sense. To find trace evidence, someone would have to be looking for it in the first place.

With each pass of the makeshift sponge, Blake could see Haeli through the pattern of shattered glass. Snuggled under the suit jacket he had draped over her, she was an artistic vision. A portrait captured in mosaic. Her dormant face, swollen, scratched, and stained, was still impossibly beautiful.

He made another trip to the water. Rinse and repeat.

The dress shirt had come in handier than he thought. Once in the concourse at Dulles International Airport, Blake had decided he needed to ditch the gym clothes. It was how he ended up looking like a walking Brooks Brothers advertisement. The options were limited. It was either that or Vineyard Vines, and he figured it wouldn't be a pastel polo and dock shoes type of trip.

In case he might need a quick change, he bought two suits, two dress shirts, two pairs of socks and a pair of shoes. Plus, there was a half-off special if he bought two. Even he had a hard time passing up a good deal. They were off the rack, but they fit well enough.

He donned the dark blue sharkskin out of the dressing room and stowed the other pieces in his knapsack. His original ensemble—gym shorts, T-shirt, sneakers—was deposited in the nearest trash bin.

The Glock? Unfortunately, by the time he got into the cab, it had already found its way to the bottom of the Potomac.

There was nothing worse than wasting a perfectly good, gently used firearm. But he couldn't take it with him, and he most certainly couldn't return home. Fezz and the others weren't around, otherwise he'd have offloaded it with one of them. For a moment, he did consider hiding it somewhere to be retrieved later, but he couldn't risk the chance of a kid stumbling upon it. No, it needed to go. Luckily for him, assuming the inner vault remained secure, he had many, many more where that one came from.

Blake climbed the embankment and went to work on a final wipe down.

As he swiped the windshield, he could see Haeli. Her face reanimated. Her mouth drawn up in a thoughtful smile.

Blake smiled back.

After a last pass, he balled up the shirt, tossed it into the water and watched it float downstream. He put on his socks and shoes before returning to the driver's seat.

"You're awake. How're you feeling?"

Haeli put her hands behind her head and arched her back. She yawned. "Better."

Blake leaned over and kissed her. She popped her hand out from under her improvised blanket and took his hand, weaving her fingers through his.

"Where are we?" she asked.

"Nowhere. Just looked like a good place to get off the road for a few."

"It's good to see you, Mick."

Blake laughed. "Yeah, it's good to see you, too. And in one piece, no less."

"Did they come for you?"

"Oh, they came for me. But I'm guessing they regret it now. Thanks for the heads up. I read your texts, you know."

"I figured you would. I mean, I hoped you would." She paused. "So then you know why I left? It wasn't because—"

"I know. I know. It's okay. You did what you thought was best. But what I don't understand is—well, any of it. Sokolov? Germany? And what is this about diamonds? What does any of it have to do with you?"

"It's a long story, but basically I'm sort of Sokolov's last ditch effort. A few years ago, my team and I worked a mission for the Israeli government. One of their assets was supposed to be delivering a large quantity of diamonds to Botswana on Sokolov's behalf. We were there to provide protection and to gather intel. The asset went rogue, and things went south. We fought our way out, but the asset managed to disappear himself. With the diamonds."

"And that's somehow your fault?"

"Sokolov ended up finding him. I'm guessing pretty recently. Apparently, he tried to save his own ass by putting the blame on us. It didn't work. Well, not the saving his own ass part. Sokolov's a real bad guy, Mick. I mean, bad."

"So I've gathered."

"He's not going to stop. The rest of the team, they're all dead, Mick. He killed them. All of them."

Tears welled in Haeli's eyes.

Blake reached over with his free hand and stroked her hair, then kissed her on the head. "I'm sorry."

"I went to Israel to warn them. I thought if I could get to them in time..." She turned her head and stared out the window.

Blake gave her a moment.

"I'm sorry I dragged you into this." Haeli retracted her hand from Blake's and manipulated the jacket so she could put it on.

"There's also a pair of pants in my bag you can wear for now. Until we can get you some clothes. They'll look ridiculous on you, but it's better than nothing."

"Okay. Thanks."

"And as far as dragging me into this, I wish you had sooner. The whole thing's ridiculous to begin with. Even the accusation. That you're some kind of thief. It pisses me off. I'd like to get ahold of those diamonds just so I can shove them down Sokolov's throat."

Haeli chortled. "They're worth tens of millions of dollars. Seems like an expensive meal."

"I don't care what they're worth. He can choke on them." He smiled.

"So what do we do now?"

"The first thing is to take care of this car. We'll have to stage a little accident. Find a spot, out of the way but within walking distance to civilization, and send it into a tree or something. We'll find a motel, get cleaned up, and I'll call in the stolen car report. Then we'll figure out how to get back to the States."

"That's all fine, but I told you already, he'll be there. He'll be wherever we go. Sokolov runs one of the largest crime syndicates in the world. It's not like we're just going to go home, and everything goes back to normal."

"Then we don't. We stay and finish it. Go on the offensive."

"If we could even find him, we'd never get near him. When we were working with Mossad, back in Botswana, they said no agent had ever gotten close enough to Sokolov to lay eyes on him in person. The fact that he came to interrogate me himself, instead of just sending his people, it's unheard of. For some reason he's got some kind of personal vendetta."

"He was there? At the trash place?"

"Yeah. He had me drugged. Sat right there in front of me."

Blake thought back to the two men he had seen on the cameras. They had mentioned his name. "Does he happen to have a deformity?"

"No. That would be his psycho sidekick. The guy's missing an ear."

"Damn it. I had them."

"What do you mean?"

"I mean, Sokolov was still there while I was there. I watched him drive away before coming after you. I could've ended it right there."

"You could have gotten yourself killed."

"Maybe, but now what? He's in the wind, and we're chasing our tails."

Haeli slapped the dashboard. "So then we draw him out. We send him a message that I have the diamonds, and I'm willing to hand them over. I can reply to the text he sent. I'm sure it will get back to him. Except, I don't have my phone."

Blake reached under his seat. "This one?" He handed it to her. "Don't turn it on. I've got the number on my laptop, anyway. From the backup."

"Okay. That's the working plan then. Ditch the car, find a room, get some new clothes, and then figure out how we set him up and get the upper hand."

"I've got an idea," Blake said. "We need to get to Stuttgart. We can ditch the car once we're close. If we're going to do this, we'll need help. I've still got a few contacts there I can reach out to. There's one in particular. Let's just say he's got a unique set of skills." Blake turned the ignition. "I'll explain what I'm thinking on the way. Sound good?"

"Sure."

Blake hooked his arm around the back of Haeli's chair and looked out the rear window as he backed away from the embankment.

"I'm thinking we keep the Calvin Kline underwear-ad look though. It's kinda sexy."

Haeli twisted a finger to her cheek. "Awww, you think I'm sexy? Are you comin' on to me Blake Brier?"

Blake threw the car in drive. "You bet your ass I am."

31

FRESHLY BATHED AND SPORTING NEW, MORE COMFORTABLE ATTIRE, BLAKE and Haeli walked hand-in-hand through the square, which teemed with tourists and locals alike.

Schlossplatz, roughly translated in English as "Castle Place" or "Palace Square", was one of the focal points of Stuttgart. Situated in front of an eighteenth-century palace, the square was once used for military parades. These days it was used for art exhibits, fairs, and general lounging about. On this day, lounging about seemed to be the activity of choice.

People sat on blankets, played hacky sack in the grass, and sat hip-to-hip around the central fountain. Blake was surprised and amazed. Not by its charm—he had been there many times before—but by the realization that hacky sack was still a thing.

The palace itself had been restored after incurring heavy damage during World War II. It was what set the square apart from its surroundings.

Much of the city had been destroyed beyond repair as a result of Allied bombing. The majority of the rebuild had occurred when the economy began to recover in the late seventies and early eighties. As a result, the place had an eclectic aesthetic that appeared frozen in time. Old world European meets postmodern disco.

Being there brought back memories. Some good, some bad. Mostly, it reminded him of Anja. They had met in this city, and it was where her and Christa's parents had lived. In a way, he was glad he could re-experience it with Haeli. Launder the memories a bit. There was, after all, some enjoyment to be had. Even if the current circumstances were a bit tenuous.

Blake had once called Stuttgart home, but the truth was, he was just as much a visitor then as he was now. The home of the United States European Command and African Command, it was, among other things, a hub of operations for the U.S. Special Forces. While thousands of U.S. servicemen and women lived and worked there, for Blake it was merely a jumping off point. A launch pad to places unknown.

Sometimes he wondered why he had chosen to leave it all behind. Even though, in his heart, he knew the answer. It had been time. Time to reclaim some semblance of a life. Time to make way for the next nineteen-year-old kid, full of piss and vinegar.

It was the cycle of life.

That night, somewhere in the city, a ten-year-old army brat with an astute eye would be sneaking out in the middle of the night to catch a glimpse of the blacked-out cargo planes coming or going, their only mark the sound of their engines and the flashing of the stars they eclipsed. Watching and dreaming. And thinking, *One day I'm going to be on one of those planes.*

"This place is great," Haeli said.

"It is."

And it was. But while the square was a nice place to visit, it wasn't exactly an ideal place for a clandestine meeting. Unfortunately, his contact had insisted, and he knew, as well as anyone, that beggars can't be choosers.

"To your left," Blake said, "on the bench. That's Oli."

Oli. Short for Oliver, he assumed. But when it came to made up names, did it really matter? Whoever Oli was at birth, they were long since dead and buried.

"See him?"

Haeli nodded and they sauntered in that direction. Looking around, pretending to take pictures. Once they were close, they milled around for a few more minutes. The plan was to ask him if he minded if they sat, then pretend to strike up small talk. In case anyone was watching.

"What are you doing?" Oli shifted on the bench to call over his shoulder.

Oli was a character. Wild, curly hair. Coke bottle glasses. A socks with sandals type. Born in the Black Forest region and raised in the United States, he had started with the CIA before Blake had even graduated primary school. When he spoke English, he did so with a bit of New York swagger. But when he spoke German, he channeled the Swabian accent flawlessly.

In Stuttgart, like much of the south, the Swabian dialect prevailed. It differed from standard German. Words were spelled differently. Pronounced differently. It was a distinct subculture. But Oli, he was a subculture of his own.

Blake and Haeli approached.

"Incremental insertion," Blake said.

"Please. This isn't a James Bond movie. Sit down."

They sat.

"You got old," Oli said.

"You haven't changed a bit."

Blake slapped him on the back of the shoulder. Oli met it with a blank stare.

"Schlossplatz?" Blake questioned.

"The best place to hide is right out in the open. Always served me well. Anyway, no one out here knows who I am or what I do. Hell, most of the people I work for don't know what I do. But you do, right Blake? Which, I'm guessing, is the reason you called." He leaned around Blake. "And you are?"

"Haeli." She offered her hand.

"Pleasure." Oli pinched Haeli's hand as if she were Duchess Cecilie. "The fact that Blake has brought you here tells me he vouches for you beyond all possible reproach. Am I correct in this assumption?"

"You are correct," Blake said.

Oli was an odd bird, always had been. In his line of work, Blake guessed one would have to be. But he and his team had been there when Oli needed something. When Oli came to him asking for a favor. A task, about which no questions could be asked. Now, he only hoped that the cantankerous old man would return the favor under the same conditions.

"So what can I do for you?"

"I need one of your items, small enough to fit in a case about this big." Blake bladed his hands horizontally, then vertically, to approximate a one-foot by four-inch box.

"A bomb is what you need. You can say it, we're all adults here. Right Haeli?"

Haeli nodded and then looked behind her, presumably to see if she was being filmed as part of a hidden camera television show.

"And the person or persons you intend to kill are a threat to the security of the United States or her allies?"

"Actually," Blake said. "We don't intend to use it at all. But we need it to be fully functional. With remote arming capability."

"You need an explosive device with remote arming capability, but you do not intend to use it?"

"That's the gist, yes."

Oli leaned forward again to look Haeli in the eye. "The pitch is not very convincing. It's lacking a bit of—what am I thinking of?—logic. Common sense. A justifiable reason of any kind."

"We know," Haeli said. "But it's better you don't know."

"Ah. Yes. And so it might be." Oli took his glasses off, rubbed them on his AfB Stuttgart football jersey, and then put them back on. "And when would you need this device?"

"As soon as possible," Blake said.

"You know, there are few people I trust."

Oli left it at that. Blake knew what he meant. It was a reference to the past. A quid pro quo about to be made good.

"There's one other thing." Blake pulled several small square photographs from his pocket and handed them to Oli. Self-portraits. "We need passports."

"I don't do passports."

"I know. But you know who does."

"Tell me something," Oli said. "On a scale from 1 to 10, what are the chances this blows up in both our faces? No pun intended."

Blake could have said "Zero," but it would have been the wrong answer. There was always a chance. Every operation had some risk. Some more than others.

"Eh," Blake said with a grin, "a Muggeseggele."

Oli let out a hardy laugh and, this time, slapped Blake on the shoulder.

Muggeseggele. The smallest unit of measurement in Stuttgart. It was a Swabian saying that literally translated to "Housefly scrotum." But it wasn't used in a vulgar way. In fact, it was commonly used by old women and school children alike. More importantly, it was one of Oli's favorite sayings.

"I'll have it to you tomorrow." Oli stood up. "And I dare say this makes us even."

And so it did.

32

BLAKE PUSHED THE PAPER HANDLES OF THE BAG UP HIS FOREARM AND pinned the tray against his body so he could turn the doorknob. It hadn't occurred to him before, but the antique, clear glass knob was cut to look like a giant diamond. Ironic, under the circumstances. He pushed his way in.

"Mornin'."

Still in bed, Haeli turned to her side and rested her head on her hand and her elbow on the mattress. The light streaming through the horizontal slats of the wooden shutters striped her. She was beaming from ear to ear.

"Come back to beds," she said.

Blake laughed. *Beds.*

The no-frills room had come with two twin-size beds. The night before, they had removed the small table from between them and pushed them together to make one, big uncomfortable mattress. Luckily, comfort wasn't what they were going for.

"It's nine o'clock."

"I thought you said I could sleep for weeks."

"That was a one time offer." Blake placed the paper bag and

metallic case on the bed, then popped a paper cup from the tray and handed it to Haeli. She sat up.

"Coffee. Didn't know what you'd want so I got eggs, sausage, some rolls with marmalade, and potato pancakes."

"Yes, please."

"Which one?"

"All of it." Haeli swung her feet to the floor.

"Someone worked up an appetite." Blake dragged the table to the edge of the bed and pulled up the lone chair next to it. He sat on the bed and started to dig into the breakfast stash.

Haeli pulled on Blake's t-shirt from the day before. It hung to mid-thigh. "Is that it?"

"It is."

He abandoned the food for a moment, lifted the metal case, and placed it on the table. Haeli walked around and sat in the chair across from him.

"When he said tomorrow, I didn't think he meant the crack of dawn." He unlatched it and lifted the top on its hinges.

Inside was a row of cylinders, a small black box, and a bunch of wires.

"Are we sure it's safe?" she asked.

"I'm sure. Oli's a master. This thing's not going off unless we want it to. Unless we drop it really hard." Blake slammed it closed. "Boom."

Haeli jumped. "Stop it."

Blake slapped a blue booklet onto the case. "Your new passport, Ms. Katlyn Richards. And, oh yeah." He reached into his pocket. "I picked up a prepaid. We've just gotta figure out what we want to text him."

Haeli took the passport and examined it. "Can you move that?" She pointed to the case.

He moved it to the bed, grabbed the paper sack, and started laying out the Styrofoam containers on the table, opening each with a flourish. He took the passport from Haeli, exchanging it for a pack of utensils. "Dig in."

Haeli popped a plastic fork through its cellophane wrapper and dug into a potato pancake. "Hmmm. So good. I like this little breakfast date. Very romantic."

"Making up for lost time."

Haeli finished chewing a bite of sausage and went back for another. "I don't know what I was thinking. When I got those pictures, those texts, the only thing I could think of was getting as far away from you as I could."

"Wow. Really?"

"That's not what I meant. I thought if I left—I mean, I was who he wanted. Once I was gone, he'd have lost interest in you. And you wouldn't even know about it. It was my way of trying to protect you."

"And what if you were killed and I never knew what happened? Never even had a chance to help. Did you even consider that?"

Blake realized how selfish it sounded. *If you were killed, how would that affect me?* But he was just being honest.

"You're right. I should have waited for you. Or gone to you. We could have figured it out together. God knows I only made it worse."

"You didn't make it worse. If you hadn't gone to them, they would have been killed just the same. Only sooner. You know that's true."

"I know it is. But I can't stop feeling responsible. It's like once I get it in my head that it's my job to protect someone, it's all consuming. I loved those guys. They were my friends. You know what I'm talking about, I know you do. I could hear it in your voice when you talked about Christa's daughter. You had attached yourself to her, a girl you never met, and you took it personally."

"That's exactly right. And there's nothing wrong with you taking it personally. We're not robots, Haeli. People like us, we can turn off that sense of human empathy when we need to. To bring extreme violence when it's warranted. But you've got to be able to turn it back on. And you can't let it eat you alive. I've been down that road. And that's exactly what I wanted to tell you. When I got back home. I wanted to tell you that it was over."

"What? Us?"

"No, not us. Me being an ass. Wallowing in the past. I realized something out in Rhode Island. Actually, I realized a lot of things. But the most important was that I love you. And that I hadn't been able to get out of my own way to tell you or to show you what you mean to me. I didn't need a shrink to tell me I'm screwed up. I'm screwed up. But I know what's important. You are important. To me."

The words hung in the air for a moment. He had spewed off more than he intended. But he meant every word of it.

Haeli looked at him with the most cavalier expression he had ever seen come across her face. "I know."

"You know?"

"Mick, come on. You're crazy about me."

God damn, she was cute when she wanted to be.

"Okay, fine, enough of the heart to heart, then. How about we figure out this plan?"

Haeli formed her mouth into an oval of mock surprise while clearly fighting back a smile. She poked at the potato pancakes with her fork while she sang an improvised song. "He loves me. He really loves me. He even said so. He even said so."

"You're ridiculous," Blake said.

She repeated her song, only louder. And instead of the pancakes she poked him with the fork. "You love me, you really, really love me."

On the fourth poke, Blake snatched her wrist, pulled her over the table, and kissed her. A long, passionate kiss that could have easily drawn him back into the bed. Which, he knew, was her evil plan all along.

"Seriously," Blake said. "We've gotta hash this out. What's the plan?"

Haeli dropped her fork and sat back in her chair. "We blow Sokolov to smithereens?"

"No. Not the plan. We send a message that you're done running and that you're willing to make a deal. The diamonds for your freedom. That part's been established. We tell him we're in Stuttgart and that the diamonds are here. In a bank safe deposit box, right? I'll stake out the outside, while you go in with the case. When he arrives, you make like you just retrieved it and hand it off to him. Once you do, I make a call reporting a man with a bomb, threatening to blow up the bank. I give a good description. Make and model of his car, direction of travel, the works. By the time he leaves the bank, there'll be a welcoming committee waiting for him outside. Or at least stopping his car a block or two away. Did I miss anything?"

"Yeah, the part where he blows up."

"We're not blowing up a bank, Haeli. And we're not getting any cops hurt. Once the cops take him and separate him from the bomb, once we know the bomb squad is going to address the case, then we'll arm it. Just so it's operational when they go to neutralize it. The criminal charges wouldn't mean much if the thing is inert."

"The plan's fine, but I don't like sticking around here. Too close to his turf and we have to choose a bank out of a hat. I know a bank in Zurich. I've used it before. Perfect layout, and it will make sense. If he's to believe I have the diamonds and hid them in a safe deposit box, it wouldn't be here. Switzerland, on the other hand—"

"That's not a bad idea. Three-hour train ride, tops. And if we can get down there first and set up, it could be an advantage. Saves us from scouting a bank around here and puts some distance between us and Sokolov in the meantime."

"See. Aren't ya glad I'm here?"

"Wouldn't be here without ya, that's for sure."

"As long as Sokolov takes the bait, I'd say it's a solid plan."

"He'll take the bait. But are we confident he'll show up, himself? It doesn't help us if he sends earless or another pack of blockheads."

"Oh no, he wouldn't send someone else. I guarantee you, he wouldn't miss it."

"Okay, then." Blake stood up and started tidying the remains of breakfast. "We'll text him when we're on the train."

Haeli stood up as well. She slipped the t-shirt over her head. "But in the meantime, I'm sure we have a few minutes to spare."

33

As they walked, Blake swung the silver case by its handle, depriving it of the reverence it deserved. And it was by design.

Blake had learned long ago that a person only became suspicious when they themself believed they were. He figured he could pretty much walk into an opera house with a bazooka, as long as he acted like it was perfectly normal. Conversely, hyper awareness was what led to mistakes.

It was akin to walking on the edge of a hundred story building. Not many would attempt it for fear of losing their footing and plummeting to their death. But they walked to the building, climbed the stairs, crossed the roof, all without managing to fall once. All of a sudden, the ability to maintain balance was called into question. Why?

The stakes.

Men like Blake, the top tier operators of the world, can do what they do, not because of some superhuman ability, but because they're able to ignore the stakes and focus on the task. The future of the free world on the line? Better cancel those dinner plans. Outmanned and outgunned, three to one? Another day at the office.

This was no different. Just two people on holiday. And aside from an X-ray machine or possibly a specialized dog, who could say otherwise?

When Blake had met with Oli to pick up their order, Oli had rattled on about the makeup of the device. Most of the technical details had gone in one ear and out the other, but Blake got the gist of it. The core compound was a proprietary mixture, like composition 4, or C-4, in that it used RDX as the explosive agent and included binders and plasticizer. But there was one major difference. Commercial C-4 included taggants. Chemicals that acted as an identifier, used in detecting its presence and tracing its origin. Oli's version contained no such thing. At the time, he hadn't thought to ask if bomb-sniffing dogs would still be able to smell it. He assumed they were trained to hit on the RDX, if it had a scent, but knowing Oli there was a chance he had a workaround for that too.

Sixteen hours earlier they had breezed through the Stuttgart Hauptbahnhof station without so much as a second glance. Luckily, police presence was minimal, and there hadn't been any bomb-sniffing dogs to contend with.

A month prior and it would have been a hit-or-miss proposition. Stuttgart was insane about their football. During the season, whenever there was a game at the Mercedes-Benz arena, the riot police would come out in force to try to prevent the inevitable brawls between fans of AfB Stuttgart and the devotees of whatever club had dared challenge them. Part of the police effort included locking down the train stations and physically separating the rivals as they arrived. The exercise may have been effective in lowering the number of stabbings, but as far as he and Haeli were concerned, that kind of attention would have only served to cramp their style.

It was much the same when they arrived in Zurich. People going about their daily lives, oblivious to the couple carrying nearly five pounds of plastic explosives and armed with a half-cocked idea.

Since then, the idea had solidified itself into a proper plan. Three-quarters cocked, Blake would say.

The route they walked now was not haphazard. They had walked it before. Run through each step, over and over throughout the morning, in anticipation of the arranged meeting.

It hadn't taken much convincing on their part. Once they had boarded the train, the message was sent. Within two minutes, they had received a response. Within five, the time and place were set.

Now, twenty minutes away from go time, they would get themselves into position. From there, a chain of events would be set into motion that would determine the quality and quantity of their collective future.

As they approached the staging point, a narrow alley across the street from the Zurich International Bank, Blake broke their mile long silence.

"All right, here we are. Are you ready?"

"I'm ready." Haeli gazed out toward the bank, no doubt running through her own mental checklist.

They had chosen that spot because it offered an unimpeded view of the ornate pillars and archways of the building's main entrance, while still being out of camera range. If all went well, the wide steps, which spilled away from the building and onto the sidewalk, would be the scene of a spectacular production, written and directed by Haeli Becher and Blake Brier.

"Here." Blake handed her the wireless earpiece. "Give it a whirl."

Haeli inserted it into her ear, as he did the same.

"Can you hear me?" she asked.

Blake removed the device, turned a minuscule dial with the tip of his finger, and reinserted it. He pointed at her.

"Can you hear me now?"

"That's better."

Blake had configured the system to give Haeli an open mic. That way he could hear everything that was going on inside the bank without her having to press the tiny button each time she wanted to talk. Constantly sticking her finger in her ear wouldn't have been a good look, whether she was on comms or not.

If Blake needed to communicate with her, he only needed to key up.

"You'd better get in there."

"I know." She shook out her hands and exhaled through pursed lips. If he thought about it, Blake couldn't remember ever seeing her so stirred up.

"It's going to be fine. Easy peasy. Let me know when you're at the safe deposit boxes. If you can't get near the vault, find a bathroom or somewhere out of the way to wait. Once I give you the signal he's walking in, count to sixty before coming out. After you make the hand-off, get the hell out as quick as you can. I'll meet you at the rendezvous point."

"I've got it, Mick. Nothing's changed."

"Just don't dilly dally. Once you're out, don't look back. I'll manage the rest."

"I said I got it, didn't I?"

"Okay, okay. Well, then, good luck."

"Wait. You have the remote right?"

Blake reached into his back pocket and produced the small black clicker. He waved it in front of her before stashing it back in his pants.

"Give me a hug." She wrapped her arms around him and squeezed. He squeezed her back.

Loosening her grip, she leaned back and looked him in the eyes.

Their lips drew together. Oppositely charged magnets, helpless to the invisible force that bound them.

As they sank into the kiss, Haeli slid her hands to his buttocks.

"I love you." She separated from him.

"I love you, too."

Blake handed her the case.

Not but a second after her fingers closed around the handle, she was on her way.

34

Haeli forewent the revolving doors, using the traditional entry to its right instead.

As she stepped inside, she moved a few feet out of the path of travel and scanned the cavernous lobby. With organized methodology, she passed her gaze over every customer and employee in the place.

"He's not inside," she said.

The earpiece clicked. "Still clear out here as well."

The bank was a marvel. The outside, with its stone columns and palatial footprint, existed in direct contrast to the modern interior. Not just in its decor, but in its technology. It was one of the reasons why she had used this particular bank in the past. The main reason she kept her safe deposit box there.

Security was of utmost importance to her, yes. But so was anonymity. And the level of automation the bank had incorporated provided an ample amount of both.

She needed no direction on how to proceed.

The kiosk, positioned at the end of the long teller counter, would handle her needs with no other human intervention. She moved to it.

As she approached, the motion sensors engaged the prompt and the friendly greeting played in English, German, French, and Italian. "Welcome, please enter your personal access number."

She punched in the twelve-digit code from memory. The first three represented the box number. The other nine, the private key.

"Thank you. Your card has been activated. You have thirty minutes until expiration."

A plastic card appeared in the slot, lit by green LEDs. Haeli plucked it from the machine and, after another quick look around, headed for the vault.

From the entrance to the short hallway, the vault opening was visible. Wide open, the two-foot-thick door sat snug against the hallway wall.

A guard sitting behind a small podium nodded as she passed into the vault. His job was one of appearances. But she noticed he was armed.

The typical safe deposit vault, whether in Israel or the United States, was a single room housing rows of locked compartments. For this reason, only one person could access their box at a time. Here, this was not the case.

Once inside the main vault, there were smaller rooms to the right, left, and straight ahead. When occupied, the locked doors showed a red X on the exterior of the door. Inside, there was only one drawer. By inserting the temporary magnetic card, internal mechanisms retrieved the appropriate box from somewhere beyond view and delivered it to the requester.

It was private and efficient. But most importantly, it did not require a name, fingerprint, or photo identification. Anyone with the twelve-digit code could access it.

None of the rooms appeared to be occupied. She chose the first one on her right.

Once inside, she remembered how spacious they were. Even with the high rectangular pedestal in the center of the room, it could have accommodated three or four people without having to crowd together.

She approached the drawer mechanism and inserted her card into the slot. Following a digital tone, a whirring and ticking sound continued for thirty seconds or so, before ending with a metallic clunk. The handle of the drawer lit green.

She placed the case on the counter and then pulled open the drawer. With two hands, she removed the safe deposit box and set it down on the counter next to the explosives.

"I have eyes on him," Blake said.

Haeli reached into her ear and removed the communication device and let it slip from her fingers to the floor. With her heel, she crushed it.

* * *

"Haeli, do you read me? I think I've lost audio. If you're reading me, the target is moving to the front doors. He's got 'Earless' with him. Stay alert. Plus, there are two more posted out front. Do you copy?"

Blake waited for a response. There was nothing but static.

* * *

Haeli unlocked the door and stepped into the vault corridor, empty handed except for the magnetic keycard.

As she passed, she flashed the guard a friendly wave, then turned her attention to the faces of the patrons in the lobby. She spotted them immediately.

Sokolov and Nikitin. They really did look like brothers.

Both dressed in gray suits, white shirts with no ties. They earned no points for originality.

Haeli made a beeline toward them, ending up nose to chin with Sokolov.

"Now you have your diamonds, you leave me and Blake and everyone else I know alone."

"Where are they?"

Haeli held the card in front of his face with two fingers. "They're in the safe deposit box. Go get them yourself."

Sokolov snatched the card from Haeli's hand. She pushed past him, but before she could take another step, the fingers of Nikitin's left hand clamped around her upper arm.

"No so fast," Sokolov said. "You're not going anywhere until I have them in my hands."

Haeli noticed Nikitin had shoved his hand into his jacket pocket. She could see the barrel of the pistol pulling taut against the fabric.

"What are you going to do, shoot me? In the middle of a crowded bank?"

Nikitin sneered.

But not Sokolov. He seemed to find amusement in the question.

"I am a valued customer here. I am sure I can smooth it over. Or do you think the police will arrest me? It hurts that you underestimate me so. After all that we have been through together. You need to understand something. I could shoot everyone in this bank and burn it to the ground and still walk right down the middle of the street. No one will touch me. How do you like that for power?"

"You're a sick man."

"I am. But not as sick as Pavel. And I promised him he can have you if you do not deliver. So, I tell you one more time. We go together. If you are lying to me, you will live the rest of your short life in Pavel's basement. Let us go now, yes?"

Sokolov started walking toward the vault. Nikitin forced Haeli behind him.

As they passed the guard, she considered flagging him down. Screaming for help. But she knew it would only get the poor guy killed along with her.

Inside, Sokolov moved by several vacant rooms, finally settling on the last one on their right. He opened the door and waited, while Nikitin shoved her inside.

* * *

"HAELI, CAN YOU READ ME?"

The silence was deafening. Blake looked at his watch. She should have been out by now. It was a simple handoff. Half a minute, tops. No, something was wrong.

"Haeli, I'm gonna come in after you. Talk to me."

Nothing.

If things had gone to plan, he would have already made the call and the police would be on their way. Now, with no communication and no visual, it was anyone's guess what went awry. Did Sokolov open the case immediately and stop her from leaving? Was everyone in the bank frozen in a hostage protocol?

The only good news was the bomb hadn't been armed. Even if things had gone south, no innocent people would be hurt.

He reached into his back pocket.

What the—

He tried the other.

Haeli! What'd you do?

Why would she lift the remote? What was she planning on doing? They had a plan. They agreed. He couldn't wrap his head around it.

There was only one way to find out. He would have to go in. The only problem was, he'd have to get through the two goons first. And chances were, that was going to cause a scene in itself.

Damn it. I'm going.

Blake eased out onto the sidewalk and crossed the street. He fell in a few feet behind a family of three, who didn't appear to be in much of a rush.

There were two possibilities ahead. One, the men hadn't been instructed to look for him or were too dumb or distracted and he could just slip by, unnoticed. Two, well, all hell would break loose. If that were the case, he'd have to get close enough before they noticed him to have any chance at neutralizing them both.

Head down, he inched his way toward the steps.

* * *

SOKOLOV INSERTED THE CARD. THE MACHINERY DID ITS WORK AND THE handle turned green.

Haeli made it a point to remain optimistic, even when things looked bleak, but there was no bright side to this scenario. Whatever happened, it was hard to see how she would end up as anything but dead.

Sokolov removed the box and placed it on the pedestal. He swung the lid open to reveal the shiny metallic case inside.

"How did you think you would get away with stealing from me?" As he spoke, he lifted it out as if removing the stone tablets from the Arc of the Covenant.

Haeli raised her voice. "Take them. Take them and leave. I don't ever want to see your face again." It was a last-ditch effort, and a weak one at that.

"Let us not get ahead of ourselves." He placed his thumbs on the latch levers.

"No!" Haeli reached for the case.

Nikitin swooped in, grabbed her by both arms, and slammed her onto the floor.

She hit hard, landing on her hip. It throbbed.

Then, from her pocket, she heard a faint beeping.

The remote.

Sokolov released the latches.

It's armed.

"No!"

As Sokolov lifted the lid, Haeli threw herself onto her stomach and covered her head with her hands.

Then, nothing.

She sat up.

Sokolov stood staring at the tubes and wires. He ran his hand along the inside of the empty safe deposit box as if he had somehow missed a pile of diamonds in the visual inspection. Then he lifted the empty box above his head and smashed it onto the ground by his feet. "You bitch!"

Haeli sprang to her feet and dove at the handle of the door. It swung open, and she tumbled into the vault corridor. Nikitin darted after her.

Back on her feet, she sprinted past the guard and into the lobby, Nikitin a few feet behind.

The guard hopped off his stool and started to give chase.

As she glanced over her shoulder, Nikitin crashed into her, tackling her to the ground. He straddled her and blasted her in the face with a right jab. She put her hands up to try to protect her face.

"You stupid bitch." He hit her again. "You tried to kill him? Blow him up? But you failed."

The guard pulled his gun and pointed at Nikitin. "Get off of her. Hands up. Hands up."

Nikitin stopped and raised his hands. As he stood, he wound up and delivered a football kick to Haeli's abdomen. The force slid her a body a foot across the marble floor.

"You're wrong about one thing," Haeli coughed. "I didn't fail."

She reached into her pocket and pulled out the remote. Her finger hovered over the button.

Haeli could see the realization appear in his eyes. Then anger. Then horror.

What Nikitin did next, she would never have expected. He took off in a sprint. Not for the doors, but toward the vault.

"Olezka! Get out! Get out!"

Haeli brought her knees up, curled into a tight little ball, and pushed.

Click.

Boom.

Haeli's eardrums rattled. A wave of heat and air assaulted her. A cloud of smoke enveloped the room. And then, it was over.

Ears ringing, Haeli looked to her left. The guard laid on the floor, next to her. Blown off his feet. He slowly got himself into a seated position.

Haeli staggered to her feet. She orientated herself, the light coming through the blown-out doors, a beacon in the murky haze.

Her lungs revolted against the fumes. Pined for a breath of fresh air. She pushed forward toward the daylight.

* * *

BLAKE REACHED THE STEPS. LEAVING THE COVER OF THE MEANDERING family, he would have to close the remaining gap in the open. They hadn't noticed him yet. Maybe he could get the drop.

He scratched his head, covering his face with his hair and his forearm. All the while, moving closer and closer.

Four feet, three, two. He cocked his fist at his side.

Boom.

The building rumbled. The glass doors shattered, pelting Blake with stinging shards and sending debris raining down into the street. Smoke billowed from the void.

Haeli.

The buzzing of the fire alarm lingered in the strange silence.

Sokolov's men ran toward the building.

Blake followed. "Haeli!"

As he passed the enormous columns and under the arch, Haeli appeared through the smoke. A phoenix from the ashes.

Blake triaged her from a distance. She was tattered, but otherwise did not appear to have any catastrophic injuries.

He ran to her. Hugged her. "Are you okay?"

"I'm okay."

He put his arm around her back and helped her toward the steps.

"Mick, I'm fine. I can walk."

Reluctantly, he let go.

Haeli picked up speed, hustling down the steps.

Blake caught up. "We've gotta get out of here. What happened?"

"Sokolov's gone. It's over."

As they turned the corner at the end of the building, they ran. As fast as their legs would take them.

35

"I THINK WE'RE FAR ENOUGH," BLAKE HUFFED. HE WASN'T SURE HOW FAR they had run, but he figured it was at least a mile. They needed to regroup, and they weren't going to be able to do it on the move.

"I'm with ya. Let's find a place to duck out for a few." Haeli's speech was unaffected by the physical exertion. Not a hint of elevated respiration. It was annoying. The woman was nearly blown up, and then ran a six-minute mile. The least she could do was pretend to be winded.

"Follow me."

At each intersection they had taken turns calling their next move. Haeli preferred cutting through courtyards and parking lots. Whenever Blake had his say, he chose to continue straight. To his mind, the more distance, the better.

He figured they had gotten far enough away from the melee that they could blend in. Here, somewhere in the seemingly endless swath of a commercial district, people on the street went about their business, oblivious to the fact that the explosion had occurred.

But they would know soon enough. Everyone in proximity to a television, radio, or internet connected device would know in a matter of minutes.

By now, the circus would be arriving. Police, fire, news media, the works. There would be initial speculative reporting about the explosion, but it would take some time to determine the actual cause. By the time information started to flow, he and Haeli would be back in the United States, tuning in to BBC World News.

"There." Blake pointed out a storefront cafe. Max, it was called. Max Cafe. There were tables set up on the sidewalk with plastic chairs, some yellow, some green. All of them were empty. The front door was held wide open by a stopper, leaving no guesswork as to whether it was open. It looked inviting, and it was as good a place as any.

Inside there were a few tables, also empty. Blake chose one by the window. Even though they would be visible from the street, it was the furthest table away from the counter. There were things they needed to discuss. In private.

The TV mounted on the wall played a daytime talk show. A Swiss knockoff of The View unless it was the other way around. The volume was turned up loud enough to provide some cover while they talked.

Haeli sat while Blake went to the counter.

"Two coffees, please."

The young woman walked away and returned with two heavy mugs on saucers and a stainless-steel pitcher of cream.

"Black's fine, thank you." He dug out whatever cash he had, then separated the Swiss francs from the euros.

"Säch einefüfzg." Six fifty-one. The woman spoke Swiss German. Quite different from standard German, but he was able to decipher her meaning.

He handed her ten. "Keep it." He picked up the coffees by the saucers and balanced them over to the table.

"Coffee?"

Blake shrugged. "We can't just sit here without ordering."

"Obviously, but I was thinking something with chocolate. This is Switzerland."

"Are you serious right now?" Blake lowered his voice. "You're going to sit here and act like nothing happened. What the hell is going on, Haeli? Why did you detonate it? You could have been killed. Not to mention go to prison. You probably just created a freakin' international incident."

Deja Vu.

It was like watching a rerun of the day they met. Running from the Las Vegas convention center, dipping into a small empty bar to regroup. To access the damage. He remembered sitting across from her and wondering who she really was and what she was really up to. Now he wondered the same thing.

"Don't be mad, Mick."

"Don't be mad? The whole time you acted like you were good with the plan, but you lied to me."

"I was, at first. Even when we got here, I intended to stick to it. It's just—"

"What? Not crazy enough for you?"

"No. Too crazy. Too convoluted. It wasn't going to work. He was never going to prison, Mick. I'm sorry, but it wasn't gonna happen. And as long as he was alive, we would have been in danger. I know it seems like I tricked you but—"

"It doesn't seem like you tricked me, you did trick me." Blake looked toward the counter to see if the worker was eavesdropping. She had retreated to somewhere in the back. He kept his voice low, regardless. "Look, it was a little over-reaching, I'll admit, but half of it was your idea. You're the whole reason we're in Zurich in the first place."

"There's a reason we're here, Mick. You know how I said that I was familiar with that bank, that I had used it before? Well, I still had a safe deposit box there. That's the reason why it had to be that bank."

"Okay, I get that. I mean, I get the reasoning. It made it easier to get into the vault. Made it look like you were legitimately getting the diamonds, all of that, but—"

"Mick. You don't get it." Haeli twisted her head toward the counter. Then back again. "I was getting the diamonds. From the safe deposit box. *My* safe deposit box."

The statement hit him like a twelve-gauge slug. Was she saying what he thought she was saying? She hadn't left much room for misinterpretation.

"Haeli, no. No. No. You are not telling me this. After everything, now you're saying Sokolov was right? That's bull. I don't believe it."

She stared him in the eye. Her face placid, lacking any of the appropriate emotion. She dipped her hand below the edge of the table, below Blake's sight line, and shifted her body. Then, with a smirk, presented a palm full of large, jagged, colorless stones.

"My god." Blake covered his face with his hands and then ran his fingers through his hair. "This can't be happening. Why didn't you tell me?"

"I don't know. I thought about telling you. But the way you got so upset that Sokolov was accusing me, like it was absurd to even suggest I would have anything to do with it. I felt like you'd be disappointed with me."

"Well, you were right about that. I am disappointed. Not that you stole them—well, that too. But mostly because you lied to me. If I had known you had them all along, we could have taken a whole different approach with Sokolov."

"Exactly. You would have wanted to give them back. As if Sokolov would have just said 'Oh, I've got them back, we're all good now, have a nice day.' Tell me you wouldn't have."

"So instead, you were willing to die so these pieces of rock could sit in a safe deposit box forever?"

"Listen to yourself, you're being delusional. He was going to kill me either way. I wasn't going to let him have the satisfaction. I wanted him to go to his grave knowing that he got burned. It was the reason I decided to take them in the first place. To stick it to the bastard."

"I came out here to help you, not to be an accomplice in a jewelry heist."

"It's not a jewelry heist, Mick. Sokolov was an evil man who committed horrible crimes. These diamonds were paid for by the blood of innocent people. Wouldn't it be fitting for them to be put to good use? In honor of the people Sokolov terrorized. Are you saying they'd be better in his hands than ours?"

"That's not what I'm saying. You're trying to twist this around on me."

"I'm not, but I just want you to think about it. With Sokolov gone, we can sell them. They're worth fifty million dollars, Mick. Even on the black market. Don't you realize what that means? The team. The mission. Your big idea. It's all possible now. Fezz and Khat and Griff. Money will never be an issue. Ever. We'll have the resources to help people who have nowhere else to turn, just like we envisioned."

Blake swallowed hard. He wanted to feel repulsed by the suggestion. He wanted to be able to tell her that she had lost her mind. But his own brain had already started to rationalize the proposition. She was right about Sokolov. She was right about a lot of things.

Haeli flicked her head and shifted her eyes. The woman was back behind the counter. He wondered how long she had been standing there. And how much she had heard.

Blake took a sip of his coffee and looked out the window. He waited until the worker wandered off again.

"How?" He whispered.

"How what?"

"How did you guys pull this off?"

Haeli's eyes widened, and her eyes welled. Something about the question had triggered her.

It took a moment, but she regained her composure.

"They didn't know. Michael, Ricky, Chet. They never knew. It was only me."

"But, I mean, how? You said Mossad was monitoring and the asset fled. How were you able to get a hold of them?"

"At the hotel, before we even left for the mine. I swapped them out for a handful of gravel and hid them in the room. Behind the baseboard, like in Vegas. Goldmann was acting squirrely. I—I don't know. I started getting the feeling that he was up to something. I don't know what came over me, but I saw an opportunity and I took it."

"That was incredibly stupid."

"It was. And I regretted doing it for the longest time. It was one of the reasons I left Techyon. I felt like I was losing my way. Like my moral compass was getting completely flipped upside down. Took me a little while to convince myself to go back to Botswana to get them. But I eventually did, and I came here and hid them in the safe deposit box. I regret what happened to my guys, beyond words, and I'll have to live with what happened to them forever. But I no longer regret taking them. Not anymore. Not after seeing what Sokolov was capable of. What we're going to do with this money will set everything right."

Haeli didn't get it yet. Nothing was ever going to set it right. No matter how many people they helped. No matter how much justice was served. It would never be enough.

Blake took both of her hands in his and rested them in the middle of the table. "Look, I don't know what to think about all of this, but what's done is done. There's no changing it. At this point, it's about moving forward."

Haeli smiled. From the tapping of her shoes, he knew her knees were bouncing. A little dance she would always do when she was excited. "I knew you'd come around. Can we call the guys? Griff is going to lose his mind when we tell him. Tell 'em to put in their papers. It's finally on."

"Slow down. We'll sit down with them when we get back. See what they have to say about it. Right now, we need to focus on getting out of here."

"How bad do you think it is?"

"You mean the exposure? Depends on what happened in there. Was the box under your name?"

"No, it's anonymous. But I'm on camera."

"Yeah, but there's no crime in visiting your safe deposit box. As crazy as it sounds, the whole thing might line up perfectly. Sokolov's remains will be identified, eventually. If we're lucky, it will look like he was the bomber and he inadvertently blew himself up. I don't know how I'll explain it to Oli, but I'll cross that bridge when I get to it."

"They'll see I went with them to the vault."

"So, they may end up looking to talk to you. If they can identify you. And if that happens, you'll have a story prepared. They tried to take you hostage. We'll figure something out. Anyway, once we're home, it's not likely they'll track you down. Sokolov and his guy are known terrorists, they're not going to look much further than that."

"True. And the guard saw Nikitin tackle me when I was trying to escape. It fits the narrative." Haeli paused. "Wait. The guard."

"What about him?"

"He saw me with the remote. He saw me detonate it."

"He saw you unlocking your car. That's all."

Haeli drifted into thought. No doubt, recounting the events, trying to tease out any details she may have forgotten. How could one look so angelic and so mischievous at the same time? There was an allure to her devilish side. It drew Blake in. If anyone else had pulled what she just did, he would have walked away in a heartbeat. But not with her.

"Ahhh. I'm so pumped up," Haeli said. "I really, really can't wait to see the look... On. Their. Faces." Her speech slowed until each word popped out, one at a time, as if without her knowledge. Then her lips ovaled and her eyes became wider than Blake thought they could go. She pointed over his shoulder. He turned, expecting to see a ghost.

While they were talking, the German language talk show had been preempted by the news of the explosion. Blake expected to see live footage from the street. A montage of broken windows, flashing police lights, and crime scene tape. But instead, he saw a single image. A high-definition frame of surveillance video. Zoomed in on Haeli's face.

Shit.

The German caption translated as "Wanted."

Blake checked the counter. Thankfully, the woman wasn't there to see it.

They listened to the commentary.

Haeli spoke over it. "They're calling it terrorism. They're saying I'm a terrorist. I knew it. It was the guard."

Blake stood up and pulled on Haeli's arm.

"We've gotta go. Right now."

36

As Haeli slid across the back seat of the cab, Blake took out his phone and tapped the map application. He knew as soon as he got in, the driver would ask the obvious question. Where are you going? It was a question he didn't yet have the answer to.

Blake climbed in and closed the door. There was an overpowering chemical fragrance. Some kind of air freshener, although he couldn't imagine it being intentional.

From the screen, he picked a place at random. A city, close enough that the driver wouldn't laugh at them, and far enough to be in a different local jurisdiction. Then they would pick up another ride, leapfrogging their way toward the border.

Lucerne.

It looked to be close. A half-hour away, he guessed. If that were the case, he didn't think the driver would balk.

The man came out with the obligatory question. He spoke in German, but not well. Blake looked at the posted ID.

Andrej Milošević.

He was young, maybe thirty. Tall. So tall that his head almost touched the ceiling of the Toyota hatchback. He had a goatee, but it was mostly underneath his chin, with only a few follicles creeping up to the front.

"Do you speak English?" Blake asked.

"Yes, of course." His English was better than his German. From his accent, he guessed he was from Serbia or somewhere in the Baltics.

"Great. We're going to Lucerne."

"Lucerne? Are you sure?"

"Yes."

"But it will cost four hundred or five hundred. We charge for the trip back to Zurich, too. I will take you, but you know you can take the train for thirty."

This was a first. They had found the most honest cab driver in the world.

And he was right. It was cheaper and probably just as quick to go by train. In fact, they wouldn't have to stop at Lucerne. They could get clear out of the country.

The problem was, they would run the risk of being recognized. Police were probably already swarming the stations, and Haeli's face was all over the media. Andrej clearly hadn't seen the news.

"That's all right. We'll pay," Blake said. "When we take the train, my wife just complains the whole time that it's uncomfortable and there are too many people."

Haeli covered her mouth with her fingers. He wondered if she found amusement in the idea that she was a complainer, or that he had called her his wife. If he was being honest, it kind of felt good flowing off his lips.

"What address?"

Blake poked at the screen and called off the random address that popped up. He hoped it wasn't a police station.

Andrej put the address into his GPS and pulled out. They were underway.

Normally, Blake liked to have a broader plan. Several steps already lined up. But the shock of seeing the bulletin had forced them to act quickly if they had any chance of finding a taxi driver who didn't know who she was.

Because criminals move freely between countries, European nations rely heavily on Interpol. Contrary to the myths propagated by Hollywood movies, Interpol has no agents, nor any power to arrest. The organization essentially manages information, allowing it to be shared between the law enforcement communities of member countries, much the way the FBI's NCIC database unifies information in the United States.

A 'Red Notice,' as it's called, is basically an international APB. A request by one jurisdiction that a suspect be held if located by another jurisdiction. Typically, the record includes name, date of birth, and other identifiers. In Haeli's case, the authorities didn't have this information. But it didn't mean they were in the clear.

For an incident of this type, classified as domestic or foreign terrorism, it was a good bet that Haeli's picture had already been disseminated to all one hundred and ninety-four countries who participate. Including the United States.

It was also a good bet that it was on the radar of non-law-enforcement agencies. The kind Blake once worked for. The kind he'd like to avoid at all costs.

"Are you on vacation?" Andrej asked.

"Yeah," Haeli said. "It's our first time here. We just love it."

"What will you see in Lucerne?"

"We thought we'd find a place on the lake, do a little hiking, you know, see the sights. Like the Chapel Bridge, I hear that's cool. Oh, and that cog-wheel train up the mountain. Definitely. Have you been?"

Blake was glad Haeli had taken over the conversation. Beside the fact that he hated small talk, she sounded like she knew what she was talking about. He, on the other hand, did not.

"Yes, I have, of course. More when I was young. My father would take us when we first moved here from Serbia."

Serbia. Nailed it.

"That sounds great, Andrej."

Blake took Haeli's hand and settled in for the ride. It had only been a few minutes, but he was hopeful that Andrej had exhausted his small talk repertoire. He needed some quiet to think. In forty minutes, they would need to make another move.

Andrej pulled the car over to the side of the road, in front of a "k kiosk" convenience store, which occupied a standalone building, belonging to a different century.

"What's wrong?" Blake asked.

"Nothing is wrong, only I have to use the bathroom. Very quickly. Is that okay?"

"We'd really like to get there before it gets too late. Are you sure it can't wait?" It was hard to make a case for the rush. Haeli had already indicated they had nowhere to be.

"It's okay. I'll hurry. I know the owner here. I can use the bathroom. Two minutes."

What were they going to say? No? Not that it mattered, anyway. Andrej hadn't waited for the answer before slamming the door and darting off toward the store.

"Don't encourage him," Blake said.

"I'm just being polite."

"I know. I just don't want him to get too nosy. Before you know it, we'll have to keep track of a whole backstory about your sister's Aunt Suzy, who went to school in Zurich."

"I kinda like the story. Never been a wife before."

"Yeah, I thought you might have got a kick out of that. But somehow I doubt this is your first wife cover story."

Haeli laughed. "I couldn't even begin to count them."

"Did you ever think about it, for real?"

"What? Getting married?"

"Yeah, I mean did you ever think, 'I could see myself settling down one day'?"

"Not really, have you?"

Blake shrugged. "I don't know. It was never really an option for me. Not with what I did for a living."

"I guess I just don't understand why people want to. I mean, it's a piece of paper. It means nothing. Doesn't change anything. Right? Anyway, why do you ask?"

"Just rambling. Wondering if the internationally wanted cat burglar and secret weapon of war had any dreams of domestication in her youth, that's all."

"Do I look domesticable?

"I'm not even sure that's a real word. And no, you don't." Blake looked at his watch. "What's taking him so long."

"Maybe it wasn't number one."

"Number one? Really? What, are you in preschool?" He gave his best five-year-old impression, facial expressions and all. "Ha ha. He had to do the dookies."

Haeli laughed. "I'm just sayin'. Who picks up a fare knowing they have to pee?"

"True. Unless..."

Unless he didn't have to.

It had been too long. Something wasn't right. Had Andrej recognized her? Were they sitting there waiting to be captured?

"Come on." Blake opened the door. "We've gotta leave. This isn't right."

"Are you sure?"

"I'm sure. Just—come on."

Blake got out. Haeli followed. They started walking.

"Keep moving." Blake looked over his shoulder. "Do you see that parking garage up there? When we make it there, we'll cut through. There's usually an exit on the other side. For now, just walk normally."

"You sure he's just not using the bathroom?"

"At this point, it's not worth the risk. If he's not, we should be hearing sirens real soon."

No sooner did the words come out of his mouth, he heard the wail of a siren in the distance.

"Never mind," Blake said. "Run."

They took off toward the parking garage. When they reached it, he looked back at the taxicab, still idling in the street. They weren't there yet.

Through the ground level, they weaved between the parked cars, heading for the opposite exit as soon as they found it.

The sirens warbled closer. Three, four, maybe more.

They peeked out the other side of the garage.

"Cops."

They retreated and stepped behind a concrete pillar.

The police car flew past, the doppler effect winding the siren up and down.

"Now."

They darted across the street and between two buildings. Ahead, there was light at the end of the narrow alley. A street.

Another police car flashed by the gap. This time in the opposite direction.

"They already know we're on foot." Blake pushed Haeli along. "They're searching the area."

"We should get back to the garage, get into one of the cars."

"No, too close. They'll be all over that place."

They reached the next street. Blake poked his head out. It looked clear.

"Go."

Across the street, they slipped into what looked like another alley between two apartment buildings.

Only it wasn't.

What looked like a separation between two different buildings was actually a design element. An indentation which jogged inward only twenty feet or so. Straight ahead, an electrical box filled the space from side to side, rising to just below an apartment window. They had cornered themselves into a ten story, three-sided box.

"Get down." Haeli dropped to a pushup position, then lowered herself flat.

Blake followed suit, just as the police car whizzed by.

The frenetic pace of the search was working to their advantage. If the officer, or officers, had slowed it down, methodically checked either side of the street, laying down or not, they would have been caught out.

"There's a street about fifty yards to the left. We're going to have to pick our moment and make a break for it."

"We'll be way out in the open."

"I know, but we can't stay here. This position is indefensible."

Haeli rolled onto her back and levered herself onto her elbows. "What about the window? That one. It's already cracked open. I say we go in through there."

"And if someone's home?"

Haeli sighed. "Then we'll figure it out. Unless you've got a better plan?"

He didn't.

Haeli sprung up onto the electrical box and pushed the window all the way open. She leaned her head and shoulders inside for several seconds, then back out again.

"A kitchen," she whispered. "I don't hear anyone. I'm going in."

Haeli climbed through. A big cat, sneaking up on its prey.

Blake did the same. A round peg in a square hole.

Pressing his lips against Haeli's ear, he barely emitted a sound. "Get to the hallway, find the stairs and get to the roof."

She nodded.

From the kitchen, there was a hallway. The first opening on the left was a living room. Inside was what looked like the main door.

Blake waved Haeli into the living room.

From somewhere around the other end of the hallway, they heard a woman's voice call out. It was weak and raspy. Most likely elderly. "Henry, is that you?"

Haeli opened the door. As he guessed, it led to the common hallway. They both slipped out, and Blake closed the door, trying not to make a sound.

They headed to the stairwell and hiked the ten flights to the top. The door to the roof was unlocked.

"Okay, now what?" Haeli asked.

Blake walked to the edge of the roof and kneeled. He turned and motioned for Haeli to come next to him.

"We've got a good view of the activity from here. As long as we stay low, they shouldn't see us up here. Unless they have a helicopter, then we'll have to hide out in the stairwell."

"And if the dogs track us here?" Haeli asked. "We'll be trapped."

Blake looked to the right. The next building over was twenty times too far to jump. To the left was the corner and another street. Haeli was dead right. They would be trapped.

"All we have to do is make it until dark," Blake said. "Then, as long as they aren't camped out down there, we'll move. The more time that goes by, the further they'll assume we travelled. It'll widen their search radius and make it unmanageable."

Haeli spun and sat on the roof with her back against the two-foot ledge.

"You good?" Blake squeezed above her knee.

"Sorry, first time getting chased by the cops."

"Something tells me that's not true either."

Haeli leaned her head back on the lip of the ledge, and chuckled. "Nope. Couldn't begin to count."

37

BLAKE UNLOADED ITEMS FROM THE GREEN PLASTIC BASKET. TWO BOTTLES of water, four energy bars, two phone chargers, two pocket LED flashlights, and a package of bobby pins.

With all the disinterest of a part-time college-aged cashier, the kid scanned the items and waited for payment.

There hadn't been much concern in the decision to make the pit stop to the chain drug store. It wasn't Blake's picture that had been released, after all. But that wasn't to say there wasn't some risk.

After the cab driver called police, the authorities would have considered Blake a possible accomplice. Of course, Andrej would have provided a physical description. But even if the description was broadcast, there was little danger of being recognized. Without Haeli standing next to him, he was out of context.

While the freedom of movement was helpful, he hated leaving Haeli alone. Curled up behind a dumpster at the back of the building, she might as well have been on an island, a thousand miles away.

Blake entered the cash-back amount. The cashier handed him the money, closed the drawer, and then wandered off. People didn't seem to be much for, "Bye now, have a nice night," in this country.

Outside, he made his way around the building and found Haeli where he left her. Tucked into a shadow, she melted into the background. For a split second, he had felt a surge of panic that she was gone. But no, there she was, looking up at him with eyebrows raised.

"Found everything," Blake said.

"The bobby pins too?"

"Yep."

Neither had been sure bobby pins were a thing in Switzerland. Funny how people tended to view other cultures as somehow lacking in the conveniences of their own. The people of Switzerland couldn't possibly possess such advanced technology as bobby pins. What's next, McDonald's?

"Here, these had the most protein." Blake handed her two of the bars and a bottle of water.

They both dug in, forcing down each chalky bite with a swig of water, until both bars were consumed. Unsure if they would get another chance, it was much needed fuel for what lay ahead.

"Ready?"

They pocketed the remaining items, discarded the bottles and wrappers, and hit the road. Their destination was within a five-minute walk.

On the roof, he and Haeli had come up with a decent working plan. They knew where they needed to go next and why. And by the time it got dark, police activity had fallen off dramatically.

A helicopter did patrol the area for about an hour, but the chopping of the rotor blades gave them ample warning before each pass.

Two hours after sunset, they decided it was time to move.

Almost every hit-and-run mission Blake could remember was conducted at night. The moonless kind, when possible. The darkness always provided an advantage to the one who knew how to use it.

As they neared the address, they could already make out the sign. *Arabesque*. Theatrical supply.

Like the rest of the shops in the strip, it was dark and shut up tight. Having closed six hours earlier, its employees were long gone.

When Haeli suggested the idea, it seemed a bit unhinged. But the more Blake thought about it, the less absurd it became. They were savvy enough to get themselves out of the country. They had the experience and the resources to pull it off. The only thing they had to worry about was being recognized in the meantime.

So, a disguise.

And what better place for that than a professional costume shop. Wigs, clothing, makeup, accessories. The sky was the limit. They just needed to get in and out, undetected.

Around the back of the strip, they located the door for Arabesque. There were no cameras visible. But it didn't mean there weren't any inside.

Haeli went to work bending the bobby pins into shape, while Blake located the electrical meters.

There were two things which concerned him. Cameras and alarm. Cutting the power to the shop would help mitigate, but not eliminate them. While it was uncommon for consumer grade camera systems to run on battery backup, alarm systems were often equipped with the feature. If that were the case, and they tripped the alarm, they'd be forced to abandon the plan. This they wouldn't know until they got inside.

Assuming the meters were arranged in the same order as the shops, Blake counted over four from the right and yanked it. The light above the door blinked out.

Haeli waited with pins inserted into the deadbolt. There was enough ambient light from the other shops for her to still operate. Blake gave her the thumbs up.

Two minutes, manipulating the pins and tumbler, was all it took. Then they were in.

As they slipped inside, they fired up the pocket flashlights and listened for the beeping prompt of a security system, demanding the disarm code. There was none. Blake was hopeful that cutting the power had been enough to disable it.

"You look for the panel, I'll map out the cameras," Haeli said.

Blake ran along the wall, through the main showroom, into the small sewing room, office, and bathroom, until he had circled the entire perimeter and reached his starting point. No panel.

Haeli found him by the rear door. "Only one camera. Above the till."

"You sure?"

"I'm sure. Looks like they're more worried about the employees stealing than about us."

"Unbelievable. And who has a retail business without an alarm system? I'm gonna put the power back on."

Blake went outside, seated the meter, and then returned. Haeli was already flipping through a rack of clothing.

"What should we be?" Holding her flashlight with her underarm, she lifted a fist full of red fabric and white lace. "Seventeenth century British royalty?"

He chuckled. "Yeah, should be able to breeze right into the airport with that."

"How about a mermaid?"

Blake ignored her, flipping on the light switch just inside the sewing room. An overhead light came on, spilling into the showroom enough to make the flashlights unnecessary.

Haeli passed Blake carrying a small black purse. Something out of the nineteen twenties, perhaps. She placed it on the worktable, next to the sewing machine, then began emptying her pockets. He watched as she shoveled handfuls of raw diamonds into the bag. She was loaded up with them. Front pockets, back pockets, even in her bra.

When she was done and had double checked each location, she began to strip off her clothing, until she was down to her bra and her thong.

"What are you waiting for?" she asked. "Let's go, drop 'em."

Reluctantly, Blake stripped down to his jockeys and socks.

Careful to avoid the area of the cash register, he selected a few pieces of clothing and tried them on. Nothing that fit.

Haeli had already donned a full ensemble. Black halter top, with a long sleeve fishnet shirt over it. Pants with chrome studs running along the seams. She stuck her thumbs through the holes in the end of her sleeves, such that the fishnet covered her knuckles.

"What are you supposed to be?"

"I'm a goth girl. Just wait, you'll see, the look's not complete yet."

"Can't wait."

Haeli thumbed through a rack of men's clothing. "We should match. I mean, it should make sense that we're together. Here, try this." She pulled a black long sleeve shirt from the rack and handed it to him. Then a pair of black pants.

Black shirt and black pants. That he could handle.

"Put those on and then we'll accessorize."

Great. Accessories.

Haeli walked over to the wall where rows of plastic heads modeled wigs of every color and style. She selected one. Jet black, shoulder length hair with bangs.

"Come here, Mick, pick one out."

Blake perused the selection. As he looked closer, he was amazed at how real they looked, even on the plastic dummies. The hairline wasn't stark like a Halloween wig. Fine hairs were woven into a mesh that made it look like the hair was growing out of the plastic. After looking at the price tag, he knew why. Three thousand francs for a wig?

Blake didn't really want to choose any of them. Haeli knew it, which was why she had already chosen for him. He pulled her selection onto his head.

He looked into one of the several mirrors and burst out laughing. The shaggy black mop of hair looked ridiculous. Realistic, but ridiculous.

Haeli flitted about, collecting costume jewelry and makeup, then led Blake to the sewing room for a little extra light.

He put his boots back on.

"Bend down." She lassoed his neck with a pile of five or six silver chains of varying lengths, then pulled out a black eye liner pencil.

There was no use fighting her.

Haeli colored his eyebrows and added thick lines around his eyes.

"If we're questioned, I'll just tell them I'm one of the members of Motley Crue." Blake tried not to move. Getting stabbed in the eye with the point of a pencil was just about the only thing that would make the situation worse.

"Done," she said. "No, wait. One more thing." She picked up a black ring off the table and clipped it to his lip.

Blake looked in the mirror again. He had to hand it to her, he was a different person.

Haeli did her own makeup and clipped one of the rings to her nose.

When she was done, the transformation was amazing. She looked completely different. And strangely sexy.

"We should have a backup in case we're blown. Something we can switch into on the fly."

"Agreed," Haeli said.

They worked together to select the various pieces. Haeli picked out a tight blue dress and a blonde wig, Blake, a tweed suit that was big enough to fit over his current clothes, a brown seventies style wig, turtle shell frames, and a bushy walrus mustache.

"How does this thing stick on?"

"Spirit gum." Haeli ran to the makeup section and brought back a bottle of the skin-safe glue. "Good thing you shaved."

"You're not kiddin."

Haeli completed her look with a pair of thick heeled dance shoes, which was the only style of shoe the shop seemed to carry.

"We may not mesh together as well," Haeli said, "but we'll make it work if we have to. See if you can find something to carry this stuff in."

While Blake ripped the guts out of a makeup caboodle, he heard Haeli firing up the sewing machine in the back room.

It wasn't until he finished loading up the gray plastic carrying case with their chosen items and joined her at the sewing table that he realized what she was doing.

Cutting a slit in the edge of the purse's lining, she had created a hidden pocket. Which, she was now sewing closed.

She spoke over the machine. "How is it that you're all bent out of shape that I stole, yet here we are helping ourselves to thousands worth of stuff."

"This is different." He would have thrown out a sturdier argument if he had one. But the truth was, aside from value, it was the same thing.

They made a choice to do what needed to be done. Because they could. Because they wanted to.

"Uh huh." Haeli formed her lips into a line and puffed out her cheeks. "Right."

"So what's your name, goth girl?"

"Stormy."

"Eww, Stormy. Sultry." With dramatic flair, he lifted the back of his hand to his face and peered through his fingers. "I'm Draven."

They laughed. A deep, stress-relieving, life-loving laugh. Hey, if the costumes didn't work like they hoped, at least they'd have some fun with it.

"All set." Haeli shutdown the machine and picked up the purse and the caboodle.

Blake gathered their clothes, to be discarded in one of the trash bins out back.

"I'd say we're ready to hit the station." Blake fingered the light switch and gave one last look to make sure they hadn't left anything out of place.

"Yep. Paris, here we come."

38

BLAKE AND HAELI MILLED AROUND THE PLATFORM. THE TRAIN WOULD BE arriving in four minutes.

They had arrived at Zurich HB station by a quarter to six. Although there was a train leaving for Paris at 6:01, they decided to wait for the later, but faster train.

The 6:01 was a nearly seven-hour trip and would require them to change trains. The 7:20 high-speed express was direct to Paris Lyons. Four hours and four minutes. It was a no-brainer.

On top of the direct path and lack of a change, the route had only three stops. Basel SBB, Mulhouse Villa, and Dijon-Ville. Which meant, including Paris, there were only four opportunities for law enforcement to intercept them once they were underway. Four may have been three too many, but it was the best they would get.

When they arrived, they secured their tickets within minutes, which left them with another hour and a half to kill.

Blake had been to this station before on several occasions, but only in passing. He remembered thinking it impressive at the time, and that hadn't changed. Doubling as a multilevel high-end mall, it was organized, modern, and beautiful.

Initially, they had spent a few minutes wandering around and popping in and out of the stores. But after spotting the third officer, they decided it would be better if they stayed further out of the way.

On a mission to become inconspicuous, Blake bought a pack of Parisienne cigarettes at one of the newsstands. Outside, among the smoking crowd, they melded in nicely. Although their outfits were unique compared with the other degenerates hanging about, they only added to the variety of counter-culture style. Just another couple of weirdos.

In a way, it was liberating. Dressed up as the kind of person he would have probably beat up in high school, he felt a freedom to do and say whatever he wanted. As if taking a step away from normal society was a free pass to completely disregard its expectations. The way he saw it, he had reaffirmed a few things he already knew about himself. First, while Haeli could pull it off in spades, he was way too old to be wearing eyeliner, even with the aging punk rocker vibe. Second, he was just as much a misfit as the rest of them. And lastly, he never had, and never would, beat someone up who was minding his own business, no matter how weird they were.

"Behind you, by the stairs," Haeli said.

He didn't have to look. They had been alerting each other to the location of the cops for the past hour.

"Just one?"

"Yeah, but he's looking for something."

"It's fine, Haeli. Train will be here in another minute."

The platform was crowded. Hundreds-of-people crowded. In his opinion, the chances of being picked out of the herd were slim to none.

Haeli kept her head low, and a screw-the-world look on her face. Her black lipstick, punctuating her pout.

Blake had to admit, she was good at being Stormy. And committed. A method actor who refused to break character between scenes.

She shoved her hands in her pockets and her eyes flitted between the ground and a distant part of the platform. "There's two of them now. They're definitely looking for someone."

"I know angst is part of the character, but you might wanna dial it back." Blake said, only half-jokingly. "Remember the mantra. You're only suspicious—"

"—if you believe you are."

The truth was, underneath it all, Haeli was a block of granite. Every bit as much as he was, and probably more so. Clutch, as they'd say on the teams.

For them, there was a threshold. A certain level of stress at which they stopped operating as living, breathing human beings and became more relatable to the trains flowing in and out of the station. Relegated to a single set of tracks, emotion, empathy, and fallibility became foreign concepts. A robotic arm, oblivious to the world outside its programming.

Pick up bolt, insert bolt, ratchet bolt, next.

Haeli hadn't yet hit the threshold.

The nose of the train broke the daylight at the opening to the tunnel. As it squealed to a stop, the blank LED screen lit up with a number. 9222. To Paris.

The doors opened. People began funneling inside. Blake took a step.

"Wait. I'll get on, you hang back for a minute. Watch what they do." Haeli gave him a peck on the lips and boarded, pausing for a moment to wave a fake goodbye.

Blake hung back and watched. There were still only two officers, and they hadn't moved.

Haeli was being overly anxious. Under the circumstances, he couldn't blame her. Anxiety is often defined as an exaggerated attention to threat. For the average person, this unwarranted threat bias is detrimental. For Blake, it was just the opposite. Threat bias is what had kept him alive all these years.

When the platform was almost empty, Blake boarded and found Haeli. She clutched her purse with both hands. The caboodle saved his seat. He moved it to the floor.

"We're good," Blake said. "Smooth sailing from here on out. I'll book the flights on the way. As long as we get through the airport without any problems, Kaytlin Richards and Cody Hodson will be home free."

The last few passengers trickled in. The visible section of the platform was empty, and everyone was seated. Blake checked his watch.

One minute and twenty seconds off schedule.

The doors remained open.

Across the aisle was a blonde woman and her young child. Blake made eye contact with her. Her mouth twitched the beginnings of a smile and she looked away.

A low murmur filled the car. Hushed conversations, for now. Until the rattling would force everyone to raise their voices to the level of a barroom brawl.

From the next car forward, a kid with spiky hair, wearing a dog collar and a worn Beatles t-shirt, came through the adjoining door and continued down the aisle. As he passed Blake, he looked right at him, extended a thumb and pinky from his closed fist, and stuck his tongue out, as if trying to lick his chin. Blake wondered if it was some kind of punk rocker code, like the way people who drive Jeep Wranglers wave at each other on the street. Blake responded with an air fist bump. The kid plopped down in a seat a few rows behind.

Blake leaned toward Haeli. "Are the Beatles cool again?"

She looked in no mood. "Why aren't we moving yet?".

Blake didn't have an answer. The doors sat open. The whole train and platform, idle. Technical issues, maybe?

A moment later, they got their answer.

Two policemen entered at the front of the car. A third lingered on the platform, just outside the door.

Haeli reached over and squeezed Blake's leg.

The officers moved down the aisle, row by row, swinging their heads back and forth as if scanning the faces of each passenger.

When the first one reached Blake and Haeli, he paused. Gave them a harder look than the rest. Blake had a feeling it was about to get ugly.

From behind, he heard a commotion. Dog collar kid had sprung out of his seat and was sprinting for the rear door.

The officers gave chase. Out onto the platform, they disappeared.

Voices yelling, keys jingling, boots pounding—a whirlwind of sound and fury, all receding into the distance.

After a second of eerie silence, the car erupted. Passengers whooped and chattered about the show they just witnessed, until being hushed by the crackling of the loudspeaker.

"We apologize for the delay," the announcer said, in German. "Standby for departure."

Doors closed, wheels turned, and two pairs of lungs exhaled.

39

"How long to Dijon?" Haeli asked.

"Twenty minutes or so, why?"

"Maybe we should get off there."

"Get off there? Why? Dijon's the last stop. After that, it's straight through to Paris. What would be the upside?"

Haeli wrapped her hand around the inside of his bicep and pulled him closer. She spoke to his ear. "That couple, three rows ahead, on the right. The woman keeps stealing glances at me. I think she knows."

Blake had noticed them coming in from the next car, about fifteen minutes after stopping in Mulhouse, but hadn't paid them much attention since. The man, who sat on the aisle, was clean cut and wore an untucked Oxford shirt. The woman, to his right, wore her hair pulled back tight and a collared button-down blouse. There was nothing unusual about them.

For the next few minutes, he devoted more attention to the pair. He decided they did fit the profile of police detectives or agents, but that didn't mean anything. If they were cops, they'd probably have acted already. And even if they were civilians who simply recognized her, they most likely would have left the car by then to alert someone.

The only peculiar thing Blake could nitpick was the way they were interacting. Or not interacting.

When they entered the car, they were talking. Chummy, like they'd known each other for a long while. Once they sat, they were stiff and quiet. But that didn't necessarily mean anything either.

He wavered back and forth. Now Haeli was getting into his head.

"Na. I wouldn't worry about it," he finally told her.

She seemed placated.

Blake took her hand and they sat in silence for a while. Blake's mind wandered. He thought about Haeli wrapped up in his jacket, asleep in the car. He thought about Fezz and Khat and Griff and wondered if they were home safely. And he thought about his lab. How he had pushed the big red button.

"Whatcha thinkin' about?" Haeli asked.

"Nothing."

"Ya know what I was thinkin' about? Our conversation in the cab. When you asked if I ever thought about marriage."

"Yeah?"

"I told you no. I feel like I wasn't being completely honest. I have. I mean, there've been a few times I thought I might be open to the possibility. Like when I was a young girl, before I knew what my life would really be like, I'd fantasize about the beautiful white gown and all of that. But then, before I knew it, I was neck deep in a world where that kind of attachment wasn't even feasible. As time went on, I guess I started telling myself that getting married was pointless and stupid, just to make myself feel better about not having the option."

"Believe me, I get it. We tell ourselves a lot of things."

"I don't know why I thought of it. I guess just to set the record straight. I don't really think it's stupid."

"Okay."

Blake wasn't quite sure what she was getting at. Was she trying to nudge him toward a proposal? How else could he read it? The truth was, he'd propose to her in a second if it was what she wanted. The diamond ring shouldn't pose much of a problem, anyway.

He let his gaze float toward the couple. For a split second, he caught the woman's eye. She looked away with furtive flair.

Not good.

"Ya know what? I think you were right. The station should be coming up in a couple minutes, we should be prepared to get off."

"I knew it," she said. "I told you."

Blake grabbed the caboodle and her hand. They got up and moved to the front of the car near the door, keeping the suspicious pair in his peripheral vision.

The woman leaned over to her left to say something to her partner. Blake caught a glimpse of something in her right ear.

They're agents.

Blake levered the handle and slid the connecting door. He walked through, knowing Haeli would follow. Another door and they were in the next car. It slid closed behind them.

"She has an earpiece," Blake said. "I saw the look in her eye. They know. Keep moving."

They moved through the aisle until they reached the front of the car.

"So when we hit the station, we run?"

"We'll have to. But you can bet there's gonna be more waiting for us."

The shush of the outside air filled the car as the rear door slid open and the agents stepped in.

Even across the length of the crowded train car, there was an unspoken acknowledgement. A head tilt, a blink, the rise and fall of their chests. A "we know that you know that we know that you know" kind of vibe.

Ready. Set.

"Go."

Haeli pushed open the forward door and they ran. Dodging wingtips and computer bags poking into the aisle.

The agents burst into the car, behind them. Tense mouths and narrow eyes.

Blake and Haeli blurred through the next car. And the next.

The agents kept pace.

In the fifth, a man stood in the aisle, reaching for the rack above his empty seat. A small child stood next to him. Without stopping, Haeli shouldered the man out of the way, scooped up the child and deposited him on the seat. As they crossed into the next car, Blake could hear the agents trying to get around the irate man.

Then there was a groan. Blake could feel the floor shifting beneath his feet, the change in momentum making each step less stable.

"We're stopping. Get ready."

Another car. The columns along the platform ticked by the windows. Slower and slower.

The loudspeaker. "Dijon-Ville"

Haeli grabbed the handle of the next connecting door. It was locked.

"End of the line, Mick."

Through the forward window, Blake could see the steel skin of the engine.

The train rocked and then settled.

The agents burst through the rear door. They pulled their guns.

There was screaming and yelling. Both from the agents and the passengers, who covered their heads and ducked below their seats.

With a chime, the main doors opened onto the platform.

Blake and Haeli made a break for it. Pushing through a group already trying to board.

Haeli stayed close, the front of her shoulder against the back of his.

They cut through the crowd at a diagonal and joined a group heading toward the train.

Blake pulled the wig from his head and stashed it under his armpit. Haeli took the cue and did the same.

They pressed up against the group as tight as they could.

Others crowded behind them as they funneled back on board, one car away from where they exited.

Haeli dropped into a seat and scooted over toward the window, facing the platform. She slouched. Blake shoved in next to her, bending at the waist to peer through the window beside her. From the outside, two foreheads pasted to the glass.

Blake picked out at least two other agents, carrying walkie-talkies and pushing their way through the thinning crowd. He pointed them out to Haeli.

One of the men intercepted the agents from the train. They spoke. He pointed at the stairs. They started to move. A play in three acts, performed in under an instant.

Then, as if by magic, all three descended, vanishing into the station.

Over the thumping of his heartbeat, Blake heard the chime.

The doors closed. And two pairs of lungs held their breath.

40

"Paris Gare de Lyon." The announcement blared.

Blake and Haeli stayed seated. This time they'd file out in an orderly fashion.

During the final leg, they had walked back several cars to find an open restroom. Luckily, the man Haeli had crashed into must have gotten off at Dijon.

It had been a trick, dressing in the three-by-three restroom, but they were able to manage it. One at a time, they'd gone in as one person, and returned as another. And since it was located at the back of the car, no one took notice. Had the restroom been at the front, it would have been a whole different, more public event.

Strangely, Blake felt more comfortable in the new role than his last. Although he had grown into it, "Draven" was the kind of character that sought to attract attention. This new guy was just the opposite.

The sum of the overly large suit, seventies hair, glasses, and mustache had an instant wallflower effect. Or at least that's how it felt.

Haeli wasn't as inconspicuous. Tight dress, blonde hair, supermodel makeup. No, she was going to turn some heads.

After the completion of their transformations, they slipped into the next car back, one at a time. Some of the passengers, who started in

Zurich or Mulhouse, would have seen them running past earlier in the trip. The fact that no one seemed to make the connection was affirmation the disguises were doing their jobs.

The train stopped, and the passengers began gathering their belongings and making their way to the platform. Blake took the caboodle. They had packed out the old costumes, which they would toss in the trash at the earliest opportunity.

Next to Blake, an elderly woman struggled to tip her bag from the rack above her head. He helped her, throwing in a little good-natured flirtation. She gave it right back to him.

As she made her way down the aisle, Blake and Haeli trailed behind her. Slowly but surely, they reached the platform.

"Ol' Pari." Blake smiled.

"I would kiss the ground if I could."

"Just keep your eyes peeled. We should have no problem walking right out of here. I'm guessing every gendarme within a hundred-mile radius is bearing down on Dijon as we speak."

"It's not the Gendarmerie we've gotta worry about here, it's the National Police."

They followed the droves into the main terminal. In a lot of ways Gare de Lyon was similar to Zurich HB, but with less retail.

"If for whatever reason we get separated," Haeli said, "we'll need a meeting spot. How about the Lufthansa ticket counter? Four o'clock."

"That's fine. But there won't be any need. Look at those guys." He pointed. "No one's looking."

Several officers stood by the turnstiles leading into the terminal, but they seemed to be focused on their normal duties.

"Good, 'cause I've gotta use the bathroom."

"We were just in the bathroom on the train, didn't you go then?"

"I didn't have to go then."

"Uh." Blake looked around. The signs were easily visible. *Toilettes.* They headed that way. "Hurry."

Haeli trotted away and disappeared into the tiled maze marked "Femmes."

Blake waited impatiently for ten seconds before he remembered he was still carrying the caboodle. He took it into the men's restroom with the intention of burying it in the trash.

Unfortunately, the slender metal trash slots wouldn't allow that to happen. Instead, he opened the case and, when no one was looking, removed the pile of hair and fabric, and stuffed it through the slot. He'd leave the empty case somewhere else. Now that it was empty, it wouldn't matter if it was found.

As he was leaving, he walked by a full-length mirror. It caught his eye as if it were a doorway through which a complete stranger was approaching. He gave himself a once over. Yep, he really did look ridiculous.

To make matters worse, he noticed that the right side of the mustache had come unstuck and was flapping outward when he moved his mouth. He felt his pocket. The bottle of spirit gum was still there. But he decided this particular beauty regimen was better done in private.

Locking himself in a stall, he removed the cap and brush and dabbed the gum on his upper lip by feel. He pressed the mustache flat and held it until it felt secure.

With makeup touched up and a passing grade on a final mirror check, he headed back into the terminal.

By the water fountains between the two restrooms, he stood with a group of men who took turns looking at their watches and at the entrance to the ladies' room. A kind of male purgatory, to which all men with wives or girlfriends are eventually relegated. Waiting and waiting. And waiting.

Blake gave it a few minutes before starting to worry. Then another few minutes passed.

This isn't right.

Haeli was always quick. Hell, he'd seen her incapacitate a group of armed men in less time. At any other time, in any other place, he'd have wandered off to entertain himself with something or another. But under the circumstances, he had good reason to worry. It was nearly ten minutes since he'd watched her go in.

His mind started to play the worst-case scenario game. What if something happened while he was in the men's room? Had she come out to a garrison of police officers waiting to haul her off? Not possible. There would have been a ruckus. The terminal remained status quo.

That's it, I'm going after her.

There were some things that struck fear into the hearts of all men. The women's room was one of them. Going into an Al-Qaeda compound in Kandahar was an easier decision. And less dangerous.

Blake broke away from the group, stashed the caboodle on the floor by the fountains, and slipped into the abyss. Whatever was about to happen, his new group of friends weren't to blame. They tried to warn him. Shouts of "Wrong one, buddy," and "You can't go in there," echoed off the tile walls and were summarily ignored.

Inside, there were a handful of women at the sinks. Although there hadn't been any screams or slaps, he was met with a fair helping of shocked and dirty looks. Other than the women who were inside the stalls, the place cleared out in a matter of seconds.

Blake moved down the line of stalls, checking the insides of open ones and banging on the doors of the closed. "Kaitlyn, are you in here?" After receiving no response, he bent down and checked under the doors for Haeli's clunky dance heels.

She's not here.

He retreated as fast as he could, but it was too late. One of the fleeing women had fetched an officer, who intercepted Blake as soon as he emerged.

The men's club looked on in horror.

The officer spoke in French. "What's the meaning of this?"

Blake responded in a British accent. Why? He didn't know. Who was to say Professor Peabody wasn't English?

"I—I—I'm so sorry. I seemed to have gone into the wrong loo. I'm terribly embarrassed. Mortified, really. Pass on my apologies to the ladies, would you, chap?"

Inside, Blake was shaking his head at himself. Chap?

The officer responded in broken English. "Pay attention for next time."

"Oh no. No next time. Won't happen again. I can tell you that."

In the end, the official response consisted of a disgusted look and a cold shoulder as the officer returned to his post.

Blake took several passes around the station, first inside, then out.

She was gone. Of that, he was sure.

She wouldn't have left on her own, would she?

He was at a loss. But then something she had said reached out from the recent past and smacked him across the face.

If for some reason we're split up...

The statement hadn't seemed odd at the time. But now—

Oh, Haeli. What are you up to now?

41

Sweat streamed down Blake's glazed forehead. It dripped from his nose and chin onto the conveyor belt below his feet. Under the wig, his hair was drenched. But from an onlooker's perspective, his seventies quaff was bone dry. The only outward explanation, a rare forehead-sweating condition known as 'Get-this-crap-off-me' disease.

At seventy-seven degrees, it was a typical June day in Paris. But clad in two layers of heavy clothing and a half-pound of someone else's hair, even the mild French climate became sweltering.

But it wouldn't be long before he would have to ditch the getup, anyway. In order to use their passports to clear security, they were going to have to look like their pictures. In other words, they were going to have to look like their fugitive-selves.

First, he would have to find Haeli. Then, before pulling the trigger, they would make sure the coast was clear. It would be a calculated risk, only to be acted upon at the last possible second.

Of course, all of this was assuming Haeli hadn't run into any trouble in the city. She had set the time and place of their meeting before sneaking off. He figured it meant she knew what she was doing. Or at least that she had every intention of showing up.

Still, Blake hated the idea of her being out there alone. He couldn't, for the life of him, understand why she'd run off with no explanation. Was she still trying to protect him? Limit his exposure? Or was there more to the story than she was letting on? Whatever the case, she must have had her reasons.

For the moment, he operated under the most hopeful premise. That she believed they would both be safer if they travelled separately. If he stretched it, he could almost justify the thinking. Having already been spotted together twice, the authorities would be looking for a couple. And she probably knew he would have shot down the idea as soon as she suggested it.

Having left the train station, she'd have to rely on buses or taxis to get to the airport. After their experience in Zurich, he hoped she'd avoid the taxi at all costs.

For him, there hadn't been any issues. After searching every corner of Gare de Lyon, without being further accosted by law enforcement, he felt confident staying within the commuter train system. He hopped on the A line to Chatelet Les Halles, where he was then able to transfer to the B line, a direct route to Charles de Gaulle Airport, Terminal 2.

Once on site, it was a short jump on the light rail to Terminal 1 where, if all went well, he would meet Haeli at the Lufthansa ticketing counter.

Now, as he rode the escalator from the shopping level to the departure level, he had a three-hundred-sixty-degree view of the terminal. Through tall split-panel windows surrounding him, he scanned the floors for a blonde bombshell. There were a few candidates, but none of them were Haeli.

The architecture of the terminal was bold. An enormous ring, the concentric floors looked out into the open air core, crisscrossed by belt-escalators wrapped in glass tubes. From the perimeter, it looked like a giant hamster cage. From inside one of the tubes, it was like being inside a giant jet turbine. Which, he figured, was the intended effect.

More than anything, the design meant exposure. Any given point, visible from every other. Until they were past security and at the gate, they would be in the constant public eye.

When the escalator dumped him off onto level three, he circled around until he saw the familiar Lufthansa logos on the wall behind the counter. A line of people carting rolling suitcases and small children snaked through a maze of nylon straps. But no Haeli.

He checked his watch. Ten minutes to four.

Pacing the length of the Lufthansa section, he turned his focus to the wall of windows. He watched the hordes of people being pushed through the hamster tubes. He checked each floor for a flash of blonde hair and a tight blue dress. When he was done, he started over again.

Nine minutes to four.

There was a good chance she was already there. Like he had done, she was probably getting the lay of the land. Watching from a distance until she was sure the meeting spot was safe. He made himself visible in hopes she'd see him waiting there.

Eight minutes to four.

Seven.

Six.

Then, across the expanse and on the same level, he saw a woman. A blonde woman in a blue dress with her back to the glass. He stopped pacing and pressed his forehead against the window.

"Turn around."

As if she could sense him, she turned.

Haeli.

Blake gave an inconspicuous wave. She didn't see him.

Her head swayed back and forth as if she were scanning each floor, the same way he had been. He stood firm. Eventually, she'd see him.

Her expression changed. Emoted recognition. Only it wasn't one of delight, like he had expected. And it wasn't directed at him.

He followed her gaze up to the fourth floor, a quarter of the way around the circumference. There, he saw two men. One with a walkie talkie to his mouth, the other pointing down toward Haeli.

Blake squinted. He knew this man. Even from a distance, it was unmistakable.

Levi Farr.

He wanted to yell out. To warn her. "It's a trap, Haeli. Run." But she wouldn't have heard him. And based off the look on her face and the fact that she had vanished from her original spot, she already knew.

By the time Blake found her again, she was pushing her way into the escalator tube. Packed with travelers, the conveyer slowly moved her toward the second level.

"No, Haeli. Turn around," he said to himself out loud.

What she likely couldn't see from her vantage point were the uniformed men converging around the bottom of the tube. The moving belt was bringing her right to them.

He banged on the glass. "Turn around!" But there was no way she would hear him.

The suspended escalators couldn't have been the only way to get between floors. There must be emergency stairwells. He looked around. Nothing stood out.

She was halfway there.

At the top, several more men gathered. Some uniformed, some in plain clothes. They talked amongst themselves.

She was pinned. Trapped in a hamster tube with no avenue of escape.

Above, Levi Farr looked on. He was still nodding and pointing. His finger following Haeli's path.

With no time or means to get to her, there was nothing Blake could do but watch the scene unfold below. If she could just see them waiting for her. If she would just turn around and come back to the third, he could get to her.

He watched as she neared the bottom. He willed her to be ready.

Then her head jerked. She glanced up toward the departure level. Toward the Lufthansa ticket counter. Toward Blake.

Blake waved his arms above his head.

She looked down, then back up. Their eyes connected.

"Go back up." He mouthed the words while swinging his arms and pointing. "Go. Back. Up."

Haeli looked away again. Then she turned and started moving.

"Good. Good. Yes. Go."

She fought against the motion of the belt, pushing people out of the way as she inched her way back toward the third level.

Blake took off and began sprinting around the perimeter. If he could reach the top of the ramp before she did, he could create a diversion. He could try to overwhelm their forces. Give her a chance to escape.

Haeli moved faster as the density of the people thinned.

Blake's legs burned. He wasn't going to make it.

As the windowpanes blurred by, he could see her reaching the top of the tube.

Hang on. Almost there.

The silent movie played out beyond the glass, each frame flickering at an increasing speed. A nickelodeon, cranked by a turbocharged engine.

The men pounced. Arms and legs flailed.

No!

Blake rounded the corner and froze.

Ten men and women had descended on her. More were coming out of the woodwork. Fifteen. Twenty.

She was on her stomach. Three knees jammed into her back. Her arms were wrenched high behind her and her cheek was glued to the floor.

One of the men, wearing a suit with a laminated card dangling from a lanyard around his neck, had snatched her purse and was rummaging through it.

His mind swirled. He would fight. All of them if he had to.

No, he would take the blame. Confess to the bombing. Trade himself for her.

He had to do something, and fast.

Pushing against the weight of the men piled on top of her, Haeli managed to turn her face to the other cheek.

She looked at Blake. Past the bushy mustache and the sweaty tweed suit, her eyes connected with his soul. Barely perceptible, she shook her head and mouthed a word. "No."

His stomach cramped and his eyes welled. He knew what she was saying. And worse, he knew she was right.

There was nothing he could do to help. Not then. Fighting was as futile as falling on the sword. The most he could hope from a confession was to include himself as an accomplice. But that wouldn't help her. It wouldn't help anyone.

He nodded. A flood of emotion came over him. He would die for her. But dying wouldn't free her. If he were to be of any use, if he were to somehow fix it, he'd need to walk away. He'd need to leave her to the wolves. He knew it, and she knew it, too.

Looking her dead in the eyes, he sent his thoughts to her. "Be strong. I will come for you." He put his hand over his heart.

She smiled.

Blake swallowed hard, struggling to keep his emotions contained.

Then, conjuring every last bit of strength, he backed away. Slowly melding into the curious crowd of onlookers until their locked gaze was broken.

He lowered his head and made his way to the opposite side of the loop, fighting and losing against the compulsion to glance back at her.

From the Lufthansa ticket counter, he watched as they lifted Haeli off the ground and escorted her down the escalator.

A floor above, Levi Farr was gone.

He must have seen the news. Offered his help. Maybe even his resources. He knew her better than anyone. He had anticipated her movements. Personally picked her out of the crowd.

Blake imagined his smug self-satisfaction. It disgusted him. And it wouldn't stand.

He wished he could touch her. Smell her. Kiss her. Hear her laugh.

Why? Why did she have to do it? If she had never touched the diamonds in the first place, she would be with him. She would be free.

In the end, it had all been for nothing. The diamonds were gone. She was gone.

And he was alone.

On top of everything else, there was still a task at hand. He needed to get out. To see the plan through. For Haeli's sake.

Blake made his way to the restroom. At the sink, he wet a paper towel and wiped the coating of sweat from his face. He waited for the man next to him to dry his hands and leave.

Peeling the mustache from his lip, he stared at himself in the mirror.

This isn't over.

From this day forward, he wouldn't waste one single second. Haeli would be free. And Levi Farr would pay.

If it was the last thing he ever did.

42

"IF THIS IS A JOKE. IT'S A BAD ONE," FEZZ SAID.

"I wish it were." Blake hadn't been smiling. In fact, at this point, he wasn't even capable of it.

"I thought we were coming here to have a few drinks and a couple of laughs," Khat said. "Ya know, to celebrate a successful mission. Then you show up and tell us Haeli's been arrested and is gonna spend her life in prison?"

"No. I'm telling you I need your help to make sure that doesn't happen."

Fezz rubbed his cheeks. "How do you figure we're gonna do that, huh? This is bad, Mick. You know she'll be charged with terrorism. Not to mention a couple counts of murder. Khat's right. She's probably looking at life, if not worse."

"Not necessarily," Griff chimed in. "Switzerland's criminal justice is super lenient. Served concurrently, she could be out in fifteen or twenty years."

Blake drove his fist into the table. The empty glasses clattered. "I'm not leaving her rotting in prison for the next twenty years."

"Calm down, Mick." Fezz said. "You know we'll do whatever we can."

"I just can't wrap my head around why she stole the guy's diamonds." Griff directed his attention toward peeling the label away from the bottle of Miller Light. "And then to risk so much to keep them. Why not just walk away? Never pegged her as the greedy type."

"There was no walking away, Griff. And she wasn't being greedy. She did it for us. The team. She believed in the idea. Going private. Off the grid. Helping people who had nowhere else to turn. She was so excited to tell you guys you could put in your papers. I think she was just proud to be the one to make it possible."

"It's a damn good thing we didn't," Khat said. "We'd be screwed right now. I don't think the Swiss government's too eager to share the proceeds."

"That's not the point. Her heart was in the right place. And to make matters worse, if the diamonds hadn't been seized, we would have had the resources to get her out. One way or the other. I've got a couple million in investments, and I'll use every last penny of it if I have to. But I don't think it's gonna cut it."

Fezz wrapped his hand around the back of Blake's neck. "Look, Mick. I know where her head was. And we appreciate it, we do. We've been talkin' about it a lot, and we all agree, we'd jump ship as soon as it's possible. We believe in the idea as much as she does. But we've gotta be smart about it. We've all gotta live."

"I know." Blake held out his fists and squeezed. "But it was right there. Within reach. We were going to start fresh. And I was going to propose—"

"Wait, you were gonna what?" Griff scoffed. "Are you serious?"

"Yeah, I'm serious, Griff. She's the one, I know she is."

"Don't listen to Griff," Fezz said. "I think it's great. Congratulations."

Congratulations.

A ridiculous notion. The woman he loves, ripped away from him. His home compromised. His life's work, destroyed. And then, there was Levi Farr.

"I should've killed him when I had the chance."

"Who, Sokolov?" Fezz asked.

"No. Levi. I'm a fool for thinking he was just gonna go away. He's the reason Haeli was captured. He was there, in Paris. He made it a point to be there in person."

Fezz shook his head. "I don't mean to be a jerk but—"

"Another round, gentlemen." Arty leaned the tray against the table and offloaded his payload. "This one's on the house. Happy to see you all back in one piece."

"Maybe we should make this a new tradition," Khat said. "Before and after, then you'll get to look at our ugly mugs twice as much."

"Good with me." Arty shook the tray, letting the residual liquid spill to the floor to be sopped up by the layer of peanut shell dust, and headed back behind the bar.

"Such a good dude," Griff said. "We really should come here more."

"What were you gonna say, Fezz?"

"I was gonna say, as much as I hate Levi Farr, we can't really put this on him. Yeah, he went out of his way to stick it to you, but it's part of the game. We always know the risks. Look at Vegas. How we're not all in prison, I'll never figure out. Haeli knew the risk when she detonated that bomb. She decided to accept the risk. Don't take that away from her."

Blake let the words sit for a moment. Fezz was right, he wouldn't make her into a victim. She was strong, and she knew what she was doing. He could see it in her eyes, right there on the floor of Terminal 2. She was at peace with the consequences.

It was funny, really. He had this drive to protect her. But it was the other way around. She pushed him to be better. She put herself in harm's way to keep him out of it. And in the end, she had separated herself from him to protect him. She sacrificed herself.

"So what's the first step, Mick?" Griff said.

"Research. And I'm gonna need your help with that part. I had to hit the button."

"*The* button?"

"Yep. It's all gone. Starting over from scratch. Which is going to make this a whole lot harder."

"You'll rebuild, Mick," Griff said. "Bigger and better."

"I will. But not here. I put the house on the market."

"You're leaving?" Fezz asked. "The bombshells keep comin'. Where you goin'? Switzerland?"

"I'm sure I'll be seeing Switzerland again soon, but no. I'm looking at the Newport area. Rhode Island. Been thinking about it for a while. Just need to get away from D.C. I can look in on Lucy occasionally. Regroup, recenter, that kinda thing."

"Man, you really liked it up there," Khat said. "I'm gonna have to go check this place out."

"It's like a different world. Ya know, the funny part is, when it looked like we had the resources, I had this vision of going to Rhode Island and building a base of operations. There's this house out on a peninsula, near a lighthouse. It was a military installation, some kind of communication command, but it was built to blend in. It got me thinking. What if we built a state of the art facility with the same concept? Just another waterfront estate, from the outside. Right? We could have lived in the lap of luxury but have everything we'd need to operate. It'd be perfect. Underground bunkers, high tech security, boat access. Hidden in plain sight."

"Damn." Khat laughed. "Wayne freakin' manor. Count me in. I'll go to Switzerland and get the diamonds back myself."

"Yeah. Good luck with that," Blake said.

Fezz raised his glass. "How about this? A toast. To things that could have been."

Blake raised his glass, but he didn't know why. A lot of things could have been, but weren't.

"How about, to bringing Haeli home?" Blake said.

Fezz slapped the table. "I'll drink to that." He guzzled the entire beer.

"So, you planning to stay with me in the meantime while you figure it out where you're going?" Griff asked.

"I appreciate the offer, Griff, but no, I'm good."

"Wasn't an offer. I just figured changing your mailing address was a subtle hint."

"What do you mean?"

Griff reached down and picked up his knapsack from under the table. "I mean, why am I getting your mail?" He pulled a small box from the bag and tossed it to Blake. "Blake Brier, that's you, right?"

Sokolov?

Blake punched through the paper packing tape and tore open the flaps. He reached in and pulled out a velvet bag and a folded scrap of paper.

No way.

He unfolded the handwritten note and read it out loud. "I hope these find you well. Please know that I love you all. You'll do amazing things. I'd do it all again in a heartbeat. I know we'll see each other again. I have faith. P.S. Mick, make sure you save one. In case you finally ever work up the courage to ask. -Haeli."

"Mick," Fezz said. "Is that what I think it is?"

Blake tipped the bag, pouring a few of the raw stones into his open palm.

The four of them sat, dumbfounded.

"Gentlemen," Blake said, "it's time to go to work."

***

The Blake Brier experience continues in CONTRAIL, available for pre-order now!

https://www.amazon.com/dp/B0983T62RN

Or turn the page to read a sample of *CONTRAIL.*

Want to be among the first to download the next L.T. Ryan book? Sign up for my newsletter, and you'll be notified the minute new releases are available! As a thank you for signing up, you'll receive a complimentary copy of *The First Deception (Jack Noble Prequel) with bonus story The Recruit: A Jack Noble Short Story.*

Join here: http://ltryan.com/newsletter/

I enjoy hearing from readers. Join us in my private Facebook group https://www.facebook.com/groups/1727449564174357 or drop me a line at contact@ltryan.com.

If you enjoyed reading *DRAWPOINT*, I would appreciate it if you would help others enjoy these books, too. How?

Lend it. This e-book is lending-enabled, so please, feel free to share it with a friend. All they need is an amazon account and a Kindle, or Kindle reading app on their smart phone or computer.

Recommend it. Please help other readers find this book by recommending it to friends, readers' groups and discussion boards.

Review it. Please tell other readers why you liked this book by reviewing it at Amazon, Barnes & Noble, Apple or Goodreads. Your opinion goes a long way in helping others decide if a book is for them. Also, a review doesn't have to be a big old book report, Amazon now allows for a simple star rating. If you do write a review, please send me an email at contact@ltryan.com so I can thank you with a personal email.

CONTRAIL

BLAKE BRIER BOOK FIVE

by L.T. Ryan & Gregory Scott

CONTRAIL PROLOGUE

"Do you see her?" Christian Krehbiel peered over the railing and scanned the vast rotunda of the Charles De Gaulle International Airport terminal.

"Not yet," Levi Farr said. "Be patient, she's coming."

"Can't you call your people? The ones with access to the tracker."

"Won't matter. The chip reacts to a satellite signal. As long as she's inside the building, it won't register. For that we'd need the mobile unit. But her last location was on the premises. She's being careful, but she'll pop out. She'll have to if she wants to get to her flight."

"Unless we already missed her." Krehbiel scoffed.

"We didn't miss her. I'm sure of it. I could pick her out anywhere. Believe me, we are well acquainted."

"My people on the train said they were heavily disguised. I wouldn't be surprised if they changed their look again."

"It doesn't matter. I'll know her when I see her."

"What is it with you?" Krehbiel asked. "Why are you helping me on this? What's the angle?"

Levi turned to Krehbiel. "Why? What are you worried about? What I'll want in return? Don't worry, you've already sold me your soul, this one's a freebie."

The statement stung Krehbiel in the gut. It was the way Levi put it. *Sold his soul.* But that's exactly what he did. He didn't know what was worse, what would have happened to him if Levi didn't intervene, or being indebted to a depraved maniac—never knowing when he was going to come to collect.

"Just keep your eyes on the escalators," Krehbiel snarled.

In all the years he'd known Levi, he'd never liked him. No. Hated him. But until this week, he had almost forgotten how much.

"But since you mentioned it, there *is* one thing I'm going to need from you in return. One minor little thing. For my trouble."

Here it comes.

"I knew it. What?"

"The name I've given you, isn't her real name. I made it up. In fact, when you capture her, you can be sure she will have rock-solid identification on her. That will not be her real name, either. But, even knowing that, you will process her under whatever information she gives you. You will not question it. You will not mention it. To anyone. Agreed?"

"Why?"

"That is my business. I'm giving you the win on this, don't look a gift horse in the mouth."

"What's her real name?"

Levi let out a snide laugh. "Haeli. And there she is, right on schedule." Levi pointed at one of the glass tubes, crisscrossing the center of the terminal.. "Right there. Blonde wig. Getting on the escalator."

Krehbiel keyed his radio and shouted into it.

"We've got a visual. Escalator D. All agents, move in. Move in!"

CONTRAIL CHAPTER 1

Ninety-Nine. One Hundred.

Haeli collapsed and rolled onto her back, sprawling her arms out to her side. The rubberized concrete floor was cool and it felt good against her quivering triceps.

In her opinion, there was nothing like five sets of a hundred push-ups to clear one's head.

There were more than a few things weighing on her mind. Being incarcerated, not the least of them. But the truth was, adjusting to being locked up wasn't as difficult as she'd imagined. Then again, she had to admit, two weeks wasn't exactly "hard time."

A few more years, or decades, were likely to change her perspective. Right now, the only thing she could do was take one day at a time.

After she was apprehended in Paris, she was transported back to Switzerland, where she was taken to the Canton Police headquarters to be processed. The lead investigator, a guy named Christian Krehbiel from the Federal Criminal Police, had tried to question her, but she refused to cooperate until she had secured a lawyer. Judging by his reaction, he didn't get that type of response very often.

She was brought before a judge, who remanded her to pre-trial prison, as it was called, until the conclusion of the trial. Krehbiel had made a strong argument that she was uncooperative, a danger to society, and a flight risk. She couldn't give him too much credit for his success. All of these things were a hundred percent true. If she'd had even a sliver of an opportunity, she'd already be a ghost, never to be seen again.

So, here she sat. Gefängnis Zürich—Zurich Prison.

Halei had been to many prisons, both official and not so official. Compared to those, Zurich Pre-trial prison was like a seaside resort. Clean, spacious and laid back, it bordered on the edge of comfort.

Her room had two beds, two desks, a shelving unit and a half-bath that was partitioned off by a half-wall for privacy. It looked like one of the staged kids' rooms at IKEA. And the best part— as of yet, she didn't have a roommate.

The guards were easy-going, by prison guard standards. Many of them were males, who moved back and forth between the small women's wing and the much larger men's portion of the prison. From overhearing bits of their conversations, she got the sense the men's side was a less desirable assignment, which meant the ones who nabbed the post were generally in a good mood.

As a testament to a low crime rate or a reluctance about incarcerating violators, there were only accommodations for eighteen women at this facility. The current occupancy was sixteen, but the numbers changed on a daily basis. When Haeli first arrived, there were only ten.

The first few days were bleak. Mandatory quarantine, following a series of medical exams and tests, kept her in her cell around the clock. But then she started to settle in.

After the first week, Haeli was given phone time. Ten minutes per day. She had used hers to call Blake, of course. Every day, like clockwork.

Hearing Blake's voice boosted her confidence as much as her mood. Especially after getting a cryptic confirmation that he had received the package with the diamonds. It would have killed her to learn that her sacrifice had been for nothing. And knowing they were received allowed her to dream of all the things the team would be able to do with the money.

Blake continued to assure her that he was working on finding the best lawyer for her situation. He had told her to "sit tight." As if there were any other choice.

She trusted Blake, more than anyone in the world. He had travelled halfway around the world to rescue her. Turned his life upside down to include her. He was the smartest, most tenacious person she knew, and she had no doubt he would come through.

So, she would sit tight. Until there was something solid. A plan to set in motion.

Beyond the more creative approaches, there remained one base option. She could take her chances with the judge. Or judges, in this case.

In Switzerland, she had come to understand, there was no jury system. The accused stood trial before a judge or panel of judges, depending on the severity of the crime and the jurisdiction. Haeli wasn't sure if this was a positive or a negative. Or a little of both.

Once she was able to meet with the attorney, she'd get a better sense of what her chances were. She had a few ideas about how to play it, given what she believed the police had on her, but she wouldn't be talking to anyone until the plan was fully hashed out.

Shaking out her arms, she flipped to her stomach to start her next set.

One. Two.

A buzzing signaled that her door was about to open. Haeli sat up as a female guard, with a tight bun on the top of her head, entered.

"Let's go, it's meal time."

"I'm not hungry."

"Then don't eat. But you're going. Everyone goes, no exceptions. You know this, Katlyn"

"All right," Haeli sighed. "Let's eat."

Haeli got to her feet and followed the guard to the cafeteria area at the far end of the ward.

The room had six tables, each with four stools, all bolted to the floor. A large open window allowed workers inside the kitchen to serve trays of food to the inmates, lined up in the sitting area. Based on the frenetic activity inside the commercial sized kitchen, she figured that the men's cafeteria was on the other side.

Haeli fell in behind a red headed girl who arrived in the queue at about the same time. The girl turned to face her.

"I wonder what's on the menu today," the redhead said.

"Does it matter?" Haeli replied.

"I guess not." She giggled. "Here, you go ahead of me, you were here first."

"That's alright, I'm in no rush."

"I insist. Please, go ahead."

Haeli decided not to engage in an argument. She stepped in front of the redhead and kept her back to her.

After picking up her tray of what looked like some type of mashed potato concoction, she picked an empty table and sat.

Thus far, she had managed to limit conversation and keep to herself, whenever possible. For the most part, the other women had left her alone. That was, until now.

"Mind if I sit with you?" The redhead sat without waiting for an answer. "My name's Gigi, what's yours?"

Uh.

"Haeli. Well, Katlyn. But everyone calls me Haeli. It's my middle name."

Haeli had taken on so many aliases in the last month, she was starting to lose track.

"Nice to meet you, Haeli. First time?"

"Yep." Haeli met Gigi's stare. After an awkward few moments, she gave in to the pressure to reciprocate. "You?"

"Here? Yes. But I won't be around long. Already plead guilty. They gave me a bonny deal. Six months. Wouldn't have got that back home."

Haeli knew the woman would expect her to ask the obvious question. And although Haeli didn't want to encourage further conversation, she was curious about what kind of crime garnered a six month sentence. "What'd you get pinched for?"

"I set fire to my ex-boyfriend's apartment. And his car."

"You got six months for burning down an apartment building? I'm guessing no one was inside."

"No. He was inside. Which is how he put it out before it could really get going. No one was hurt. But the car burned to a pile of soot. Black as the Earl of Hell's waistcoat, I tell ya. He loved that car too. Bastard."

There was a moral to the story. Haeli wasn't sure what it was to Gigi, but to her, it meant there was still hope of getting out of there before she was ninety.

"Anyway," Gigi continued, "he was an arse and he deserved it. I moved all the way out here for him and then I come home to find some filthy little lass in my bed."

"Ah." Haeli smiled. "I'm surprised they locked you up at all."

"Right?" Gigi laughed.

Gigi's personality was unnerving. How could she be so bubbly? If this were an episode of the Twighlight Zone, there would be a sorority house somewhere with stinky, dark cells and rusty iron bars. In some ways, she felt she'd be more at ease getting beaten and thrown in "the hole" on a daily basis.

"How 'bout you? What'd you do?"

"Well, Gigi, I haven't decided if I've done anything yet. But if I make one of those sweetheart deals, I'll let you know."

Gigi's eyes squinted. After a pause, she giggled again. "Oh. Of course."

Haeli poked at the pile of mush with her spork, still undecided if she was going to eat it. For the first time since she arrived, she felt the magnitude of how long even one more day in this place would be.

"Don't look now," Gigi said, "here comes Hilda."

"Who's H—"

"Look at this." An enormous woman approached. Tall, busty and blonde would normally be the traits used to describe a bombshell babe, but not in this case. Hilda was—how would she say it in polite terms?— hard to look at. Maybe the most homely woman Haeli had ever seen. A true brute. And her thick German accent only added to the effect.

"Hilda's my new roommate." Gigi swallowed hard. "Just came in this morning. She's a regular. Right Hilda?"

Two other girls had filed in behind Hilda. The intimidation squad, Haeli figured. At about a hundred pounds a peice, the two crackheads, or tweakers, or whatever they were, presented as more pathetic than anything else.

Hilda slapped her hairy man-hand on the table and leaned between Gigi and Haeli. "Who said you could talk to my girl?"

Haeli smiled. "You got in this morning and she's already your girl?"

"She is if I say she is."

"Well aren't you a charmer," Haeli goaded.

Gigi shifted her eyes toward the table. It was subtle, but it spoke volumes about the situation she was dealing with.

"And here I thought I was your girl," Haeli said.

"You've got a big mouth, newbie. Where you from? You're an American, aren't you."

"I'm from a lot of places. And you? No, let me guess. Indonesia?"

"You think you're cute. But you've messed with the wrong bitch. Now you've gotta make it right."

Finally. Now it's almost a proper prison.

"And what did you have in mind?"

"I'm reasonable. And I'd hate to mess up such a pretty face. How 'bout we make a trade. Her, for you."

Haeli couldn't help but let out a chuckle.

Hilda's lips twisted.

"Are you sweet on me? Haeli grinned. "Is that what this is about? Well, I'm flattered. Really, I am. But unfortunately, I'm spoken for, so, it's not gonna work out. Tell you what, you can have my meal and we'll call it even."

The two minions behind Hilda looked equal parts shocked and amused.

Hilda planted her other hand on the table and, with straight arms, leaned in close until she was nose to nose with Haeli. A disgusting noise emanated from her throat as she hawked up a wad of phlegm and let it pour from her mouth into Haeli's dish. "Watch your back bitch."

Haeli feigned a frown and placed her hands on the table just behind Hilda's. With all the nonchalance she could muster, she said, "See now, you've ruined a perfectly good meal. I was really looking forward to enjoying it."

In one fluid motion, Haeli slid off the stool, dragging her hands under Hilda's and knocking out her support.

Hilda's center of gravity shifted, sending her downward and driving her face into the pile of cold potatoes, ground meat, and phlegm.

By the time Hilda righted herself and cleared the paste from her eyes, Haeli had already walked to the guard by the entrance, indicated that she was finished with lunch and politely requested she be allowed to return to her room.

Haeli had no doubt the guard had witnessed the events unfolding only fifteen feet in front of him, but his sly smile told her it wasn't going to be an issue. Apparently, she wasn't the only one Hilda had rubbed the wrong way.

The first guard motioned to another to escort her back to her room, while he maintained his post.

Haeli never looked back, but she could hear the cackling of the crackheads and the growing chatterings of the others.

She imagined Hilda's rage, and it gave her a warm, fuzzy feeling.

She knew it wasn't the last time she'd have to deal with Hilda—by humiliating her, she all but guaranteed it. But, truth be told, she was always up for a little good spirited fun.

CONTRAIL CHAPTER 2

"Can we, can we? Please." Ian Thorne's bottom lip jutted out in a forced pout. Wet with saliva, it glistened against the desert sun, streaming through the dirty apartment window.

Ima Thorne didn't turn away from the laptop's screen to see it. "Mommy's working, honey."

Fighting to stay focused, Ima tapped at the keyboard. It had already taken her fifteen minutes to get into "the zone," as she called it, and the interruption threatened to reset her train of thought. She tried to ignore him, but she should have known Ian's ten-year-old, one-track mind wasn't going to let it go.

"You promised. Just for a few minutes. Please. Please. Please."

Ima snapped the screen of the laptop shut, then tried to soften her initial annoyance. "Fine. A half-hour."

A smile erupted on Ian's face before he scampered out of the room..

"Get your shoes on," she called after him.

Ima didn't have to tell him which ones. He only owned one pair. One pair of shoes and three changes of clothes.

It wasn't that she didn't have the money to buy him clothes, or anything else he might have wanted. After all, her work had brought in enough to pay Kadeem for the privilege of staying with him in the two bedroom flat for the past nine years, and to stash away a considerable sum for the future. Ima's reluctance lied in the logistics.

Over the years, she had learned to make do with only the bare necessities. Diapers, toys, and child sized clothing being delivered to a single man with no children on a regular basis was sure to raise a few eyebrows if anyone happened to notice. And Kadeem wasn't one volunteer to run kid-related errands. Likely for the same reason.

The level at which these things were monitored in the United Arab Emirates was up for debate—one she and Kadeem had engaged in on several occasions. No matter the truth, for Ima, it wasn't worth taking any more risk than necessary.

Ima's transition to becoming an unofficial, permanent resident of Ajman, UAE, was rooted, in large part, in its lack of an extradition treaty with the United States. It was convenient enough, but the country posed its own unique set of problems. Governed by Sharia law, something as simple as accidentally showing her shoulders or knees in public could have brought the kind of negative attention she had worked so hard to avoid. Or maybe her nose, eyebrow and tongue piercings would be deemed offensive. It was hard to tell who would take issue with what.

When she arrived, her jet black hair was shaved on one side and bleached and dyed neon green on the other. It had taken the better part of two years to grow it out to something less—indecent.

But, in the end, it wasn't the decency laws that concerned her. It was another archaic law—the one that made it illegal to have a child out of wedlock. Of that, she was as guilty as middle eastern days were long, and no amount of time would change it.

Neither she nor Kadeem were sure whether the law would be enforced, or what the penalty would be. Deported. Jailed. Worse. But for her, it didn't make a difference. Just getting documented into the system was enough to end her life as she knew it. No, she couldn't afford to take any chances.

For nine years, neither she or Ian had left the apartment complex property. In fact, it was rare for either to even step outside the four walls of the small flat, with the exception of the occasional visit to the playground behind the twin buildings. Even then, it had taken her several years to suppress her better judgement enough to venture that far.

She remembered the first time she led Ian down the stairs and into open air. He was five years old. Smart, well-mannered and as cute as a button. The moment he laid eyes on the two-story, wooden tower, with its colorful tube-slides, cargo netting and rope bridges, he began to sob. Overcome by unadulterated joy. Not yet sure about what it was or what it was for, he seemed to know it was something wonderful. Magical, perhaps.

Within minutes, Ian was playing with the other children. Emulating them. Socializing with them—despite having never met another child in his life. It was a sight to see, and it made her proud. He was every bit as strong and resilient as she'd hoped he'd be.

Afterward, Ima reiterated her instructions that Ian never talk about who he lives with or where he was from. And, above all else, that he never, ever, speak to an adult.

"I know Mom, I'm not stupid," he had replied.

Ima remembered chuckling at his response. Even at five years old, his mannerisms were that of a full grown man.

But it was what he said next that tore at her heart and gave her a turn at sobbing.

"Mom, do you know what I learned today?"

"What, honey?"

"The world is so much better than I thought it would be."

"Oh, honey," she wanted to say, "that wasn't the world. That was a mediocre playscape in a godforsaken city. There's so much more out there for you. So many wonderful places to explore. Opportunities to be seized. Real life to live." But instead, she pulled him close, hugged him tight, and said, "It's nice, isn't it?"

Throughout the years that followed, Ima devoted much of her time to homeschooling Ian. He learned geography, history, science, and politics. He grew to understand a world he had never seen, at a level most children his age couldn't absorb. But they never spoke about the outside world after that day. Not in terms of the present. Or the future.

This is no life for a child.

It was a theme that nagged at her.

Maybe it was selfishness, but she loved him more than life itself, and couldn't bear the thought of being apart. But, despite her devotion, not a day went by that she didn't question whether she was doing the right thing. If she was caught, arrested, locked up forever, would he finally have a chance at a normal life? Was he better off without her?

"Ready!" Ian bound into the room. The laces of his Nike sneakers laced up tight.

"So am I!" Ima picked up her laptop and let Ian lead her to the door. "Hang on, let me tell Kadeem we're going."

Ima hurried down the dank hallway and rapped on the closed door at the end.

"Come in," Kadeem's gruff voice answered.

Ima cracked the door.

Bathed in the light of several computer monitors, Kadeem Sarib stared at her, fingers resting motionless on the keyboard. "What's wrong?"

"Nothing. I'm taking Ian outside to the playground."

"You don't have to tell me when you want to go outside."

"I know. I just wanted you to know where we are in case anything happens."

"Has anything happened before?"

"No."

"Right." Kadeem's fingers sprang back into action, then paused again. "Where are you with the Tesco data?"

"I'm working on it. Almost there. They have pretty tight security. It's not as easy as you make it out to be."

"If it were, I'd be doing it myself."

Ima couldn't argue with that. "Okay then, we're going. We'll be a half-hour. If we're not back by then—"

"What? Call the police?"

"No. Just— nevermind. Be back in thirty."

Ima closed the door and made her way back to Ian, who had opened the front door and was pacing around the common hallway.

"Can we go?"

"Go ahead," Ima said.

Ian ran toward the stairs, then stopped and waited for Ima to catch up.

At the bottom, Ian pushed through the outer door. A surge of one-hundred-seven degree air singed Ima's lungs. She held her complaints but, inside, she was thanking the gods of pity for the two working air conditioner window units Kadeem had in his apartment.

To Ima's disbelief, the playground was bustling. Children laughed. Mothers chatted or played on their phones. It was as if the Emiratis were impervious to heat.

"Go ahead," Ima said, even though Ian was already half-way to the swings.

Choosing the shadiest portion of bench she could find, Ima sat and flipped open her laptop. If all went well, at the end of the thirty minutes, she'd have captured the personal data and credit card information of over five million Tesco customers. A score that would buy her another full year's rent.

A woman in a black hijab sat down beside her. "Marhaba. Ma 'asmuk?".

"I'm sorry," Ima said. "I don't mean to be rude, but I'm on an important work thing."

The woman's eyes, peering through the slit in the headdress, looked confused.

"Work. Job," Ima enunciated, pointing at her laptop.

Without another word, the woman stood and sauntered off to join several other women who had congregated around an orange plastic table.

Ima wondered how the woman could survive the blistering heat, fully covered in heavy black fabric. Maybe the outfit insulated her, she thought. Or maybe she was hiding ice packs under there. Whatever the case, Ima found herself feeling jealous of the anonymity the covering afforded the woman.

Once upon a time, she had considered getting a hijab for herself, but she nixed the idea when Kadeem reminded her that she couldn't speak a lick of Arabic.

"Mom, look at me!" Ian swung himself into the tube and, a second later, popped out from the bottom.

"That's great, honey."

All of the other children were younger than Ian. Most of the other ten year old boys were off playing soccer with their friends or playing video games. Ian enjoyed playing video games on occasion himself but, because he wasn't allowed to connect with others online, he would tire of it quickly.

The only times Ima could detect any excitement in his face was when he was here. But she knew it wouldn't last forever. Soon he would be a teenager. Hormones would kick in. And the cocoon Ima had created wouldn't cut it anymore.

But for now, Ian was occupied and she intended to utilize every moment of it. She dove back into the task at hand.

Gaining access to Tesco's computer network had been easy. All it took was a blanket company-wide email and a little luck that someone would click the embedded link. Really, luck had nothing to do with it. The content of the email was socially engineered to be irresistible. Click-bait, the Internet called it. And it worked frighteningly well. The blast had garnered a whopping sixteen percent click-through rate.

Once inside, the hard part began—exploiting the servers' code to leak the connection string to the company's customer database. She hadn't gotten there yet, but she was confident it was only a matter of time.

And once she had it, she would have enough information to produce hundreds of thousands of fraudulent, physical credit cards.

While she and Kadeem wouldn't produce the cards themselves, they would sell the information on the Dark Web to someone who would. Semantics.

A score this large, especially if undetected, would bring in over a hundred thousand dollars in profit for each of them.

Ima tuned out the chattering women and the giggling children, and immersed herself in the lines of textual output, scrolling by in the terminal window. She visualized the vectors of attack, as if she were inside the circuits themselves. Launching attempt after attempt, she crept closer to cracking the shell. And then, after what seemed like the blink of an eye, she was snapped back to the here and now.

The screech of her phone's alarm cut through the thin dry air. She fumbled to retrieve it and shut it off.

Thirty minutes. Not enough time.

She could have disregarded it. Let Ian play for longer. Squeeze out a few more minutes. It might have been all she needed. But she was always strict with the schedule. Thirty minutes meant thirty minutes.

Just as it wasn't enough time for her to hit paydirt, she knew it was never enough time for Ian either. But, to his credit, he never complained when it was time to go.

Ima closed the laptop and stood, leaving a wet sweat-stained patch on the seat behind her. "Ian, honey, time to go."

There was no response.

Scanning the playground, she didn't see him. Her heart skipped and a surge of adrenaline shot through her veins.

"Ian. Come out. Right now."

He didn't appear.

Ima checked each tube slide. Slowly at first, but with increasing urgency.

"Ian? This isn't funny."

Ima darted around the park, checking every shadow. Her mind jumped to every horrible conclusion. She circled the perimeter, now almost in a full run, looking out beyond the buildings.

Oh my god, he's gone!

Part of her railed against the obvious. There was no place left he could be hiding. But there had to be an explanation. He wouldn't leave. There was nowhere to go.

Tears began to flow. Her legs went numb. "Ian! Ian!"

In full desperation mode, she barreled toward the group of Emirati women, almost crashing into one who was turning to walk away from the group. She gasped to catch her breath.

"My boy. Ian. Did you see where he went? I can't find him."

The women shook their heads. Either because they hadn't seen, or because they had no idea what she was saying.

Wait. He went upstairs. That's it.

It was possible. Maybe she had gotten so wrapped up that she didn't hear him telling her he was going inside. It was hot. Yes, it was too hot for him. She would find him curled up next to the air conditioner, reading one of his books.

A smile crossed her face. It was accompanied by a slight tinge of embarrassment over her panicked reaction.

"Sorry, nevermind."

The group of woman fell back into their conversation as Ima sprinted to the door and up the stairs. She flew through the door and into the flat.

"Ian, you scared me, honey."

But he wasn't there to respond.

"Ian?"

Kadeem stood in the kitchenette, holding a spoon and a dumbfounded expression.

"Did Ian come in?"

His quizzical look only deepened.

"Kadeem! Did Ian come back here?"

"No. He's not with you?"

Ima felt the blood draining from her face. "No, no, no" She barged into the room she and Ian shared, overturning the mattresses from their frames. She continued her tirade through every closet, behind every piece of furniture, and every other square foot of the two-bedroom apartment before returning to the spot from which she started.

Shoulders slumped and arms dangling to her sides, she had all but lost the ability to think rationally. A limp marionette, waiting for someone to lift her up and move her in the right direction.

Then, with a surge of energy, she straightened her back and screamed.

"He's gone, Kadeem. He's gone!"

CONTRAIL CHAPTER 3

Blake pulled the orange juice bottle from the otherwise empty fridge and guzzled down the last few ounces.

Ring. Knock. Ring. Knock. Knock. Ring. Ring. Ring. Ring.

"Coming."

It was no mystery who was at the door. Forever impatient, it could only have been Fezz.

He opened it.

"Hey, Mick." Fezz walked past him and made his way to the kitchen before Blake had time to close the door.

"Come in." Blake met Fezz with a smile.

"I know you're leaving for your fight in a bit. I just wanted to stop in and give you this." He handed Blake a business card.

"Mateo Pfister. So, this is the guy, yeah?" Blake pocketed the card.

"He's definitely the guy. Let's just say he's a *friendly*. Time tested, too. I actually spoke with him. He's willing to do whatever you want. Thing is, he's actually a damn good attorney, too."

"Haeli will be happy to hear that. He knows I'm comin'?"

"Yeah, he said he's available for you to meet tomorrow."

"Thanks, Fezz."

"My pleasure. How's Haeli doing? Have you talked to her today?"

"I have. About two hours ago. She's still good. Apparently mixing it up with the other inmates a bit. Shocker. But she seems to be in good spirits."

"Man, I feel horrible for her. Here we are selling off the diamonds that she went to jail for. Doesn't seem right."

"I know. But we'll fix it. She knows we're not giving up on her. And I let her know we got her package safe and sound. Speaking of the diamonds, how's it been going with your contact?"

"He's Khat's contact. And it's going well. Very well, actually."

Within two days of receiving Haeli's package, Khat had hooked the crew up with a person who was profilific at brokering deals on the black market. The guy was a heavy hitter, and over the years, he and Khat had cultivated a mutually beneficial relationship. Khat was unusually guarded about it—he hadn't even provided the team with the guy's name.

"He's already offloaded another hundred carats. The coffers are fillin' up fast."

"That's what I like to hear. We'll be in business before we know it. I've just gotta find the time to shoot up to Rhode Island. I've spoken with the agent and she's got a few lots for us to look at. Depending on what happens in Switzerland. I mean, I have no idea when I'll be back."

"Well, helping Haeli's the most important thing right now. The rest will come together in time. Anyway, if you need one of us to go up for you, that wouldn't be a problem."

"I know, but I've gotta do it myself. In these small towns, everyone knows everyone. We need everything to look normal. Just me, legitimately buying land to build a normal house. Upstanding member of the community."

"You really do wanna be Bruce Wayne." Fezz wandered around the kitchen then leaned into the dining room. "Seriously, this place looks even more organized than normal, if that's even possible."

"I've moved everything into storage. Except for the furniture, the art and stuff like bedding that the real estate agent wanted to keep for staging the place. Even the cupboards are empty.

"Downstairs, too?"

"Yep. Come down. Check it out."

Blake led the way down the staircase at the far end of the kitchen. The heavy vault door was already cracked. Blake swung it open and Fezz stepped inside.

The once noisy, cluttered computer room was empty. Nothing remained but the desk, a single chair, and an eerie silence.

"Wow. End of an era, Mick."

"Sure is. Whoever buys this place wouldn't believe the stuff that happened in this room." Blake chuckled.

It was an understatement. The basis for several high profile and very public operations were formed in that room. If not directly, then as a result of software tools Blake had built and perfected there.

"Forget believing it, they wouldn't be able to understand it. I know I don't." Fezz ran his hand along the closet's molding. "What about the bunker?"

The "bunker" was Fezz's name for the secret basement, accessed by a false wall in the closet, which had once served as Blake's personal shelter and armory. Fezz had the distinction of being one of two other people in the world who knew about it.

"Empty."

"Imagine when a buyer gets a load of the secret passageway. It's like something out of a movie. All cloak and dagger. They'll eat it up."

"I haven't told the agent about it. The place next door was vacant when it was built. I sort of commandeered a portion of their basement, if you recall. The new owners were never the wiser. It's best it stays that way."

"Well, if you get your way, I'm sure the new bunker will put this one to shame."

"You have no idea, buddy. It's already in the works. You remember Skittles?"

Fezz pursed his lips and shifted his eyes as if trying to access his memory banks.

"Yes you do. Come on. He used to do all the schematics for the ops plans."

"Oh yeah, the little guy with the glasses."

"Yes, him. He does some freelance work on the side now. Architectural drawing. Other CAD stuff. Anyway, I have him working on some preliminary plans. I'll show you when he's got something solid. Get your input on it. Right now we're looking at around four thousand square feet, subterranean. Under a legitimate basement. Twelve thousand all together. Wait 'til you see what I'm thinkin'. You're gonna soil yourself."

"Can't wait." Fezz drifted toward the stairs and started slowly climbing.

Blake followed him back to the kitchen. "What about work? You break the news, yet?"

"No, not yet. I was talkin' with Khat and Griff about it. We all agree, we should wait until the last possible minute. Right now we've got access to resources and information that might be helpful while figuring out how to help Haeli. Seems like a gamble to give that up until absolutely necessary."

"I agree. There's no rush. Plus, you can use the time to compile information on your contacts, in case we need them later."

"It's gonna be weird. I know you've already been through it, but I have a hard time imagining being on the outside. I mean, I'm ready. Just don't know if I'm prepared."

Blake slapped Fezz's midsection. "Shake it off. I felt the same way when I left. But I knew it was time, and I was right. It was easier than I thought. There was this instant sense of freedom. You'll see. Don't get me wrong, I loved my job, at the time. But what's next for us, it'll take that feeling to a whole new level. All the good parts of the job *and* freedom. Anyway, everyone we know who left is better off today than they were then. Look at Kook."

"Oh yeah, Kook. Did anyone tell Kook what's going on?"

Blake nodded. "Spoke to him two days ago. He's pumped. I mean, he'd be pumped anyway because his five year divorce is finally official. But he's very excited about the plan coming together. He said he's got a guy running the airline full time now, so he's been taking some time.

He rented a place in Santa Cruz and has been doing nothing but surfing. But he said he's willing to do whatever he can to help Haeli if we need him."

Knock. Knock. Knock.

"Who's this now?" Fezz asked.

"What time is it? Three? That's going to be Cindy. The agent. She's set up a few showings today."

"Okay then, that's my cue." Fezz started toward the front door. " I'll catch you later. Have a good flight. Give me a call after you meet the lawyer."

Fezz opened the door, greeted Cindy and continued down the steps toward the street.

"Who's your friend? Is he single?"

"Yes, actually, he is. I'll put in a good word for you. Please, come in."

Cindy stepped in and closed the door, then started looking around. "The place looks great. I don't expect it to be on the market long. I've got five showings today, now. First one will be here in about twenty or so. I'll bet you'll have at least one offer by tonight. Fingers crossed."

"That's great. Just want to remind you, I'm traveling overseas this evening. Actually, I'm just heading out for the airport now. I don't know how long I'll be away. You should be able to get me by phone, no problem. If there's any paperwork to sign, you'll have to email it for a digital signature."

"That's not an issue. We use Docusign for most of our contracts now."

Blake picked up his bag from the floor by the front door. "Keep in mind there's a seven hour time difference."

"I've got it. Have a good trip. With any luck, this will be all locked up before you get back."

"You're the best."

Blake took one more look around. One more breath. Soaking in the last moments he would ever stand in this foyer again. When he walked out the door he'd be taking years of memories. But not the pain. That, he'd leave for the next guy.

"Okay, bye."

"Bye"

Blake stepped outside and closed the door behind him. Forever.

ALSO BY L.T. RYAN

Visit https://ltryan.com/pb for paperback purchasing information.

The Jack Noble Series

The Recruit (Short Story)

The First Deception (Prequel 1)

Noble Beginnings (Jack Noble #1)

A Deadly Distance (Jack Noble #2)

Thin Line (Jack Noble #3)

Noble Intentions (Jack Noble #4)

When Dead in Greece (Jack Noble #5)

Noble Retribution (Jack Noble #6)

Noble Betrayal (Jack Noble #7)

Never Go Home (Jack Noble #8)

Beyond Betrayal (Clarissa Abbot)

Noble Judgment (Jack Noble #9)

Never Cry Mercy (Jack Noble #10)

Deadline (Jack Noble #11)

End Game (Jack Noble #12)

Noble Ultimatum (Jack Noble #13)

Noble Legend (Jack Noble #14 - coming 2022)

Bear Logan Series

Ripple Effect

Blowback

Take Down

Deep State

Rachel Hatch Series

Drift

Downburst

Fever Burn

Smoke Signal

Firewalk

Whitewater

Mitch Tanner Series

The Depth of Darkness

Into The Darkness

Deliver Us From Darkness - coming Summer 2021

Cassie Quinn Series

Path of Bones

Untitled - February, 2021

Blake Brier Series

Unmasked

Unleashed

Uncharted - April, 2021

Affliction Z Series

Affliction Z: Patient Zero

Affliction Z: Abandoned Hope

ABOUT THE AUTHOR

L.T. Ryan is a *USA Today* and international bestselling author. The new age of publishing offered L.T. the opportunity to blend his passions for creating, marketing, and technology to reach audiences with his popular Jack Noble series.

Living in central Virginia with his wife, the youngest of his three daughters, and their three dogs, L.T. enjoys staring out his window at the trees and mountains while he should be writing, as well as reading, hiking, running, and playing with gadgets. See what he's up to at http://ltryan.com.

Social Medial Links:

- Facebook (L.T. Ryan): https://www.facebook.com/LTRyanAuthor

- Facebook (Jack Noble Page): https://www.facebook.com/JackNobleBooks/

- Twitter: https://twitter.com/LTRyanWrites

- Goodreads: http://www.goodreads.com/author/show/6151659.L_T_Ryan

Printed in Great Britain
by Amazon

21174486R00171